Grave Error

Also by Roy Lewis

The Arnold Landon Novels

GRAVE ERROR

Roy Lewis

Constable • London

Constable & Robinson Ltd
3 The Lanchesters
162 Fulham Palace Road
London W6 9ER
www.constablerobinson.com

First published in the UK by Constable,
an imprint of Constable & Robinson Ltd 2005

A copy of the British Library Cataloguing in Publication
Data is available from the British Library.

ISBN 1-84529-222-7

Printed and bound in the EU

Prologue

The moon hung low in the sky, its pale crescent granting little light across the rolling countryside, leaving deep shadows in the inclines and casting a faint iridescent glow across the fields of wheat and barley, gently waving in the night breeze. It was well past midnight and the hills were framed by a soft red glow, the illumination of distant city lights. The man in the black shirt was helping the rest of the small group as they began to unload the spades and long metal poles from the boot of the car, while the *capo* scanned the hills and the surrounding landscape with infrared binoculars. He grunted, after a little while: there was no sign of movement, no farmers, or patrolling policemen, or young lovers meeting in the darkness of the tracks, away from the prying eyes of their elders. When the tight little group was assembled, expectantly, he waved a hand, beckoning to them, gesturing up to the steep slope of the hill.

The *capo* led the way, followed by the man in the black shirt and the other four men of the team. They stole along in silence, heading for the crest of the hill above them. They carried no torches, but the footsteps of the *capo* were confident: he had walked these tracks for decades, ever since he had been initiated into the activities of the *tombaroli* as a young boy. The men slipped quietly under the lee of the hill, moved up through a narrow gully, and scrambled their way across the summit to the flat tableland area beyond. The wheat fields rustled below them in the faint moonlight; the *capo* raised a hand. 'It is here,' he hissed softly.

He retrieved the long pole from the man in the black shirt and thrust its spade-like head into the earth at his feet. He withdrew the pole, moved sideways, thrusting the pole downwards into the crusted earth at regularly spaced intervals. When the pole struck hard rock he sighed in brief, triumphant satisfaction. His eyes flashed a confident glance at his companions as they shuffled in anticipation. The *capo* knew that the inner burial chamber lay at their feet: beneath the accumulated dust of centuries there would be human remains that had been buried and undisturbed for perhaps three thousand years.

The other, inexperienced men began to dig eagerly into the dry, crumbling earth, following the outlines that the *capo* had marked out for them. They worked silently enough, apart from the gusting breath expelled into the night air as they laboured. After twenty minutes the outline of the tomb was clearly delineated: the *capo* had the experience of thirty years to assist him in his confident identification and the men with him respected his skills. They knew that there was the expectation of cinerary urns, perhaps amphorae, bronze artefacts lying buried in the dust beneath their feet. As they dug the *capo* moved a few metres further down the hill, continuing to probe with the metal pole, plunging it more deeply into the earth until it slid inwards with more ease, less pressure. The *capo* snapped an instruction; two of the men stopped digging, scrambled down to join him. He had found the passageway leading directly to what would be a central chamber. Digging above could destroy what they sought; inside the central chamber would be the pottery and other artefacts that dealers in London and New York, Amsterdam and Berne, Munich and Vienna and Tokyo would jostle and squabble amongst themselves to acquire. The group gathered at the tomb entrance; shovels and pickaxes clinked and thudded into the earth and the breathing of the digging men grew laboured and harsh.

The *capo* stood to one side, still alert, sniffing the air, watching the dark ridges of the hills, the soft glow of the lights of the city some kilometres distant.

He was uneasy. He had seen nights like this a thousand times over the years of his apprenticeship and his training, and there was nothing new to him in these sombre raiding parties. But he knew the risks – had always known them, and tonight there was something in the air, a tension in the dark sky above the hill that troubled him. Like many of his kind, the men who walked the night slopes, he was superstitious. He dealt in the artefacts of the dead and he believed in the powers of darkness, winged evil, the shuddering thrust of the devil's spear in a man's heart, but it was not fear of the dead and the winged spirits that troubled his nerves this night. Something was not right; there were others abroad, and his usual confidence was ebbing away. He felt things were somehow wrong.

He glanced sideways to his companions. They felt nothing of the edginess that troubled him. But they were lacking his experience; they were labourers, ignorant peasants, village dullards who followed to do his bidding, men who had never acquired the wit, the understanding of the ancient past that would have allowed them, enabled them to achieve what he had achieved. There was one young man there, a man new to the village, the one in the black shirt, who had been recommended by the widow of the previous consultant to the teams operating on the Veii. He was her nephew, he was her recommendation, and the *capo* had been forced to take her confidence in the man as read, but the *capo* did not know this man, and he was reluctant to trust things or people he did not know. His responsibilities were great, to the villagers whom he led and not least to the men in Milan and Rome: he could not afford mistakes because he knew the consequences of failure. He had made a good living here among the Etruscan hills for many years; others had got rich on his efforts and there were times when he had begrudged such wealth to the faceless men in the city, but he knew he could not emulate their success. Here he was a leader, *capo*, in the hills above Rome, a man of consequence among those who knew him, but he knew also that he was merely a small cog in an organization that extended far beyond the bounds of Italy. Of this he was vaguely aware because the organization did not permit too close a knowledge of the widening ripples of information. Over the years he had accumulated information, a little here, a little there, for he was not an unintelligent man. Yet there was much he did not know, nor want to know because in knowledge there lay danger.

But here in the hills he was *capo*, and all his senses indicated to him now that something was wrong.

Confirmation came with a faint glinting, the sound of an incautious step.

He raised a hand, hissed a warning and froze, crouching in the darkness. The men about him stopped working, heads turning towards him in question. Everything was still about them as he stood there, stiffly, waiting: there was no sound on the hillside or the plateau but he remained dissatisfied. He waved his hand, motioning that they should crouch as he did, remove any possibility of their figures being outlined against the night sky, and they waited, their breathing quietening, immobile on the hill. The minutes passed, and still the *capo* made no movement. Then, just as he was beginning to relax, and was about to gesture to his companions to recommence their work, from the corner of his eye he caught the faint glimmer of light again, a shaded torch stabbing at the darkness below them. He cursed under his breath and dropped to the ground. His fingers dug into the soft, dusty earth as though seeking the tremors, echoes of movement down the hill, and he heard a hoarse, nervous whisper from one of the men, demanding to know what the problem might be.

The *capo* was cursed with incompetents; the man in the black shirt, the widow's nephew, dropped down beside him, tried to gabble something and the *capo* grabbed at his shoulder, clasped a horny, gritty hand over the man's mouth. He nodded down the hill and then the others saw what he had seen: the muted flash of lights along the dirt track.

'*Carabinieri*,' the *capo* hissed.

He felt the tension in the man's face, as he gripped the jaw. He glared into the shadowed eyes of the widow's nephew; he could make out his features only dimly in the darkness and yet he felt something other than fear in the man's tension. He felt the pulsing thud of a carotid nerve against his fingers; the sweaty panic of guilt.

'*Finito*,' he snarled in a low voice and thrust the man away from him, rolling down the slope. Even as he did so he heard a low whistle from the crest of the hill, and he was now convinced they had been betrayed. Someone shouted, the headlights of a car at the end of the dirt track lanced up the hill and he heard the sound of men running, feet stamping in the stony dust of the ridge. He rolled crazily down the hill until he thudded painfully into something hard; winded, he found himself at the foot of a scraggy olive tree and he waited there for several minutes, calculating. The *carabinieri* were on the dirt track below, but they were up on the ridge also, and running across the tableland that hid the ancient tombs of the Etruscan civilization that had flourished here millennia ago. The tomb raiders had been betrayed, the encirclement was almost complete, but the *capo* had no intention of being caught. Spitting dust from his lips, with fury in his heart he began to edge on his elbows and knees, down the hill towards the danger of the distant headlights, while behind him his companions panicked, rose up, starting running as lights flashed about them, men shouted and warning whistles pierced the night.

The *capo* dropped into a sharp decline, half covered by

scrub and straggly bushes, and he heard the sounds of battle above him. They were fools, his companions, idiots: they made their presence known with their noise, he heard the sounds of fighting, the long pole thudding into flesh and bone, spades being wielded as weapons, and then there was the echoing, cracking sound of pistol shots and a high screaming, police officers enraged at the foolish resistance, demanding surrender, and in the pandemonium the *capo* heard men rushing past him up the hill, where he lay flat, screened by the bushes, hardly breathing as he waited for the sounds of the battle to end.

He stayed in the narrow gully for a long time. The moon was declining, slipping low to the craggy horizon. The shouting had long since ceased; he had heard the tramping of boots down the hill, sharp commands, a plaintive whining from one of the men, car engines starting, coming up the hill, collecting the prisoners, and he knew that the car in which he himself had arrived with the team would have been commandeered. He waited until the silence had swept in again. An owl swooped past him in the darkness, pale in the predatory moonlight; he heard the rustling patter of nocturnal feet in the ancient dust about him but he remained still, silent, until the last watcher on the hill finally rose, giving up at last, walking down the hill in the belief that the *capo* had long since gone.

They had been betrayed. Perhaps it had been the man in the black shirt, the one he neither knew nor trusted. Perhaps it had been someone else, in the village. It had been many years since there had been such an occurrence: once, twenty years ago, a raid had been disturbed like this. A peasant had had his tongue cut out as a consequence: the men in Rome and Milan did not believe in half measures, and their rule was savage. Since then, there had been no trouble. The *carabinieri* regularly patrolled the hills of course, but had always made their presence felt in advance. Men had to live. The police did their duty, but demonstrably and hardly vigorously. They were rewarded surreptitiously by the men in Rome. The *capo* knew this; everyone knew this.

But tonight was different. The raid had been betrayed; there had been violence. Somewhere in the city, in government circles perhaps, a decision had been made, and action taken against the *tombaroli*.

It would be the beginning of trouble. It was trouble that could not be avoided; the kind of problem that only the men in Rome could deal with.

He lay there thinking about it all for a long time, considering the consequences, weighing up the options available to him. They were few. At last, despondently, the *capo* rose cautiously to his feet. The first fingers of dawn stained the hills in a red, suffusing glow. He made his way down in the lightening air, through the defile, across the rocky outcrops, and on towards the village. There was nothing to be gained by fleeing into the countryside. The others had been taken; men would talk, and it would be for the men in Rome to solve the problem. He would have to face what lay in wait for him. His reactions on the hill, hiding in the gully, it had all been instinctive. But now he would go home. He could make out the squat campanile of the church that dominated the town square and he skirted the narrow lanes that avoided it. A dog barked somewhere near the square, but otherwise the village was silent in the quickening dawn.

At the edge of the village he paused, waited for a little while, but there was a dull ache in his chest now that the pulsing excitement had gone. The *capo* was of a fatalistic disposition: he believed in the power of the men who employed him; he took what life gave him without complaint, and for thirty years he had enjoyed a good existence. And he was beyond surprise now, this night.

He gave no outward show of emotion as he approached the stone cottage where he had been born over forty years ago, and saw that a light glowed beyond the half-open door. When he reached the cottage he pushed the door wide, and saw his thick-waisted wife, white-faced and tense, standing there beside the kitchen table. She was not alone.

The uniformed man seated at the table was casual, confident. The pistol near his right hand was laid on the table, the muzzle pointing towards the door. The *capo* stood there silently, taking in the scene.

The man in uniform smiled. *'Buon giorno, Cosimo. Una bella notte, hey?'*

The *capo* entered the room and gently closed the door behind him.

Chapter One

1

There had been some files to clear on his desk early on Friday morning so the hearing had already started when Arnold Landon slipped into the courtroom and found a seat near the back of the room. He glanced around at the other seats in front of him: the public area was half empty. The case had aroused no great interest in Morpeth, partly because that week there had been more sensational matters for the press to deal with – the supermarket fire at Alnwick, the multiple pile-up in foggy conditions on the A1 near Felton, the police crack-down on a drug-smuggling operation at Amble – so that the trial of an antiques dealer for handling stolen property had largely bypassed the front pages of the local newspapers, and had brought only a brief mention on local television stations. Arnold was thankful for that: his own performance in the witness box the previous day had been embarrassing, and he was grateful that there had been little media coverage of the event.

He looked around at those people who were present, seeking faces he knew. He recognized the lean, hawkish features of the detective chief inspector who was in charge of the case, seated some rows in front of him. He had been approached by DCI Jack O'Connor when the police had first decided to bring the prosecution, and Arnold had agreed only reluctantly to appear as an expert witness. He had caught sight of O'Connor's face when he had been wriggling under the defence cross-examination yesterday: the man had been scowling in displeasure, though Arnold hoped it was directed to the insinuations of counsel rather than Arnold's own evidence. Seated behind and to the left of DCI O'Connor was Arnold's head of department, Karen Stannard. It was Karen who had suggested to O'Connor that Arnold should appear as an expert witness. He was not entirely sure about her motivation in the matter: it might have been due to a reluctance to put her own reputation on the line, although she was rarely averse to making public appearances where she could be the centre of attention. Maybe she considered a courtroom a step too far.

On the other hand, she had later expressed a certain unease at the prospect of Arnold's appearing in court, though she had not specified what her objections were. Perhaps she had had a premonition of disaster, but by then it was too late: she had already conceded there was no other person in the department who could undertake the task so she had put forward his name to O'Connor. Karen was there in the courtroom now, leaning forward with her chin in one hand, watching the proceedings intently. She was dressed in a cool, pale green blouse and light skirt in contrast to the formal trouser suit she had worn yesterday, when Arnold had given his evidence. He shuddered mentally at the recollection of the malevolent look she had given him when he had been dismissed from the witness box. He still smarted at the memory and frowned as his glance shifted to the slim young man who was rising to his feet to question the new witness: the defence barrister Quincy, with his faint Irish accent and somewhat supercilious, mincing manner, who had cross-examined Arnold so effectively yesterday.

Quincy had paused to have a quick word with his client. The antiques dealer himself, Islwyn Evans, now sat impassively, arms folded, his narrow features calm, his heavy-lidded eyes almost closed. He seemed bored, almost uninterested in the proceedings, but Arnold guessed the attitude would be merely a façade. If the prosecution succeeded in its case against Evans, the man's career as a dealer and chairman of the North-East Professional Dealers in Antiquities would be over. Arnold had come across Evans in a professional capacity from time to time over the last few years. He was a regular at trade fairs, and Arnold had visited his chain of retail outlets occasionally. Islwyn Evans was well enough regarded in the trade, and seemed to have a genuine interest and understanding of the materials he dealt in. He had visited the various sites under the control of the Department of Museums and Antiquities, but that was to be expected in view of the business he was in. And he had appeared on a locally produced television programme as an antiquities expert in auctions, but Arnold had never liked him: it was difficult to pin down exactly the cause of Arnold's dislike, but he felt there was a basic insincerity in the man – he was unctuous, self-regarding, and somewhat slippery in his manner. But Islwyn Evans had nevertheless built a considerable business and reputation in the area during the last four years, since his arrival from Manchester.

Arnold half listened as the new witness was sworn in. His attention had been caught by another woman in the courtroom, who would have been turning heads, he guessed, as much as Karen Stannard normally did. She was seated across to his left: she was lightly tanned, her red-gold hair framed an oval face of considerable beauty, and she was dressed well and, he considered, expensively. She looked a little out of place in the courtroom: he guessed her milieu would be more likely to be in front of a fashion catwalk. She seemed uneasy, and as he watched her, she said something to her companion, a middle-aged, balding man with a hard mouth; she touched his arm lightly, he turned his head to fix her with a long, silent stare, and then he nodded, she rose and, with an apology to others she disturbed, made her way out of the room.

Arnold frowned, staring at the heavy-eyebrowed man she had left. He knew the man vaguely but for a moment could not recall his name. Then it came back to him. Portland. A self-made man, who had built a fortune in the construction industry, a local collector of antiques. Gordon Portland.

He would have been one of Islwyn Evans's clients, Arnold guessed. Whether he was there in support of Evans, or sitting there as someone who might at some time have been defrauded by the antiques dealer, Arnold could not guess. He glanced away as he heard Quincy addressing the man in the witness box.

'You are Dr James MacLean, appearing on behalf of the accused as an expert witness?'

'My name is MacLean, yes. And I am called in the capacity you mention.'

James MacLean was tall, distinguished in appearance, with dark hair greying at the temples, worn rather long, swept back neatly from his broad forehead. He had an air of assurance and confidence: and there was a firm, pompous arrogance in his deep voice. He was perhaps forty years of age, dressed in a dark suit, immaculately white shirt and maroon tie. Appearances were clearly important to him. He was well built and he held his head high, perhaps aware that the elegant planes of his features were more happily demonstrated by raising a chin under which the flesh had begun to gather. He held himself well, and displayed none of the nervousness which had affected Arnold yesterday: he was clearly well used to speaking on public occasions and the witness box held no terrors for him.

'Would you be so kind,' Quincy suggested with a hint of obsequiousness, 'as to present us with your qualifications, experience and present occupation, Dr MacLean?'

'I hold degrees from the Universities of Cambridge and Yale,' MacLean intoned rather loftily. 'I am a sometime Fellow of the Department of Archaeology at Oxford

Brookes University, and am presently Dean of the Faculty of the same name at the University of Durham.'

'You have held official positions in the archaeological world?' Quincy prompted him.

MacLean nodded in agreement. 'For three years I was Chairman of the Archaeological Society in Massachusetts; I was a member of the committee set up by the government to investigate the funding of archaeological projects in the United Kingdom; for two years I was President . . .'

Arnold's attention wandered as Dr MacLean recited his litany of professional success and academic recognition. He glanced back towards Karen Stannard. She was in profile, her head held high as though she was aware of the admiration with which men in the courtroom would regard her, but as Arnold considered the thought she turned her head and caught sight of him; she stared at him now, her mouth set grimly. He saw the coldness in her green eyes, the displeasure she felt as she glared at him. She had left quickly before the end of yesterday's embarrassing hearing so he had been unable to have a word with her, and she had not been in the office when he had returned. The iciness in her glance now confirmed the clear impression he had received earlier that she had been appalled by his performance. She burned him with her eyes, then turned her head away in contempt, to focus once more on the witness stand.

'Now, Dr MacLean,' Quincy was continuing with a slight emphasis upon the 'Dr', 'you will be aware that my client Mr Islwyn Evans is charged with the handling and offering for sale of certain artefacts which have been described as stolen from the archaeological site known as the Avalon Island, off the coast of Northumberland.'

'I am indeed.'

Arnold grimaced. The site had been under the control of the Department of Museums and Antiquities for the last five years. In 1997 an amateur enthusiast in antiquities had been scrambling along the coast near Bamburgh after a violent storm when he noticed a series of wooden piles in the shallow waters just offshore. With a friend he had waded out to discover a low shelf of land – which he had later fancifully described as the Isle of Avalon – and dredging around among the rock and mud and shingle he had succeeded in recovering some thirty iron objects from the mud. He had failed to give the appropriate notices at the time and with his friend he began to investigate further. In consequence they had caused a certain amount of damage to the site, while putting some items for sale on the internet, which brought them to the attention of officialdom. There had been something of a rumpus in the local press, the police had declined to take action, but the public outcry had finally led to the involvement of the Department of Museums and Antiquities, which had been put in charge of the site. The name – Avalon – had stuck in spite of its catchpenny, over-romantic connotations. But then, there were those who firmly believed that Arthurian connections lay rooted among the ancient hills of Northumberland.

Arnold had supervised some of the work for the protection of the site. By putting up timber and concrete shuttering they had managed to protect the so-called island from the fury of the winter gales. The site had been isolated and secured so that it was possible to undertake a proper investigation of the area. Gradually the waters and the boggy land inshore had been properly and meticulously picked over and some important items had been discovered. It had turned out to be the mouth of an ancient river bed and within one hundred yards an astonishing number of artefacts had been discovered. Arnold had supervised the cataloguing of the finds: they had recovered some twenty swords, fifteen axe-heads, two cauldrons and more than a hundred ornamental objects, including a number of gold *fibulae*. There had been the usual disputations over the site. Originally describing it as a river settlement, the academic experts had then concluded, in view of the number of weapons unearthed, that it was actually an arsenal; later it was said to be a military encampment. But in Arnold's view the votive deposits challenged this interpretation: it was more likely to have been a cult centre at which first-century Celtic warriors dedicated weapons to the gods.

He thought back over the heated discussions that had arisen over the Island of Avalon. It had always presented problems to settled interpretations. He recalled the arguments over the items found, because of the fact that many of them would seem to have been artefacts that were in marked contrast to academic views of the classical art of antiquity. He remembered the professorial pontifications, the descriptions variously applied: abstract, curvilinear, non-narrative, sinuous, fantastical, shape-changing, dream-like, voluted, elusive, triadic, phytomorphic and zoomorphic. Everyone who had visited the site seemed to have a different viewpoint . . .

His attention was dragged back to the courtroom as he heard Quincy say, 'And you will also be aware that the charges relate in particular to the attempted sale of an object which has been described as a Celtic cauldron.'

'I am so aware,' MacLean replied, nodding soberly.

Islwyn Evans shifted in his seat and muttered something under his breath. Quincy glanced at his client and smiled in encouragement. He turned back to MacLean. 'Have you had the opportunity of inspecting this object?'

'I have indeed.'

Quincy waved his hand in a deprecating, almost apologetic manner. 'I am no expert in such matters, as you are of course, Dr MacLean, but this seems a strange kind of object to have appeared as a votive offering in a Celtic grave site.'

MacLean shook his head in disagreement. 'Not really. Cauldrons were highly venerated among the Celtic races. They often appeared as votive offerings not on account of their practical usefulness, but because they were seen as symbols, not only of abundance, but also of regeneration and rebirth.'

Quincy grimaced, inclined his head as though accepting the point, and smiled. 'So its presence at Avalon would not be unusual. On the other hand . . . would you be so kind as to describe the object in question, Dr MacLean?'

The expert witness raised his head confidently. 'Certainly. It is a cauldron, heavily embossed, decorated with heads of what would traditionally be regarded as Celtic deities, interspersed with groups of carved severed heads, birds of prey, chariots, warriors . . . an emphasis on weaponry which suggests a society geared for war, which is what Celtic society certainly was.'

'There have been similar finds elsewhere?' Quincy queried.

'A cauldron quite similar to this one was disinterred in 1844 at a site in Denmark. Like this one, it demonstrated a technique generally believed to be of Thracian origin.'

'Technique?' Quincy queried, in a purring tone.

'The cauldron is made of unalloyed silver embossed in high relief and partially gilded. Such work was a speciality of regions to the east of the Celtic world.' MacLean glanced in a supercilious manner around the quiet courtroom, keen to demonstrate his knowledge. 'The imagery on the cauldron is eclectic, Celtic motifs predominate, and with such artefacts there is a growing willingness among *some* scholars to accept that they were made by societies of Celtic origin, possibly in the Titelberg area, now in Luxembourg, and were perhaps part of the booty gathered by Teutonic raiders of the first century.'

Arnold raised his head, scenting danger. *Some* scholars. There was a clear question raised by the comment: did MacLean himself subscribe to this theory? He waited to hear the obvious question, but Quincy paused, then ignored the opportunity, and to Arnold's surprise, passed smoothly on. 'What were these cauldrons used for?'

MacLean rested his hands lightly on the edge of the witness box. He was at ease, confident, in his element. 'Not for cooking, clearly. They were probably used to hold the sacrificial blood of the victims of ritual sacrifice. Veneration of such cauldrons has deep roots. Consequently they often depicted or were held by important figures in the Celtic pantheon. For instance, the goddess embossed on the seventh-century Strettweg wagon holds a cauldron above her head, a vast bronze cauldron was a feature of the Hochdorf sixth-century tomb, and there have been similar discoveries at La Tène, and more locally, in the British Isles at Berwick and Kirkcudbright.'

'Strettweg, Hochdorf, La Tène . . . Berwick, Kirkcudbright . . .' Quincy repeated the names in a musing tone. He glanced at the notes he held in his left hand. 'And do you have any views about this particular cauldron?'

'I do.'

Quincy raised his head. His eyes were suddenly glittering in anticipation. 'And what would be your considered, *expert* view, about this cauldron?'

MacLean paused, raised an eyebrow, lifted a contemptuous shoulder. 'It is clearly a fake.'

Arnold tensed in astonishment, a warning finger of ice touching his spine. There was an electric silence in the courtroom; the hush was shortly followed by a rustling of muttered conversation. He saw the stiffness in DCI O'Connor's back, was aware of the swift, puzzled glance that Karen Stannard sent in his direction.

The barrister was smiling thinly. 'A *fake*? Why do you say that, Dr MacLean? After all, you've just told us that other, similar cauldrons have been found at the places you mention.'

MacLean raised his hand in a supercilious gesture, expressing a warning. ' No. I said that other cauldrons had been found, but I did not say they were exactly the *same* as this one. I was merely emphasizing the fact that it is not uncommon for cauldrons to appear as votive offerings at Celtic grave sites.'

Quincy nodded slowly, his sharp eyes fixed on MacLean. 'But this object is different?'

'This cauldron has an affinity with the one I mentioned earlier, discovered in Denmark in 1844.'

'And how is that important?'

'The Denmark cauldron is now generally regarded in knowledgeable circles as a fake.'

DCI O'Connor was leaning forward intently. Counsel for the prosecution was glaring at his brief, as though seeking succour. Quincy's tone was again almost purring. 'On what considerations was such a decision reached?'

Dr James MacLean shrugged and twisted his handsome mouth in contempt. 'The find at Denmark was hailed at the time as an important discovery. But its provenance was doubtful, and later, more informed, closer examination led to its exposure as a fake. And as far as this cauldron, supposedly from Avalon, is concerned, well, it bears considerable comparisons with the Denmark artefact. The two are similar in their manufacture. But it is now recognized that in respect of the Denmark object mistakes were made by the manufacturer, and the confidence displayed in the work was . . . over-exuberant. Similar discrepancies have appeared here.'

'What kind of discrepancies?' Quincy queried.

'In the first instance, unalloyed silver was used in its manufacture,' MacLean replied.

'Of what importance is this?'

MacLean shook his head. 'The cauldron appears genuine on first inspection, not least because of its enhancement. The Celtic affection for extravagantly fanciful zoomorphic shapes, the kind that appear embossed on this cauldron, may have originated among the Scythians. But all the artefacts of this kind that have been discovered, and which are recognized as genuine, were made from iron, bronze, gold or electrum. Unalloyed silver was rarely, if ever, used.'

'I see . . . Unalloyed silver was not used by Celtic artists of this period,' Quincy repeated for emphasis.

MacLean nodded confidently. 'That is the case. Secondly, one must look at the panels on the cauldron: the warriors blowing their trumpets, the joined pairs of heads, the stag antlers, the interlocking S-motifs and the swastikas . . . It is like an amalgam of every Celtic motif that has ever been identified. It is, in common parlance, somewhat over the top. In brief, it is all too *rich*, to be believable.'

'Please explain further,' Quincy requested, after a quick glance at his client.

MacLean leaned forward, with an earnest, considered expression. 'It's the *conglomeration* which is . . . suspect. There's just too much there by way of decoration. It's as though everything we know about Celtic art has been brought to bear in this one object, even though many of the forms used would have been scattered over a wide area, different sub-cultures, different periods . . . And there is an aesthetic argument also. There's been for some years considerable dispute regarding one aspect of Celtic source information: disagreement as to what extent such objects have a religious characteristic, namely, the teaching of principles of ethical living.'

'Archaeological evidence . . .?' Quincy prompted.

'Has always been sparse to support this theory. All the extant evidence suggests that with its emphasis upon weapons, its slave chains, its hints of human sacrifice and head-hunting, the Celtic religion gave little priority to compassion and philanthropy. No, Celtic religion was concerned to constrain the powers of magic and to know the will of the gods but one seeks in vain anything which can be interpreted as constituting a moral theology. But this cauldron is different: it specifically draws attention to the triad: *Honour the gods, do no evil and practise bravery.*'

Quincy smiled, and nodded. 'And do you have any other . . . problems with this particular artefact?'

MacLean hesitated. He lowered his head, appeared to contemplate possibilities. Arnold knew it was done for effect: the man was playing to his audience, milking the situation for all it was worth. 'This object flies in the face of perceived knowledge: other than in the modern anthropological sense of primitive religion it cannot be said that the Celts were at all conscious of religion.'

'I am afraid you are losing us, Dr MacLean.'

'The Celts believed in metempsychosis.'

Quincy widened his eyes, glanced around the silent courtroom. 'Which is?'

'The belief that after death the soul passes from one body to another. This was a doctrine held in southern Gaul, where Hellenistic influences may have introduced Pythagorean ideas of the transmigration of souls. But there is no evidence that such ideas were accepted in other parts of the Celtic world. This object, it is claimed, was discovered in a *cremation*.'

'Of what significance is this?'

'Cremation, leading to the release of the soul into the air, is inappropriate for believers in metempsychosis. It is for this reason that throughout Celtic history *inhumation* was preferred to cremation – more appropriate for believers in a bodily afterlife. Classically, the lavish goods deposited in aristocratic tombs were intended to ensure the dead were equipped with the means of reclaiming their privileges in the other-world.'

'So your conclusion?'

'First, the location of the discovery is wrong. I cannot believe this object can have been originally discovered at the Avalon site. Were this truly a first-century artefact it would have been found in an inhumation, not a cremation.' He picked up the photograph that had lain in front of him on the ledge of the witness box, and stared at it for several moments. 'Secondly, the article itself carries resonances that do not ring true: the arched moustache of the head here, the geometric character of this face, these are typical of Celtic art but they seem *forced* and unnatural, and there are classical influences present in the cauldron which are unsupported in the literature of the insular Celts. Irish and Welsh mythologies have much to say about the other-world: a dominant theme is the easy passage to and from one world to another. But the eschatological processes whereby mortals reach such a paradise are not even sketchily outlined in the extant literature. Yet here, on this cauldron, we see them delineated.'

'So your conclusion is that this artefact is not what the prosecution claims it to be?'

MacLean nodded confidently, sweeping the room with an imperious glance. 'Precisely. In my view it is to be compared with the cauldron discovered in 1844 in Denmark. It is nothing more than an elaborate hoax, a clumsy mid-Victorian copy of perhaps an eighth-century artefact. This is most clearly demonstrated in the fact that the copyist had access to only limited information; he bundled everything he knew and what was known at that time about Celtic art into this one object. Its provenance must therefore be suspect; its workmanship inexact.'

Quincy gave a self-satisfied smile. 'So to sum up, you are of the opinion that this artefact was actually created in the mid-Victorian period, and probably did not come from the Avalon site?'

'Avalon? No. I doubt it greatly. It may have been placed there at some recent period, to give it a provenance –'

'But we have no evidence of that,' the barrister urged quickly.

'On that issue I cannot comment. But in my view this cauldron cannot be dated in the manner it has been suggested.'

'It is a fake.'

'In my view, certainly.'

The barrister smiled thinly. 'And if, in your expert view,

it is a fake, it can hardly be the subject of a prosecution for theft of a first-century Celtic artefact, would you not agree?'

Dr James MacLean grunted in contempt. 'That conclusion would seem to me to be inescapable.'

Arnold sank back in his seat. Yesterday had been bad; today was even worse.

2

The Celts, Arnold mused, had always regarded water as a regenerative source. For them healing and ritual cleansing had gone hand in hand. It accounted for the fact that it had been common practice to deposit votive offerings in wells and streams, rivers and springs. It was why they had chosen the Avalon site, the emergence of the river into the sea, in which to leave skulls and *fibulae*, horse and bull images, bones and carvings . . . and cauldrons.

He sat on the headland looking down to the site they had been working on for the last four years, the sun warm on his back, a fresh breeze from the sea ruffling his dark hair. Arnold had felt the necessity to get away for the weekend, escape the nagging recollection of the humiliations and the tensions of the Evans trial, try to regather his thoughts and test his confidence in his own judgements again. He bitterly regretted agreeing to appear as an expert witness, now; when Karen Stannard had suggested he take on the task he should have been more stubborn in his refusal. But under the pressure exerted he had relented and agreed to appear.

He had thought he possessed more resilience, but Quincy's cross-examination had surprised him. The barrister had asked him little about the cauldron: instead, he had attacked his expertise. It had been a brutal experience. Arnold had never held himself out as an academic: he had developed his understanding of other worlds from long experience, nurtured on a basis inculcated in him by his father from the days when they had tramped the Yorkshire moors together, investigating old lime kilns, medieval pit-workings and quarries, the wreckage of an industrial age, ancient Iron Age barrows and Roman forts and roadways and battle sites. His father had talked to him about the sites, and together they had spent long hours searching over the windswept hills for signs of ancient workings.

Quincy had sneered at such experience.

'So, Mr Landon,' he had said loftily, 'you hold no degrees?'

'No.'

'In fact, your formal education has been somewhat limited, shall we say?'

'I suppose so,' Arnold replied, shifting uneasily.

Quincy persisted. 'You've held no university post?'

Gritting his teeth, Arnold had agreed that was true.

'Have you published any learned papers on archaeological subjects, or been asked to serve on national committees, or been sought out to advise on archaeological matters?'

'I have not.'

The thin, supercilious smile on Quincy's narrow lips had irritated Arnold, but he had been forced to sit there while the barrister taunted him, laying the foundation, the baseline against which his own expert witness would later be held up for praise. 'So how did you emerge into the world of archaeological study, Mr Landon?'

'By good fortune,' Arnold had snapped unwisely, goaded into retaliation. 'I had originally been employed in the Planning Department but my interests were such that I was eventually transferred to the Department of Museums and Antiquities where I've worked ever since.'

'Ah, yes, your transfer . . . Was it not the result of certain disagreements you had with your superiors?'

Quincy had done his homework. 'There were some dis-agreements, certainly,' Arnold had agreed reluctantly.

'And in your present department, you are one of the longer serving members, I believe,' Quincy had smirked.

'I believe so.'

'But in spite of your service there, you were never offered the position of head of the department when it fell vacant after the unfortunate death of the incumbent?'

Arnold was aware of the presence of Karen Stannard in the room, watching and listening. 'I never sought the position,' he had glowered.

As he sat now on the headland, looking down on the rolling tide that edged in frustration around the base of the Avalon site, protected by its concrete walls, he felt a vast dissatisfaction at the recollection of his performance in the witness box. He had been caught off balance by the thrust of the questions and had allowed himself to be needled into truculence; he had failed to defend his own personality and acquired skills; there were things he could have talked about, the offer of a university professorial post in the States, his success in dating ancient materials, the regard in which he was held by many better qualified academically than he. But under Quincy's contemptuous, dismissive questioning he had retreated into his shell, erecting a defensive carapace, allowing himself to feel he had nothing to prove to the world. But that was not the issue in reality: he had been put in the witness box to state and defend his beliefs and understanding of the ancient world, and to use that experience in the identification of the cauldron, but he had failed miserably because he had allowed himself to be trapped, denigrated, and later made to look like a foolish amateur against the muscular confidence of the defence expert witness. Quincy had not been interested in his opinions; he had wanted to expose Arnold's deficiencies when measured against the man Quincy intended calling for the defence.

Dr James MacLean.

Arnold rose, kicked disconsolately against a tuft of grass. There was a bitter taste in his mouth as he walked across the springy grass to the cliff edge and began to make his way down the rocky path that led to the beach. The ancient river that had flowed down through the gully had long since disappeared, blocked and buried by convulsions a thousand years ago, its path eroded by sea and wind, but the stony delta that had been built up over millennia was still there, a flat platform that had finally been washed over by the rising seas.

It was a matter for wonder that the riches of the Avalon site had remained over the centuries. The votive offerings that had been cast into the river mouth would normally have been ground away, leached from the rock, washed out to sea, lost for ever, but for the geological accident that had shattered some of the rock of the cliff face and dug out a gully in which artefacts had been trapped; finally, when the seas had receded again after the collapse of the cliff to the north of the site, the flat area that the fanciful had described as an island had been left to hold and protect the remains of an ancient Celtic civilization.

He had been taken aback by MacLean's observations: he felt in his gut that MacLean was wrong, whatever his qualifications might be.

Arnold stood on the narrow causeway that had been built to the site two years ago. It gave easier access to the island but there was no one working at Avalon this weekend, and the site encampment some two hundred yards away, the scattering of small wooden huts under the lee of the cliff, surrounded by a wire fence, was empty. It was clear now, in view of what had occurred, that the security had been insufficient, that access to the huts had been too easy, that site control had been lax so that when artefacts had gone missing it should have been no surprise to anyone. That they had been stolen was incontrovertible; that the artefacts were Celtic in origin was well established.

The problem was, Dr James MacLean had alleged that the one object on which the Evans trial was based could not have come from the Avalon site because it was a fake. Arnold stared around him at the site, arms folded, anger burning in his chest. MacLean had been wrong, he was certain of it, but Quincy had held out the credentials of the defence expert witness and emphasized the superiority of his judgement over that displayed by the expert witness for the prosecution.

Arnold's own counsel had done his best, tried to remedy the imbalance.

'It was you, I believe, Mr Landon, who discovered the *sudarium* some years ago.'

'It was found by the team I led,' Arnold admitted.

'And the ancient Viking sword, later identified as the *Kvernbiter*?'

'Yes.'

'And you have been proved right on a number of occasions when the dating of medieval constructions has come into question?'

'From my study of the development of wood joints employed by medieval artisans, that is correct,' Arnold had nodded.

But it had all sounded lame and unconvincing, the luck of an amateur. It could not stand up against the confident assertions of the university expert brought forward by the defence. He had seen the conclusion reflected in the eyes of Karen Stannard when counsel for the prosecution had been unable to shake the conviction of Dr MacLean, and in the hunched shoulders of Detective Chief Inspector O'Connor who could see his prosecution being shredded.

From that point onwards, it was clear the case against Islwyn Evans was doomed.

Arnold had needed to get away this weekend, to the clean, salt-tanged air of the Northumberland coast. He needed to forget the humiliation heaped upon him by Quincy, to regather his thoughts and his confidence, recover his own belief in himself, and cast to the back of his mind the implications of the thrusting questions raised by Quincy in the courtroom.

But he was also aware that the matter was not yet over for him, and he was not looking forward to returning to the office at Morpeth on Monday.

The meeting took place, inevitably, in Karen Stannard's office. She kept him waiting in his own room for two hours before the summons came; when he entered her office he was a little surprised to see Portia Tyrrel already there. Slim, dark-haired, olive-skinned, she sat there demurely, wearing a cheongsam that emphasized her Eurasian beauty, and an innocent, concerned expression. Arnold guessed immediately that the cheongsam would have irritated Karen, which no doubt was why it was being worn. But Karen would have said nothing, because it could not be argued that it was inappropriate dress for the office. She herself was given to wearing clothes that emphasized her own startling beauty. But the irritation meant that her claws would be that much sharper for Arnold, honed by her irritation with Portia.

'All right,' she snapped briskly, waving him to the chair in front of her desk. 'Let's get straight down to business. I'll be having another meeting with the Chief Executive later, after matters have been raised in committee, in view of the damage this affair has done to the reputation of this department.' She glared at Arnold. Her eyes seemed to have darkened in a reflection of her anger. 'Let's start right at the beginning. We took over the Avalon site four years ago?'

Arnold nodded. 'That's right. There was a certain dispute at the time. The site had been damaged, the Environment people wanted to get involved and English Heritage were –'

'Never mind all that,' Karen intervened impatiently. 'Let's not concern ourselves with the infighting that went on. Though perhaps it would have been better if we'd never taken on responsibility in the first place. What I want to know is what went wrong.' She turned her gaze to Portia. There was a hint of malevolence in her glance. 'Were you not involved at the beginning?'

Portia smiled confidently. 'You might remember, Karen, we were *all* involved at that period. It was not long after the death of the previous head of the department, I had just joined the team, you had not been confirmed in your present post, and everything was . . . shall we say . . . somewhat up in the air. I was put in charge at one point,' she admitted sweetly, 'but because it was felt I was perhaps too junior to take on such responsibility, you yourself moved me off the project.'

Neatly done, Arnold thought. Portia Tyrrel was not prepared to be hung out as a sacrificial lamb. He waited. There was a short silence as Karen Stannard stared at her assistant, wanting to take issue but unable to find firm ground. She turned back to Arnold. 'That puts things back firmly in *your* court.'

'Not exactly,' Arnold demurred. 'I certainly was responsible for the initial work on site, but then the sea cave project came up, we all got involved in that and you'll probably recall that we enlisted the assistance of the university at Newcastle.'

'You can't say they were responsible for the security of the site,' Karen snapped in irritation.

'No, that's true.' Arnold eyed her carefully. 'But I believe you consulted the Chief Executive at the time about our budget constraints. I think it was you who persuaded him that we should bring in a security firm from outside.'

Karen Stannard took a deep breath. Her cheeks were a little flushed. She shook her head. 'It was a joint decision. But it doesn't really matter a damn. The fact was there was a break-in at the site two years ago and a number of artefacts were stolen. The items were identified by a check on the catalogue. Who had supervised the cataloguing?'

Arnold considered the matter carefully. There was no

doubt that as the senior person personally involved it had been his responsibility. The cataloguing had actually been done by Portia, but under his supervision. Any discrepancies could be laid at her door, but that should not derogate from his own responsibility in the matter. He glanced at Portia's placid, unconcerned features and nodded miserably. 'I supervised the logging of the items found at the site.'

'And you checked the list against the items after they were stolen?' Karen demanded.

Arnold nodded. 'I listed the artefacts that had been taken during the break-in.'

'How the hell did the thieves get in so easily?' Karen asked, shaking her head.

Arnold shrugged. 'The security firm had erected a wire mesh fence around the huts, the doors were all padlocked, but it seems their own budget couldn't cover the cost of dogs, or a watchman. But to be fair, it's the first time we'd faced such a problem. Normally, there's been no great interest in such artefacts, in spite of their intrinsic value.'

'The catalogue was one of the items brought out in Evans's defence,' Karen said bitterly. 'And that damned man Quincy soon demonstrated there were deficiencies in the loggings. What defeats me is how the hell you could have allowed this to happen! The evidence you presented, the statements you made to the prosecution before this trial got under way, they all pointed to the existence of a Celtic votive cauldron in the storeroom that was broken into.'

'A cauldron had been listed,' Arnold muttered.

'But not *described*!' Karen Stannard hissed.

Portia Tyrrel coughed lightly. 'I think I should intervene at this point,' she suggested. 'It was a very busy time for the department. We had the sea cave project at Hades Gate coming up, there were two exhibitions being organized, some of the students from Newcastle who were being used to identify and catalogue items after cleaning had been withdrawn during the examination period and so it was inevitable that some discrepancies might have arisen.'

Karen stared at her icily. 'Excuses of that kind don't help us escape the inevitable facts. A cauldron appeared in the list. It was one of the objects stolen. But there was no detailed description of the artefact in the catalogue. In other words,' she added, turning her glance back to Arnold, 'everything comes back to the fact that the identification of the cauldron taken by the police from Evans's possession is down to you.'

'It *was* the cauldron that had been found at the Avalon site,' Arnold said stubbornly.

'So you told Detective Chief Inspector O'Connor! But how could you be sure it was the same cauldron?' Karen demanded.

Arnold had already thought long and hard about the matter. He shook his head. 'There was no detailed description in the log. That I admit, and I admit that it was an oversight on our part – for the reasons that Portia has already outlined. But I haven't changed my opinion.' He held Karen's cold glance steadily. 'I was up at the site several weekends. I inspected all the artefacts that had been dredged up. And I inspected that cauldron closely. All right, maybe I should have entered the details myself there and then, but at the time I was fascinated by its appearance. I cleaned it, I inspected it minutely, I marvelled at the workmanship –'

'Oh God give me strength,' Karen moaned. 'Don't start extolling the virtues of the bloody thing! It was a fake!'

'What I held in my hands,' Arnold insisted stubbornly, 'was a wonderful piece of Celtic workmanship. From my reading, from my experience, from all my instincts I knew that this was a significant find. I inspected it. I handled it. I *knew* it. And when you asked me to go to that meeting with DCI O'Connor, and I was shown the artefact that they had confiscated from Evans's showroom, I knew it was the same piece, the Celtic cauldron that I had held in my hands up at the Avalon Island site.'

The two women regarded him solemnly for several seconds. 'The trouble is,' Karen commented at last in a sour tone, 'there seems to be no one else who speaks with such conviction. And that's how you ended up as an expert witness at the hearing.'

'Only when you persuaded me to do so,' Arnold responded bitterly.

'You were convincing,' she flashed back at him.

'And I'm still convinced!'

'Dr James MacLean is of an entirely different opinion! And he's the one who's been believed!' Karen Stannard sat back in her chair, her bosom heaving angrily. She glared at her long fingernails as though they in some way held responsibility for the problems that faced the department, and sighed in exasperation. 'We can't escape the realities of this situation. The case against Islwyn Evans has collapsed; the Crown Prosecution Service has, I understand, advised withdrawal of the prosecution, and it's our departmental reputation which is suffering. I've got to make a report to the committee and then I've got to talk again to the Chief Executive. I've got to tell them that we made a mistake –'

'I dispute that!'

'The court heard MacLean,' Karen responded angrily. 'Face facts! They *believed* him! Evans is off the hook because you failed miserably in the witness box. Quincy threw the catalogue details in your face and you had no convincing answer. He asked you to describe the cauldron and you bumbled on about its provenance, only for MacLean to be called and sink the whole argument by demonstrating that the artefact held by the police was a nineteenth-century fake! The fact is, whatever you saw at the secure site two years ago at Avalon, it could not have been the item the police recovered from Evans!'

'I don't believe that. I inspected that item. I recognized it again.'

Karen threw her head back in despair at his stubborn clinging to his conviction. 'But didn't you understand what MacLean was saying? That bloody cauldron could not have come from Avalon! It is a botched-up copy of a Celtic artefact that was of the wrong manufacture and threw into the equation every possible idea from Celtic art. It's not a damned bit of use you going on about your convictions. That's all yesterday's news. What we've got to decide now is how we handle this situation. There's a lot riding on this, Arnold. Budget time is coming up; we've got three applications in for Heritage grants –'

She caught his grimace of disgust and rounded on him.

'I see you think all that's unimportant!' She glared at him, breathing hard. 'That's the difference between us, Arnold! It's why I'm in this chair and you're not! I take the politics of our situation seriously and I accept the need to make people believe in what we do! And what's happened here, allied to your damned stubbornness, your refusal to back down from your own misconceived opinions, means I have a mountain to climb!'

She sat up straighter in her chair, her eyes darkened with anger, and seemed about to add to her outburst. Then she checked herself, glanced at Portia, took a deep breath. 'All right, I think I don't need you here any longer, Portia. If you wouldn't mind leaving us now.'

Portia Tyrrel raised an elegant eyebrow then stood up, smoothing the wrinkles in her dress carefully. She nodded at Karen, smiled faintly at Arnold and left the room. Arnold caught a hint of her perfume as she passed him. After she had gone the silence gathered about them as Arnold waited. Karen seemed lost in thought. After a while she raised her head, stared at him. He thought he detected a degree of uncertainty in her glance. They had long been at odds with each other, of course, ever since she had arrived in the department. Though he had never wanted to succeed to the position of head of the department she had always continued to regard him as a rival. On the other hand, more recently the tension between them had been sharpened by something else – a reluctant regard, a closeness, a warmth that she had resisted apart from one vulnerable occasion in an hotel at Alnwick . . .

'I don't quite know what to do about this, Arnold,' she muttered in a low tone.

He allowed cynicism to gain the upper hand. 'You'll need a sacrificial lamb,' he suggested.

He had annoyed her. She frowned. 'This isn't a departmental error, I may remind you. It was your identification of the cauldron that the police relied on. And which we took on board.'

It was true. Arnold made no reply.

'I shall have difficulty with the committee,' she went on. 'You'll be aware there are certain members there who are committed to cutbacks, who are even susceptible to suggestions that the department should be merged with the library service, of all things.'

Which would inevitably put her job on the line, Arnold thought. He waited silently.

She picked up a pencil, rolled it between her fingers, began to tap it absent-mindedly on the desk top. 'I must talk to the Chief Executive. I think there's only one way forward. We must sideline the issue as far as is possible. He's already spoken to me on the phone, and we discussed suspension while further enquiries are made. On balance, however, he felt that could make things even more difficult . . . a sort of admission of irresponsibility.' She flicked a disturbed glance in his direction. 'What has come out of this, what the Chief Executive thinks . . . well, he's of the opinion that maybe your lack of qualifications –'

'It's never been an issue before,' Arnold bridled.

'And you've got an excellent track record,' she responded quickly. 'But the Chief Executive . . . he feels maybe we need to take something positive out of this situation. Do something that'll take the heat out of matters. Gloss over the perceived failings in certain directions . . .'

Her voice trailed away. Arnold waited. She was talking about what the Chief Executive thought, but he was certain it was her own feelings that were being expressed. 'I could always resign,' he said quietly.

She hesitated, struggling with the thought. He guessed she found it an attractive proposition. But maybe she had already raised it with the Chief Executive, and it had been vetoed.

'No,' she sighed, 'I don't think we could call for your resignation.' A brief smile touched her lips. 'We wouldn't want the further embarrassment of an industrial tribunal hearing for unfair dismissal, would we? No, nothing so drastic.' She looked at him directly. 'The committee meets this afternoon. You won't be called to appear but I shall have to make a report. After that, I need to speak to the Chief Executive again, of course, but I think I can persuade him that what we need to get us off this particular hook is an agreement with you.'

'Of what kind?'

She hesitated. 'We need to reach a solution that will allow things to cool down. We need you to have a lower profile. I know that you might find this a further humiliation, Arnold, but I think we need an agreement with you . . . an agreement that you would accept some form of retraining . . .'

Retraining. Arnold stared at Karen Stannard coldly. He could already hear the malicious laughter that would soon be echoing in certain dark corners of the building.

3

Assistant Chief Constable Sid Cathery was a big-shouldered, bull-necked, heavy-paunched man, and he filled the leather chair behind his desk. The hands he placed on the polished surface in front of him were like slabs of meat: he was reputed to have used them to good effect upon opposing forwards in the darker recesses of the scrums when he had played for Somerset Police as a young man. His barracuda-grim mouth rarely expressed pleasure; his sharp blue eyes seemed constantly to be seeking for deficiencies in his subordinates, and his short-cropped, iron-grey hair bristled defiantly in a reflection of his personality. He was not expected to remain in the north long: he was an ambitious man who would seek promotion as soon as he had made his mark in a force that he had already made clear was one he regarded as sloppy.

He waved DCI Jack O'Connor to take a seat directly in front of the desk. DI Farnsby, lean, saturnine, with a dis-satisfied mouth, was also present, seated slightly to one side. O'Connor wondered whether they had already been talking about the collapse of the Islwyn Evans prosecution. The Assistant Chief Constable leaned forward, fixing O'Connor with a glare. 'So the CPS have closed down the prosecution. What the hell went wrong?'

O'Connor glanced sideways towards Farnsby. He wasn't certain why the man was there: Farnsby had not been involved in the prosecution of the Evans case. On the other hand, it was well enough known that he had managed to ingratiate himself somewhat with Cathery, in the way he seemed to have been a blue-eyed boy with Cathery's pre-decessor. Maybe all the top brass were impressed by Farnsby's graduate fast-track record. O'Connor shrugged diffidently. 'We played the wrong cards, I guess.'

'This isn't a bloody game, O'Connor,' Cathery snarled.

O'Connor took a deep breath. 'I'm aware of that, sir. But the fact is we were wrong-footed by the defence. They nailed the weakness in our case –'

'We shouldn't have gone to court if we had a weak case!'

'The CPS had approved it,' O'Connor flashed back. 'And

we've been watching Evans for some time. It seemed to be the right opportunity. We got some information on the grapevine, we raided his premises, we found some stuff that seemed dodgy, and there was the one item that we were told came from the Avalon site, so we went with it. The problem was –'

'Yeah, tell me,' Cathery sneered.

'The problem was the defence expert witness, Dr MacLean, persuaded the court that the stolen artefact wasn't what it appeared to be. And the court believed the defence expert, not our own man.'

'Our own man. Landon,' Cathery growled, almost to himself. 'What persuaded you to use him anyway?'

O'Connor scratched his lean jaw in reflection. 'The Evans file goes back three years, sir. When it was first opened, it was handled by DCI Culpeper. Naturally, when Culpeper retired and the file was handed to me, I thought it best to have a word with him, get background, that sort of thing. Particularly when the Avalon cauldron came to light.'

Cathery's narrow eyes glinted with malice. 'You took advice from a retired officer? What's going on, you unwilling to stand on your own feet, O'Connor?'

'It wasn't like that,' Jack O'Connor protested. 'It seemed to me that since DCI Culpeper had held a watching brief on the Evans file, waiting for the opportunity to nail him, and with his experience –'

'Experience, my arse,' Cathery interrupted scornfully. 'You had the file, you should go with your own instincts. Hell's flames, when I came here I found I had a shit-hole to deal with. A Chief Constable just retired under a cloud of suspicion, a force that was demoralized to say the least, old men like Culpeper clinging to their chairs and hanging on for their pensions, back-biting, insubordination, some dodgy new recruitments . . .' He fixed O'Connor with his angry eyes. 'And new blood like you who, it seems to me, need their hands held, don't have the guts to go out on a limb and handle matters on their own initiative.'

O'Connor raised his head. His tone was steely; he wasn't about to lie down under such accusations. 'That isn't the way of it, *sir*. I had every right to go with this the way I did. It made sense to talk to Culpeper: I'd do it again.' He was aware of Farnsby shifting slightly in his seat. He glanced briefly in his direction. O'Connor knew there had been bad blood between Farnsby and the retired DCI Culpeper. His own relationship with Farnsby was edgy, because the younger man still felt he should have got promotion to Culpeper's job; instead, O'Connor had been brought in from outside. It still rankled with Farnsby. 'I approached Culpeper, and he advised me that I should talk to Landon. He had respect for the man; I've come across Landon before, and I had confidence in him also. Landon took a look at the artefact we suspected had been acquired illegally. He immediately confirmed it'd been stolen from Avalon. I respected that judgement, and we went with it. We couldn't prove Evans had stolen the thing, but it was recovered from his storeroom, so we charged him with handling.'

'And were proved wrong!'

O'Connor held his temper in check, his jaw muscles rigid, a pulse beating angrily in his temple. 'We all make mistakes, sir.'

'And when we do, we have to live with them,' Cathery growled. He drummed impatient fingers on the desk top, seemed to want to continue with the argument, but then thought better of it, shifted his bulk in his chair and shrugged. 'All right. Water under the bridge. The thing is, where do we go from here?' He eyed O'Connor with a certain malevolence. 'Do we now just give up on Evans?'

O'Connor considered the matter for a few moments then slowly shook his head. 'I don't think so, sir, though we may have to back off somewhat, play it a bit more carefully until a better opportunity arises.'

41

'We've shown our hand,' Cathery muttered.

'And on reflection, maybe we did that too soon,' O'Connor conceded reluctantly. 'But I think we need to keep the file open. The fact of the matter is that there's a certain history to Evans: he was under suspicion in Manchester before he removed his business up here. The odd thing is that four years ago he had a pretty big business down there, and by coming up to Newcastle he was downsizing. That puzzled a number of people. He was suspected of running some sort of racket in stolen artefacts, paintings, sculptures, an extensive range of stuff in Manchester, and from what we've been able to gather, it was a wide-ranging sort of operation. So when he upped sticks and came north it raised a few eyebrows. We took on the Manchester files, started our own investigation, but Culpeper was unable to pin anything significant down to him –'

'*Culpeper*,' Cathery muttered contemptuously. 'An old warhorse who should have been put out to grass years before he went.'

DI Farnsby shifted slightly in his chair; O'Connor suspected Farnsby would be in agreement with the sentiment. 'Anyway,' he continued, 'it's been an ongoing investigation, and when we came up with the Avalon item –'

'Which proved to be a fake.'

'– we thought it was time to move. You're right, of course, sir, when you say we've shown our hand and if we press on there's the danger Evans might start screaming harassment, but I've no doubt in my own mind that he's a villain, and we'll get something on him in due course.'

'That's as may be.' Cathery scowled thoughtfully, then nodded towards Farnsby. 'All right, you'd better tell O'Connor what you've been up to.'

Farnsby leaned forward. 'I've not been involved in the Evans investigation, of course, though I was aware of the file on him. DCI Culpeper never kept me in touch with it, kept it close to his chest –'

'Never mind that,' Cathery grunted. 'Let's not rake over old coals.'

Farnsby flushed slightly. A sensitive soul, O'Connor judged, easily pricked to offence.

'What I've been concentrating on recently,' Farnsby continued, 'is an insurance matter. I've been working with NSM, the Northern Shipping and Marine people – big insurance company up here – and in particular I've had access to their files. It seems two years ago they went to court over a claim in respect of a warehouse fire. The premises were severely damaged, and the NSM company had issued a policy to cover the building, fixtures, fittings and stock. When the claim came in, they sought to avoid the policy on the ground that the managing director of the company concerned had deliberately caused the fire.'

'An old tale,' O'Connor murmured.

'Anyway, when the case came to court it seems that on the facts the judge was not satisfied that fraud could be proved. The fire could have been caused by an electrical fault which had caused woodwork to smoulder. The managing director and other occupants of the warehouse had failed to notice the smouldering. But very shortly after they left the building the fire burst out. The NSM insurance people argued that the fire resulted from an intentional ignition of the stock. The judge commented that they had not discharged the admittedly heavy burden of proof – namely, they hadn't managed to prove fraud to a high degree of probability.'

'You're beginning to sound like a bloody lawyer,' ACC Cathery muttered irritably.

Farnsby's eyes were cold, but he directed his attention towards DCI O'Connor. 'The reality is, the managing director succeeded in his claim. The insurance company failed to avoid the policy, and had to pay out.'

'This managing director you mention,' O'Connor asked, not quite certain where the conversation was heading. 'Is he known to us? Does he have a record?'

Farnsby shook his head. 'Not really. There's a view among the team that he's had dealings with some dodgy people from time to time, but in the main he seems to be relatively clean. He's in the distribution business, commercial materials, timber, electrical goods, that sort of thing, plying between here and Europe, a few contracts with the States, the odd consignment into Asia.'

'So why have you been looking at him, if nothing could be pinned on him over the insurance fire claim?'

'Northern Shipping and Marine raised the matter with us last year because they felt that some of the items claimed in the loss adjustment were . . . unusual.'

'How do you mean?' O'Connor asked curiously.

'They'd expected to see items such as refrigerators and similar electrical goods, car parts for India, machine tools, the general run of commercial goods that the warehouse was holding for shipment. But when the list came in there were some rather expensive items that they hadn't expected to see.'

'Presumably the presence of these items could be proved.'

'They were held in warehouse manifests for shipping, yes,' Farnsby agreed.

'So what did they comprise?' O'Connor queried.

'Some eighteenth-century paintings,' Farnsby replied. 'Italian marble sculptures. A fourth-century triptych; a Greek Orthodox icon . . .'

O'Connor raised his eyebrows. 'Where were these items to be shipped to?'

'The States, it seems.'

There was a short silence. Cathery waited as O'Connor considered the matter. 'The insurance company paid out?'

'They couldn't refuse. Everything seemed to be in order on the manifests. And NSM had failed in court to avoid the policy on grounds of fraud. Yes, they paid out. But they were more than a little unhappy. So they've been talking to us.'

O'Connor shook his head. 'Don't seem there's much we can go on, if they've failed in their claim,' he suggested. 'And I don't see –'

'A good copper,' Cathery intervened, 'gets prickles at the back of his neck from time to time when things don't seem to be quite right. Maybe your neck should be feeling a bit scratchy right now, O'Connor.'

O'Connor frowned, glanced at Farnsby. 'Where is this going?'

Farnsby shrugged. 'I think the NSM claim is dead in the water. But we do have this list of items which seem out of place somehow. Moreover, the policy was a slightly odd one. It was the managing director who made the claim against these items: the real owner of the items did not. In other words, the risk of loss was borne by the shipping company: when the items were destroyed, we can presume he compensated the owner for the loss, after he'd made a successful claim against NSM. But the owner who was shipping the items to the States never raised his head above the parapet.'

O'Connor considered the matter for a little while. 'I don't think there was any reason why he should have been named. Some of these people, they like to keep their business to themselves. This managing director . . . what was he called?'

'His name is Ron Hamilton. He's still in business, though from what we gather he's drawn in his horns somewhat now,' Farnsby replied. 'He's acquired new premises at Gateshead, but he's cut back on some of his shipping arrangements. Now, he's concentrating on Europe and the States – the odd item to Japan, but not a great deal.' Farnsby glanced uncertainly towards ACC Sid Cathery. 'We've not got much to go on, but . . .'

Cathery waved a negligent hand. 'Sometimes you got to go with your instincts,' he intoned. 'All right, O'Connor, you got a bloodied nose over the Evans prosecution, but we're not going to let the little Welsh bastard get away with it. We'll nail him yet, and maybe, just maybe a little sniffing around this guy Hamilton will bring us a result.'

O'Connor frowned thoughtfully. 'You're suggesting there might be a connection between Islwyn Evans and this Ron Hamilton character?'

'From what I hear, he turned up in the courtroom a couple of times, during the Evans hearing.'

'I wasn't aware of that,' O'Connor replied. 'But I gather a few dealers came in, out of curiosity.'

There was a suspicious gleam in Sid Cathery's blue eyes. 'Something in my water tells me we ought to check it out, any possible links between Evans and Hamilton. What is it they say around here? You gan canny, all right? But you check it out. Let's see if we can find out who owned the stuff, these antiques, that went up in smoke in Hamilton's warehouse fire. Let's see if they belonged to Evans. And if they did, maybe we'll find out if some of it was a bit dodgy.'

O'Connor glanced uncertainly at DI Farnsby. 'I'll be working with DI Farnsby on this?'

Cathery leaned back in his chair and nodded. 'Get your heads together, yeah. We don't need to allocate responsibilities at this stage. Just see what you come up with. But O'Connor . . . in the meanwhile, there's someone else you need to go and see. This guy Gordon Portland.'

'Portland?' O'Connor frowned. A wealthy man who had made his money in the construction business, he had become something of a collector of antiques. The man had been helpful in the early days of the Evans investigation. 'What does he want?'

Cathery shrugged. 'He wants to have a chat with you about the Evans trial. From what I gather he's done a fair bit of business with Evans this last couple of years and he wants some assurance that the man's clean, now the trial has collapsed. He's looking for reassurance, I guess. Anyway, better make an appointment to see him.' He wrinkled his nose thoughtfully. 'He's loaded, you know. Self-made millionaire, they say. He's on the Chief Constable's dining circuit. So go see him. And wear your kid gloves.'

O'Connor nodded. He got the picture. At Cathery's level local politics tended to intrude, and the friends of the Chief Constable had to be kept sweet.

Cathery sighed, glanced at his watch, and rose to his feet. 'All right, you two shove off. I've got a meeting to organize. With an Italian bigwig. Minister of Culture, no less. Can you believe it? And I came into this business to catch villains!' He waved them towards the door. 'Catching villains . . . And what do I find myself doing? Playing nursemaid to a bloody wop politician!'

It was another two days before Arnold found himself in the presence of the Chief Executive. Powell Frinton was a careful, precise man, a lawyer by training, of a somewhat desiccated appearance and personality, a man who held his employees at arm's length, was careful in his dealings with the politicians who ruled his professional life, and was not known for his personal warmth. Arnold had known him for some years now and although he recognized the restraint of the man's personality, he had nevertheless always found him to be fair in his judgements and his dealings with the people who worked under him.

Powell Frinton was waiting in the committee room when Arnold entered with Karen Stannard, his sensitive fingers lightly brushing the leather-topped table as though polishing away intrusive marks left by the sweaty palms of his political masters. He managed a thin, controlled smile as he caught sight of Karen: he was always polite to her, Arnold considered, but remained wary as though he felt slightly nervous in her presence. He had a view about women, and particularly about beautiful women: he rarely trusted their judgement. 'Ha, Miss Stannard . . . Mr Landon. Please take seats here, on my left. I've arranged for coffee to be brought in. I am holding a meeting that I think it might be appropriate for you to attend.'

When they had seated themselves, he continued his involuntary polishing of the tabletop thoughtfully. After a brief silence he flickered a sharp glance in Karen's direction. 'I've had the opportunity to read your succinct report of the committee meeting, Miss Stannard, in respect of the . . . ah . . . difficulties arising from this recent unfortunate court hearing. I must admit I do not entirely agree with your recommendations, although I concede they have a degree of logic on their side. But before I deal with that matter . . . ah, here's the coffee.'

Two women entered with trays. Arnold noted the crockery was of the best kind held in Powell Frinton's office. It had not been purchased for the use of departmental minions. 'Are our guests on the way?' Powell Frinton asked one of the women.

'They're just outside in the corridor, sir, with the chairman. He's just saying goodbye, I think.'

Powell Frinton nodded. Arnold looked at Karen, raised his eyebrows. He had expected a private meeting with the Chief Executive, but clearly there was something else in the wind. Powell Frinton moved towards the doorway: a few moments later two men entered the room, dark-suited, carefully groomed, the leader with his right hand extended in greeting. He took upon himself the duty of identification.

'This is my colleague from the Ministry of Culture, Mr Bocaccio. My name is Gamboretti, and I am here to act as interpreter. Mr Bocaccio is personal assistant to the Minister himself.' His English was perfect, his accent impeccable.

'The Minister is here in the north-east?' Powell Frinton enquired.

Gamboretti's handsome features creased in a smile of acknowledgement. 'That is right, sir. He is attending a function at Newcastle today, but our duty is to meet certain people like yourselves.'

'Coffee?' Powell Frinton offered after he had introduced Arnold and Karen to the visitors. Both Italians seemed impressed by Karen Stannard; Bocaccio, older than his companion, balding, with predatory eyes, held her hand just a little too long, making no secret of his admiration. The visitors were less impressed by Arnold. It was to be expected, he thought to himself: Karen tended to become the centre of attention in most male company.

The small group seated themselves around the committee room table and as Arnold sipped his coffee Gamboretti talked briefly about the work they did in Rome, and expressed his pleasure and interest in seeing the north-east of England for the first time. He was a smooth operator, well versed in the niceties of social behaviour, and seemed inclined to continue his eulogies about the north-east until his senior colleague, Bocaccio, dragged his eyes away from Karen, glanced at his watch and said something in Italian.

Gamboretti smiled apologetically, inclined his head in acknowledgement. 'I am reminded that time is pressing. We have other visits to make. So perhaps we should get down immediately to the business of the meeting, the reason for our visit here to your offices.'

Powell Frinton nodded, and Arnold settled back with his coffee as Bocaccio made some suggestions in rapid Italian. Gamboretti took up his cue. 'It is necessary, perhaps, to explain that the Ministry of Culture in Italy is charged, among other duties, with the management and preservation of Italy's archaeological heritage. And we have a problem. Like so many of the so-called source countries – Greece, Egypt, Turkey, Cambodia – Italy is hard pressed to prevent the steady supply of goods to countries such as Britain and the United States where there is a significant demand, and a large market for art and artefacts of antiquity.'

Karen glanced swiftly at Arnold. Still smarting from the collapse of the Evans trial, Arnold ignored her, kept his eyes on Gamboretti.

'There is no doubt,' the interpreter continued, 'that unlike other illicit markets, such as for drugs, the trade in antiquities often infiltrates the legitimate art market. In the past, of course, works of art that came out of the source countries were not restricted – it was your own Sir William Hamilton who gave the first great impetus to the exodus of artefacts in the eighteenth century.'

Without which, Arnold mused, there would have been no great surge in the neoclassical movement in taste and design in Europe.

'But what might have legitimately been the pursuit of gentlemen in the eighteenth century is very often a crime today, however,' Gamboretti continued. 'And it has become big business, a criminal commercial activity. Many governments are now collaborating with each other to limit and if possible bring an end to this activity.' He brushed an errant lock of dark hair from his forehead, and glanced at his silent companion, whose eyes were still idly speculative as they remained fixed on Karen Stannard. 'Protective legislation has been passed in many of the source countries to restrict the loss of ancient artefacts, and it is a problem that there is no legal requirement in Britain or in the United States for sellers to publish the full provenance of objects they offer for sale in their catalogues.'

'But in this country, we often make the assumption that artefacts previously unknown in the market and unpublished in academic literature are probably the result of illegal excavations,' Arnold assured him.

Gamboretti inclined his head gracefully, conceding the point. 'On the other hand such items may come from private collections formed centuries ago and handed down over generations,' he advised, 'so it is appreciated that there are difficulties to be faced. But this is the reason for our visit.' He spoke rapidly to his companion in Italian;

Bocaccio nodded vigorously. Gamboretti turned back to Powell Frinton. 'We at the Ministry have decided to focus our attention of recent years on the demand end of the market, targeting museums, auction houses, galleries and collectors. We try to persuade collectors that the purchase of antiquities of doubtful provenance is destroying Italy's classical heritage. It is true an international consensus is growing: your country is a signatory to the UNESCO Convention, Japan has followed suit, Switzerland also. As for our friends in the USA . . .' He sighed in mock despair, raised an expressive shoulder. 'They are unlikely to do the same, although they have agreed to impose import restrictions on archaeological materials from Italy. But we now have come to the point where we wish to take the next step, and enlist more practical help at regional levels in countries such as England.'

'Help?' Powell Frinton queried, looking down his thin, pinched nose. 'Of what kind?'

He would be thinking of budget considerations, Arnold guessed.

Gamboretti glanced at his companion, then shrugged. 'The visit of our Minister to your country is part of a process: we are seeking to raise agreements for the establishment at local levels of what might be described as art task forces, or individual experts who can be given the task of tracing and identifying particular artefacts that are known to have been looted from sites in Italy. We are using, in your own country, a particularly important example. It has recently come to our attention that there is every likelihood that a certain artefact has found its way to England. The article in question is perhaps one of the most spectacular works to have survived from antiquity.'

Powell Frinton raised his eyebrows. 'What might this artefact be?'

'It is a Greek vase, known as a calyx krater, used in ancient times for mixing wine and water. This particular artefact was believed to have been painted by the artist

Euphronios, about 515 BC. It is decorated with the winged figures of Sleep and Death; together they lift in their arms the heavy, naked body of a dead warrior. According to information we have received, it was looted some three years ago from an Etruscan tomb and thereafter it passed through various hands. But from information supplied in the field, we believe it has now been acquired by someone here in the United Kingdom.'

'Are you suggesting it might be here in the north-east?' Karen asked.

'We cannot be absolutely certain,' Gamboretti conceded, with a slight, deprecating smile. 'This is only one of the areas we are targeting. Yet it is a possibility. But it provides a starting point for us, this calyx krater. It is, naturally, only one of many such artefacts that we know have been traded illicitly. What we need to do now is to establish a network of people, with whom we can maintain contact, and in whose expertise we have confidence, so that the net can tighten around these illegal dealers, and our national heritage can be protected.' He paused, glanced again at his companion. 'Funds will be made available, of course, some from the European Union, some from the Italian government, to support this project. Meanwhile, your colleagues might wish to look at this documentation . . .'

He produced from the briefcase at his feet several glossy brochures. Arnold glanced at one of them; like the others it comprised a list of artefacts, photographed in full colour, which were all known to have been taken out of Italy in recent years. He frowned. 'How is it you've been able to identify these items? If they were looted from tombs, how did you find out?' he asked.

Gamboretti's smile displayed a world-weary cynicism. 'Seven years ago we concluded an important investigation. We arrested a man called Arturo Renzo and managed to convict him. He was the head of an international smuggling organization, organizer of a highly structured underground network with far-reaching tentacles, transiting through Switzerland – exploiting a loophole in Swiss law that permits transfer of ownership in unclaimed stolen property to buyers in good faith, after five years. The organization had strong connections to the Mafia. Renzo was charged initially with *associazone mafiosa* – conspiring with the Mafia, but once we jailed him the edifice he and his predecessors had erected began to crumble. Much information came our way, and the network was smashed. Various other arrests were made, shippers, dealers, *tombaroli* – the grave robbers themselves – and to date some thirty thousand artefacts have been recovered. But there are many more important items out there in the illegal market, and in particular we wish to establish a group which can concentrate on Etruscan art. Smuggling still continues, of course, though on a less centrally organized basis. But recovery is also important, as well as closing down routes and systems.'

Bocaccio drained his coffee cup and tapped his watch, with a hint of impatience. Gamboretti nodded. He smiled at Powell Frinton. 'We have here some proposals you might be prepared to look at. The document is self-explanatory. I am afraid now my colleague and I must leave, for other appointments. The Minister . . .'

'We quite understand,' Powell Frinton said, standing up and extending his hand. 'We will look at your documentation in detail and let you have our responses very quickly. Meanwhile, may I express our appreciation of your visit, and also extend our congratulations upon your command of the English language. You speak it perfectly.'

Gamboretti ducked his head. 'My mother was Italian, but my father was English.'

'Did he work in the art world?' Powell Frinton enquired.

'You might say so. He died in prison. He was an art thief.' Gamboretti managed a slight, self-deprecating smile. 'It is the way of the world, is it not? Sins of the fathers?

I now find myself attempting to remedy some of the wrongs of the man who sired me . . .'

Powell Frinton escorted the two visitors to the hallway and waved them goodbye from the steps. He returned a few minutes later to the boardroom, where Arnold and Karen were silently studying the brochures the visitors had left. Arnold had found the photograph of the calyx krater. It was a magnificent piece of work. He guessed that its value would be inestimable.

Powell Frinton picked up the document containing the proposal from the Ministry of Culture. 'I did have some forewarning of this,' he said quietly, 'which is why I called you both in to sit in on the conversation. Miss Stannard . . . you had some suggestions to make regarding Mr Landon, in the wake of the collapse of the Evans trial.'

Taken somewhat out of her stride, Karen nodded, flashing a quick, nervous glance at Arnold. 'That's . . . er . . . that's right. We discussed suspension but you didn't think . . .' Her voice trailed away.

Powell Frinton's tone was sober. 'You did suggest, as an alternative, retraining. I remain a little unhappy about that, for a man of Mr Landon's experience and reputation, in spite of what happened at the trial.'

Arnold was surprised: he had not expected to find the Chief Executive so supportive.

'On the other hand, I am in no doubt that a period away from the department, and perhaps an element of retraining, might be best for morale overall among your staff, Miss Stannard.' He pinched his thin nostrils between finger and thumb, thoughtfully. 'It would also assist your budget if the cost of a member of staff were removed from your department, if only for a short period of time. So, in a sense, this visit from our Italian friends comes at an opportune moment.'

He fixed his glance on Karen. 'The funding mentioned in the documentation can be added to the budget of the

Department of Museums and Antiquities. Specifically to support part of the salary drawn by Mr Landon.'

'While I'm happy to receive support in my budget,' Karen said, confused, 'I don't see –'

But the Chief Executive had already turned to Arnold. 'I intend to make arrangements that you should be reassigned for a month, to undertake a course of training in Italy.'

Arnold stiffened in surprise. He glanced at Karen: her green eyes expressed shock and a degree of resentment.

'On your return,' Powell Frinton continued, 'you will thereafter assume an additional responsibility, back in Miss Stannard's department of course, for the role outlined in the documentation by our Italian colleagues from the Ministry of Culture.' He handed the Italian proposal document to Arnold. 'In two weeks' time, Mr Landon, you will fly to Rome. Miss Stannard, you will consult me regarding the necessary rearrangements of responsibilities in your department during Mr Landon's absence.'

Arnold looked at Karen Stannard. Her mouth was open. Her surprise was absolute. Whatever plans she herself might have been making for Arnold had been blown out of the water. He had no doubt that, in her mind, an Italian assignment would taste more of reward than punishment. She didn't like it, and she glared at him as though it was all his doing.

But Powell Frinton was the Chief Executive, he had made the decision, and there was nothing she could do about it.

Chapter Two

1

The house had been redesigned in the early nineteenth century for one of the coal magnates on the Tyne: the fortunes such men had made allowed them and their descendants to move inland to the Northumberland hills and attain the status they hungered after, that of entry to the squirearchy, membership of exclusive clubs, flight from the belching chimneys and dust-filled rivers, away from the dockyards and the grimy terraced houses that clung to the banks of the Tyne. Reconstructed on an eighteenth-century foundation, Belton Hall was circular in plan, its entrance containing a giant portico with Ionic columns, and a doorway flanked with marble statues of Autumn and Spring. Over the years, much of the land once attached to the house had been sold off, along with its ornamental lake, but it still remained a residence of character against a backdrop of northern hills, and it emphasized the wealth of its owner, the man DCI O'Connor had come to see.

There was an elderly resident butler. Stern-visaged, dark-jacketed, he opened the door at O'Connor's knocking, but when a voice behind him called out, he inclined his smooth-haired head slightly, and moved away on soft feet to disappear, O'Connor presumed, in the direction of the kitchens. O'Connor hesitated, then stepped into the cool hallway.

He had not expected to see the woman who stood at the

foot of the staircase which took up the central part of the house, lit by the cupola above. She had clearly just returned from riding: she wore jodhpurs and riding boots and a white, open-necked shirt. She was perhaps five feet eight in height, slimly built, and O'Connor stared at her in open admiration. Her eyes were dark, magnificent in an oval face; her skin tanned, her mouth inviting, with a full lower lip. She stood with one boot placed on the first step of the staircase; one hand on her hip, she seemed to be striking a pose for a celebrity magazine. But then she came forward, smiling slightly, her walk easy, confident. Her hair was red-gold and glossy, somewhat wind-blown, framing her oval face with its flawless skin. She tapped a riding whip lightly against her thigh as she walked, extending her hand. 'I think you must be DCI O'Connor.'

Her fingers were cool and slim; they lay in his for several seconds longer than necessary. He caught the hint of her perfume; her eyes locked into his provocatively and he was aware of the slimness of her waist, below the swelling line of her breasts.

'Have we met before?' he asked in surprise, already aware that, if they had, he would surely have remembered.

She smiled; he caught a flash of perfect, even teeth. 'We certainly haven't been introduced. But I was seated behind you in the courtroom at the trial of the antiques dealer. You were pointed out to me. I am Isabella Portland. You've come at the request of my husband, I believe. He is in the library, poring as usual over his prize collections.' She favoured him with a smile again, with a hint of conspiracy. 'It's his obsession. Collecting things.'

Her voice was low, slightly husky, melodious, with a slight accent he could not place. She raised a hand, gesturing across the hall, turned, and he followed her as she walked across the hallway. Her stride was long, a slow elegant swinging of the hips that drew his attention, the whip again tapping rhythmically against her thigh. She exuded a feline sexuality and he guessed she would be well aware of it. She opened the door, and stood to one side, leaning one hip against the wall, smiling, her glance holding his as he entered. Then she turned and headed back towards the staircase. O'Connor watched her go for a moment, and then entered the room she had described as the library.

Gordon Portland was sprawled in a leather armchair near the window. He rose as O'Connor entered, his glance straying past his visitor momentarily as the sound of his wife's retreat echoed from the hallway. Then he grimaced, came forward, held out his hand. 'You'll be O'Connor. I'm Gordon Portland.' The grip was firm and positive. He became aware of O'Connor's glance, straying around the room, taking in its high, book-lined walls, its neoclassical splendour. Portland grunted. 'Bit over the top, really, isn't it?' he suggested. 'Not exactly my taste, but I'm told it's too valuable to change. Seventeenth-century. And I'm a builder, not a vandal.' He waved O'Connor to a chair, and poured two stiff glasses of whisky without question.

'It's rather more elaborate than my own modest flat,' O'Connor replied, and took the proffered glass without demur. He preferred Irish whiskey but Scotch was acceptable, particularly of this quality. He glanced around at the decor, the grand stone carved fireplace, the elegant furniture, the heavy drapes at the windows, gold and purple. Some might regard the whole effect as ostentatious, but he did not say so. A long oak table ran the length of the room: it supported several glass-topped display cases.

'Don't think this place runs without heavy backing from finance houses,' Portland humphed as he sat down in the deep easy chair opposite O'Connor. 'I might have made a fortune in the construction business, but that doesn't mean I can afford all this without a mortgage or two.'

He had an oddly constrained manner; his mouth was hard, and a lurking suspicion seemed to lie in his eyes. His voice was gravelly. O'Connor guessed he would be over fifty years of age, with a body that was beginning to sag at the waistline. He was bald, with a hint of crinkly, pepper-and-salt hair above his ears. His features were heavy, his skin reddened and somewhat coarse, and O'Connor felt there was a glint of steel in his grey eyes. He would be a careful, controlled man: his chin was purposeful, the mouth capable of hardening with resolve. The thought of Isabella Portland suddenly drifted into O'Connor's mind: she would be younger than her husband by twenty years, he guessed. It was the kind of age difference that could lead to trouble.

Perhaps there was some reflection of his thought in his eyes for Portland said, 'You will have met Isabella in the hallway.'

'That's right. A beautiful woman.'

He hadn't meant to say the words. They hung in the air. Gordon Portland stared at him, his eyes carrying a hint of suspicion. Then he looked away, sipped at his drink. 'Isabella came along to the courtroom with me a couple of times. But she was soon bored by it: she takes little or no interest in my art collections. We've been married fifteen years now,' he added almost inconsequentially. 'I met her in Lucca, when I was there on business. We were married within a week. One must seize the moment, don't you agree?'

O'Connor nodded, detecting the hint of possessive pride in the man's voice.

'Anyway, I'm grateful that you could find the time to call out here at Belton Hall. I'm aware the request is a little unusual, but I thought it was essential that I had a word, if only to obtain some reassurance after recent events. You see –'

O'Connor was aware of the lingering hint of the woman's perfume in his nostrils. Distracted, he asked, 'Is she Italian, your wife?'

Portland paused, slightly taken aback, then nodded, his eyes glittering as he stared at O'Connor. But he would be used to men admiring his wife. He leaned across the table to take a cigar out of a silver box, lit it, and drew on it with an air of contentment. 'That's right. Educated in England, but family still in Tuscany. She goes back to see them, from time to time. I give her a certain degree of freedom; a little free rein.' His glance was cool as it rested on O'Connor. 'She needs freedom, a woman like her. Strong-willed; warm-blooded. She finds the cool winds of the north a little too much to bear, at times.'

O'Connor felt a vague unease; Portland's comments were casually uttered and yet there was an underlying tension in his tone, a sense of challenge. O'Connor shook his head, as though to clear it. 'I'm sorry, I interrupted you . . . you were saying . . .'

'The trial, yes . . .' Gordon Portland was silent for a little while, staring at the whisky in his glass, frowning. 'Well, it's simple enough really. The trial raised important concerns for me. I want to know what the future holds for Islwyn Evans.'

'He's been cleared of the charge of dealing in stolen goods,' O'Connor replied.

'That's true. But . . . what's your *view* about him?'

Jack O'Connor leaned back in his chair and watched the man facing him, studiously relaxed, the cigar held in his left hand, the whisky glass in his right. 'Is my view important?' he asked curiously.

'It could be. After all, you were in charge of the man's prosecution. It was your decision to go ahead with the charges.' Portland hesitated, calculating. 'Look, I'd better make myself clear. I'm a self-made man. I've made a considerable success out of my construction projects. The business has prospered: the recent housing booms have made me rich. As a consequence, nowadays I have managers to do most of the business: I can afford to sit back. I was late getting married – too involved with making money. My wife . . . she came to our marriage with little money also. But I give her a good life. I'm comfortable, and sensible enough now to enjoy my life, let my business run itself, relax, indulge my hobbies. But I'm the kind of man who likes to feel a hobby is not just throwing money around: there's a certain thrill in making it pay for itself, if you know what I mean.'

'Not exactly.'

Portland shrugged. 'The construction business has been my life. But it's been a cut-throat, dog-eat-dog operation. Competition has been fierce, though exhilarating at the time. It's meant a lot of scurrying around, wheeling and dealing in the City, supervising hairy-arsed builders, making sure contracts came in on time, you know how it goes. So when I married, it was time to relax, I wanted a hobby that would bring some kind of serenity into my life. My wife is a beautiful woman. I wanted to provide the right kind of backdrop to that beauty. It's why I bought this house. And it's why I started collecting. Since then, it's become different . . . I've developed a certain taste for extending my range of appreciation. Paintings; sculptures; things that have been admired over the centuries, and that I can enjoy in turn. My wife, this house, my collections, they are important to me.'

It was a curious juxtaposition, O'Connor felt. He was speaking of possessions. He wondered whether Isabella Portland might have a view about such an attitude.

'On the other hand,' Portland continued, 'I've always been a man of business and, in addition to the excitement of collecting, I like to trade as well. I sometimes keep an article until the first excitement and pleasure has gone, and then I sell it on.'

Isabella Portland once again came, unbidden, into O'Connor's thoughts. She would surely be one of Gordon Portland's possessions he would be more than reluctant to discard.

'You see what I have here in this room,' Portland said, waving his hand. 'Many of the books are rare, extended runs of nineteenth-century periodicals. I have quite a few first editions.'

O'Connor looked at the books, gleaming behind the glass-fronted shelving. They would be books that would rarely if ever be read: the bindings were magnificent, long runs of Victorian series on art, engineering and mining. The kinds of books that Victorian libraries would have stocked as a matter of course, but which since would have largely disappeared. His attention strayed to the long oak table that dominated the room, the wood dark with age. He noted again the display cases. Portland gestured towards them. 'I've managed to carry out some good deals in the States, and once or twice in Japan,' Portland went on. 'This, for instance, took a good deal of time, trouble and money to develop. And over there I have my recent acquisitions, which I find interesting. Rather different from the other artefacts I hold, such as paintings, sculptures, pottery . . .'

He rose, waving a hand to O'Connor, who put down his whisky glass and followed him. Side by side they looked over the collection in the first display case. It consisted of a group of medieval weapons, stilettos, a rapier with an elaborate hilt, daggers, a horse pistol. 'You can almost trace the history of personal violence in these sixteenth- and seventeenth-century weapons,' Portland mused. 'And in this second case, we can take it up again, in the Victorian age. This is an authentic Colt revolver; I understand this one was called the Ned Buntline Special. Some particularly nasty forms of hunting knife, and other weapons from the days when the American frontier was being extended, and won. Manifest destiny, I believed the politicians called it. Another name for genocide, some say . . .'

Portland was silent for a little while, admiring his collection. Then he sighed. 'But this kind of business – though it's no more than a side issue, a hobby – it can be expensive, and I've locked up a lot of money in it from time to time. But the kind of trade I'm talking about is based on trust. Provenance is important. And if I sell articles on, or buy new items, I need to know they're genuine. The real thing. I have a reputation to uphold. And I don't like being made a fool of by charlatans who pass off fakes as the genuine article.'

O'Connor heard the iron in the man's tone, and believed it.

'That's why I want to know what you feel about Evans.'

'Whether he's legitimate, you mean?' O'Connor asked.

'That's about the size of it,' Portland conceded. 'I'm not into throwing money away. I've bought various items from Evans over the last few years, and this trial, this prosecution has shaken me. I don't mind admitting it. At the trial, you people tried to make out he was shady, dealing in illicit materials, maybe involved in some kind of illegal trading. I need to know if that's true.'

'We brought a prosecution,' O'Connor replied easily, watching Portland with a certain curiosity.

'Yes, but was it just based on this one-off item? Does Evans have a history that I don't know about? That would maybe have come out in court if the trial had continued? To put it bluntly, am I *safe* continuing to deal with him?'

'That's for you to decide, Mr Portland,' O'Connor suggested evasively.

Gordon Portland frowned, drew on his cigar; blue smoke curled about his face, partly obscuring his features. 'I can't make such an important decision unless I know what else you might have on Islwyn Evans. Do you have any other information, of the kind that might lead to pursuing him further? Do you have any leads, any suspicions? Do you intend staying on his case?'

O'Connor hesitated. 'I don't know that I can tell you anything about that.'

Gordon Portland moved back towards his chair. He sipped at his whisky, then sat down. He pursed his lips thoughtfully. 'I've already spoken to the Chief Constable.

And to Mr Cathery. They both gave me clearance to talk to you. They told me you were in charge of the operation. And I was led to believe you could maybe steer me in the right direction. Away from Evans perhaps.' His eyes fixed on O'Connor, standing uneasily in front of him. 'Or maybe you'd be able to give him a clean slate.'

'There are other dealers, Mr Portland,' O'Connor advised in an even tone.

Portland shrugged. 'That's true. But before this whole business blew up, the trial over this damned cauldron, Evans promised . . . well, shall I say he'd been hinting at certain other artefacts that may come into his possession . . . I've had no reason to doubt him in the past, we've done several deals together, but the trouble is, I'm now not certain whether it's *safe* to deal with him. So I'm asking you directly. Is he clean? Have you got anything else on him? The prosecution you brought against him regarding the votive cauldron, is that the last of it all?'

O'Connor frowned. Portland's name had not come up at the trial, but he clearly had attended some of the hearing. 'Had you been thinking of buying that particular item from him, Mr Portland?'

'It hadn't been brought to my attention.' Portland hesitated. 'But if it had been, I would almost certainly have considered it.'

'Would you have just bought it, or would you have consulted an expert first? Someone like Dr MacLean, the man who was called for the defence.'

'Apart from checking the provenance, I usually rely on my own judgement. As for MacLean . . .' Portland's features were unreadable, lacking in expression, but O'Connor sensed turbulence in the man's voice as he went on. 'I have never placed a great deal of trust in experts: as we saw in the Evans trial, with MacLean and Mr Landon, for instance, they can disagree violently with each other. So how is a mere layman to trust them?' The question was rhetorical, but firmly expressed. Portland grimaced. 'It's better to rely on one's own instincts.'

O'Connor nodded thoughtfully. 'Perhaps you're right. Is Evans the main person you've had dealings with in following your . . . hobby?' he asked casually.

'Not the only person. He was recommended to me, not least because of his official position as chairman of the local association of dealers.'

'What about a man called Ron Hamilton? Have you had any dealings with him?'

'Hamilton?' Portland drew slowly on his cigar, inspected the glowing end, frowned, narrowing his eyes against the smoke. He shook his head. 'I can't say I've bought any items from anyone of that name. Why do you ask?'

Jack O'Connor shrugged. 'He does some dealing, but also runs a distribution business. In view of the fact you've sold artefacts from your own collection to the States, I just wondered . . .'

Gordon Portland eyed O'Connor carefully. 'I'm offered items. I make my own judgements about them. But when I decide to sell them on, I leave the organization of the sales – including shipping arrangements – to my agents. It may be that my stuff has been shipped with this Hamilton character. I wouldn't know, offhand. But to return to the main question in issue. I'm not certain whether your . . . silence is to be taken as a warning about dealing further with Islwyn Evans. Or whether it's true that you have no further information to impart . . . and that the prosecution of Evans was all a bad mistake.'

O'Connor finished his whisky and set down the glass. The taste of the malt was strong on his palate. 'We failed to nail Islwyn Evans, so to that extent, maybe the prosecution *was* a mistake. The only thing I can say, Mr Portland, is that there are other dealers out there – and maybe you'd be best advised to deal with them. You weren't bitten over the Avalon cauldron . . .'

'But you think I should remain shy . . .'

O'Connor shrugged diffidently. 'Even if experts give you advice. As you say, experts differ even over fakes. Mr Landon, for instance – he was quite convinced the cauldron was genuine, and stolen from the Avalon site. But since you were never in the market for that piece of goods it hardly matters, does it? At the time we couldn't prove Evans had a hand in the theft, so we proceeded against him for handling. Look, I wish you good luck with your collecting, Mr Portland. But there's nothing more I can give you as far as Islwyn Evans is concerned. It's all down to the matter of your own judgement. And I can't help you on that.'

It was an unsatisfactory reply as far as Gordon Portland was concerned; O'Connor recognized the dissatisfaction in the man's demeanour. 'The Chief Constable –' he began.

'Of course,' O'Connor interrupted smoothly, 'we'll always be more than willing to assist, if you have any anxieties in future. I'm sure the Chief Constable will have given you that assurance. But otherwise, all I can say at the moment is that we're keeping an open mind about Islwyn Evans and his antiquities business.'

Portland had to be satisfied with the answer. It was with a certain truculence that he saw his visitor only as far as the hallway. As O'Connor headed for the main doors Portland began to climb the stairs. The butler emerged almost simultaneously, relying upon the antennae he must have developed over the years. He held the door as O'Connor left.

O'Connor had parked his car to one side of the west wing, on a gravelled area leading down to the stables. As he walked to the car he was surprised to see Isabella Portland coming out of the conservatory to the left. She caught sight of him; he hesitated, standing beside the car door, and she walked towards him, slowly. Her air was casual.

'Your business over already, Mr O'Connor?' she called out.

'That's right.'

She stopped a few yards away. 'What was it all about?'

O'Connor shrugged. 'The Evans trial.'

She smiled distantly, raised a contemptuous eyebrow. 'Ah. Gordon's precious hobby. His obsession . . .' She shook her head. A stray wisp of red-gold hair blew across her face; she touched her red lips, pushing it away. There was boldness in her glance. 'It doesn't give him much time for other things.'

'Such as?'

'Enjoying himself. Looking after those who love him. Appreciating *all* of his possessions.' There was a certain archness in her level glance. A strange silence grew between them. There was an ache in O'Connor's chest, and his hand trembled suddenly. She smiled. 'Well, I'll say goodbye. For the moment. Perhaps we'll meet again.'

She turned, and began to make her way down towards the gardens. O'Connor remained beside the car door, watched her go. She was a beautiful woman, but the kind of woman who could be trouble for a man. As he was about to enter the driving seat of his car he looked back at the house. He caught a movement in one of the windows above the conservatory. It was Gordon Portland. He was staring fixedly towards the garden area where Isabella Portland had just disappeared.

An Italian wife, twenty years younger than he was. O'Connor shook his head. He'd heard that Landon had gone to Italy on a training course. He wondered what sort of women he might come across. He wondered whether any of them would be able to hold a candle to Isabella Portland.

The Course Director was fat, shaggy-haired and dark-moustached. He handed Arnold a glass of red wine and nodded towards the woman with the full, voluptuous figure who was making her way through the chattering group of delegates towards them. 'Carmela Cacciatore. She will be your lecturer this afternoon, and she will also be your personal guide when you do the field work. Face of an angel, *si*?'

Arnold agreed. Like many large women Carmela Cacciatore had features that were finely sculpted; her skin was soft and unlined, her mouth generous, her brown eyes softly sparkling, and her fair hair was carefully groomed. She would never grace the cover of a fashion magazine, however, for her stocky body was broad, her bosom perhaps the largest Arnold had ever seen, and her waist was thick. She had sturdy peasant arms, and no-nonsense legs: he guessed she would have the hands of a woman of the soil.

She came forward to be introduced. Her handshake was strong, the skin, as he had guessed, rough and calloused. It would have come from working with dirt-encrusted artefacts. She stood broadly in front of him, feet planted wide, a matter-of-fact woman who was acclimatized to working in a man's world. He liked her immediately. 'This is Mr Landon,' the Course Director explained. 'And this is Carmela. But everyone calls her DeeDee.'

Arnold raised his eyebrows, not understanding. The Course Director chuckled coarsely. 'It is because of the size of her bra cups.'

Arnold held her glance. He noted the raised eyebrow, the sudden, weary coolness as she awaited his response to what would have been an old male joke at her expense. He smiled. 'I look forward very much to working with you, Carmela,' he said.

Her glance softened and she inclined her head in acknowledgement. 'We will do what we can to make it a pleasure,' she replied, and the Course Director cackled his amusement before he moved off with a rolling gait to circulate among others in the group of delegates who had gathered in Rome at the invitation of the Ministry of Culture.

She watched him go. In an undertone, she murmured, 'There is a rumour that he has only one ball, but I've never been interested enough to find out if that's true.'

Arnold liked her even more.

During the next few days the delegates were treated to a mixture of cultural visits around the city: they visited the deep excavations beneath the Basilica di San Clemente to receive a striated snapshot of two thousand years of the city's activity; inspected the ancient Roman conduit and the Circus of Maxentius to view the *spina* of the chariot course, the staggered starting blocks and the tunnels from which had emerged the *quadrigae*, the four-horse chariots that the crowds cheered vociferously. They were given a whirlwind tour of the tourist Rome: the Spanish Steps, the Trevi Fountain, the Pantheon and the Villa Borghese. A requisitioned bus took them to Lazio and the Etruscan sites at Tarquinia, home of the Tarquin kings who ruled Rome before the creation of the Roman Republic, and Cerveteri, eventually destroyed by the onset of malaria and Saracen invasions. Then, back in Rome, came the object of the whole exercise, a series of lectures on Etruscan art.

Carmela was one of the lecturers. Her English was excellent, her grasp of idiom faultless: she had spent time in the States where she had managed to avoid the worst excesses of their language. In her lectures the delegates were told of the civilization that had prospered for centuries in central Italy until it was wiped out by the Romans. They were given an outline of the Italian law of 1939 which stipulated that anything found in the ground was to be regarded as state property and anyone who removed artefacts illicitly was to be held guilty of theft. They were shown important items in the state museums, and taken step by step through descriptions of bronze and gold artefacts – vases, jugs, bowls, *fibulae*, some of which had been crafted and decorated by the Greeks with whom the Etruscans had strong trading links – and given time to pore over the volumes in the art libraries, burying themselves in the history of the past civilization that had preceded the Romans, and of whose culture and way of life much still remained a mystery.

Arnold was impressed by Carmela's erudition and passion for her work. Her lectures were fascinating because she had clearly buried herself in the past. The Course Director's joke had gone the rounds, and as the week went on more and more of the delegates came to adopt her nickname. She seemed to accept it without rancour, though Arnold noted the occasional weary glance, and a bite of the lip. He remained circumspect in the manner in which he himself addressed her, however, and it was clear she appreciated his reserve.

At his invitation she joined him for a glass of wine in the hotel bar on the Friday evening. He was curious to discover what she might know regarding the artefact that Gamboretti had mentioned in the Chief Executive's boardroom back at Morpeth.

'Ha, the calyx krater,' she said in her accented English. 'We have been trying to trace it for the last three years. It is known that it was looted by *tombaroli* – professional tomb robbers – from an Etruscan tomb on the Veii. We first heard of it emerging in San Marino, before it entered the Western market: it was the time when evidence linking the Cosa Nostra to the illegal trade in antiquities became apparent. It then disappeared into a private collection.' She sipped her wine thoughtfully. 'But this artefact, it is very important, and its value is huge. It is difficult to sell, for those reasons, and when we smashed the Renzo organization the trade became . . . how do you say . . . fragmented.'

'But it has re-emerged?' Arnold prompted.

Carmela nodded emphatically. 'There is a grapevine of information, and many of the *tombaroli* who were threatened with prosecution have . . . turned their coat?' She flashed him a quick smile, triumphant at her control of idiom. 'These people have been able, from time to time, to

give us links, information, trading routes, auction houses
. . . though it is a dangerous business for them, because
revenge can be swift and deadly.'

'From the Cosa Nostra?'

She shrugged expansively. 'The Cosa Nostra, the Sicilian
Mafia . . . We have smashed the Renzo organization, but
there are still family, people who can be dangerous.'

'But you have nevertheless received information.'

Carmela nodded. 'From such men we learned some time
ago that the calyx krater has emerged into the market
again. It is suggested it has gone to England, so your own
appointment is, among other English experts, important.'
She looked at him, frowning earnestly. 'In a sense, the
calyx krater has become of symbolic importance to us at
the Ministry. It is the first step in our campaign of recovery,
a beacon for the establishment of our Ministry's group of
foreign experts. Of which you are one.'

She finished her glass of wine and put her broad hand
on his arm, gently. 'The man you will meet tomorrow, he
is one of those of the *tombaroli* who has chosen to help us.
For money, of course.'

'Where do I meet him?'

As she turned away to head for the door she said over
her shoulder, 'At Veii. Tomorrow you begin the field work.
Tomorrow we visit the city of the dead.'

2

The sun glared down out of a startlingly blue sky. The
platform of the Tiburtina train station in northern Rome
was crowded; as another train approached the station it
seemed to waver on the track, dance and shiver in the heat
haze. Carmela Cacciatore was standing by the coffee stall,
dressed in shirt and trousers and heavy boots, a pack on
her back, arms folded over her ample bosom, a fierce
knitting of her heavy dark eyebrows emphasizing her
impatience. She glanced at her watch, glared at the travel-

lers debouching from the train, her eyes flicking over them, seeking the man she expected.

'No sign of him?' Arnold asked.

She shook her head in annoyance. 'He is already one half-hour late. It will get unbearable in the sun this afternoon. I do not wish to spend too much time at the site when the day is at its most hot.'

'Do we need him as a guide?'

She twisted her mouth and shrugged. 'I know Veii well enough. But it is useful to have Cosimo with us: he is able to tell us much about the *tombaroli* and the methods they used. He has been most valuable to us at the Ministry. How is it you say in English? He was a poacher, now he is . . .?'

'A gamekeeper,' Arnold smiled. 'So Cosimo was once a tomb robber himself?'

Carmela nodded. 'Cosimo is almost fifty years old now. He has spent a lifetime looting the ancient graves of the Etruscans. By his own estimate he has broken into more than five hundred tombs in the thirty years he was active as a robber.'

'Thirty years! A long time,' Arnold exclaimed in surprise.

Carmela raised an eyebrow and shrugged expressively. 'He was never caught in that period, in the old days when it was all highly organized. He began with the *tombaroli* when he was only fifteen years old. He learned the trade from his father, who had learned from *his* father. It was a family business for generations. You have to understand, there was little work available in the villages: the men claim they did it to feed their families. To them it was never a crime; it was a vocation. And all these men, they formed almost a secret brotherhood, and regarded their membership almost as a badge of honour.'

'So how did they begin?' Arnold asked.

Carmela looked along the platform once more, checking for a glimpse of the man they waited for. 'The men joined the individual teams by invitation only: many of the *paesani* – the villagers – were *tombaroli* but they kept to their tight groups. When a leader emerged, they were loyal to him, but only a few had the leadership skills to establish their own teams. Cosimo was very proud of the fact that by the time he was twenty-one he had already set up his own team. He became a successful *capo*.'

'A leader, yes?'

'That is right. He was motivated by money as well as pride, of course. Being a *capo* meant he moved away from just getting a fraction of the profits. As a *capo* he took sixty per cent of the earnings, dividing the rest among his team. On average, he claims, they broke into a tomb every two weeks or so.'

Arnold looked about him at the train station. The crowds were thinning now, the few urchins begging for coins were beginning to disperse, a scattering of tourists under the control of an umbrella-carrying guide were gathering for instruction near the clock. The Etruscan tombs would not be something they would be introduced to. 'What sort of yield would the *tombaroli* expect to get from a tomb?' Arnold asked.

Carmela checked her watch impatiently and clucked her tongue in annoyance. She glanced up at the burning sky. 'Time passes . . . Yield? Maybe thirty vases, an assortment of other artefacts, but according to Cosimo it was often the case that when they broke into a tomb they discovered it was no longer virgin, men had been there before them, and there was little to enrich them. But a virgin tomb, ah, Cosimo told me the team could expect to earn the equivalent of maybe seven thousand euros.'

'It would have been good money in a village society,' Arnold murmured.

Carmela nodded, tapped the face of her watch and announced decisively, 'There is no more train for half an hour. We can wait no longer. We must do without Cosimo. We will visit the field site together, without him.' She

73

gestured towards the station entrance and the car park. 'Come. My car waits there. Cosimo can go to hell.'

As they walked to the car she explained that the Etruscan tomb site at Veii lay only a matter of ten kilometres from the Tiburtina train station. She removed her backpack and slung it on to the rear seat of the car, in a gesture that displayed her continuing annoyance with the absent Cosimo. She took the wheel; in a few moments they rumbled out of the car park. A car horn blared at them as she emerged into the street: she was a somewhat jerky driver, aggressive, and Arnold held his breath while she bullied her way out through the northern suburbs, but they soon found themselves cruising along quiet roads, looping past fields and through gentle valleys. When the road petered out Carmela swung left on to a narrow dirt track and they began to climb, bumping and clattering their way along a track that wound over the brow of a low ridge. Ahead of them Arnold could see a plateau rising up above the low hills. 'Veii,' Carmela said in a low voice.

'So how did Cosimo dispose of the artefacts he looted over the years?' Arnold asked curiously, hanging on to the leather strap above the passenger door as they lurched along the stony track.

'He had inherited certain contacts from his father. Cosimo's responsibilities as a *capo* necessarily included the swift transfer of the artefacts to a middleman. This was common practice: each group had its own contact, whose identity was closely guarded. No doubt they were often dealing with the same man, without knowing this, but even so . . . The middleman was, as Cosimo described him, always an educated person who had the necessary distribution arrangements, working with people higher up in the organization hierarchy, to move the treasures rapidly out of the country. They went to buyers in Switzerland and Austria, Germany, Japan, and . . .' She gave Arnold a sideways glance. 'And England also. From other sources we have been able to identify the routes used by the Renzo organization, for whom Cosimo worked. The artefacts were moved through San Mario, using Cosa Nostra contacts. They were assigned a manufactured history, fake provenance documents were provided, they were kept for a while in a warehouse in the free port of Genoa and then moved on to Switzerland.'

She pulled the car in at the side of the track, parked it under an olive tree and they both got out. She hitched the pack on to her back once more, locked the car and then led the way towards a narrow gully that climbed the steep hill, winding and twisting its way upwards. Scrub grasped at their legs as they climbed, loose stones rolled away under their feet and the sun beat down on the backs of their necks. 'We should have started this climb earlier, before it got too hot,' Arnold grumbled.

'Explain that to Cosimo,' she snapped.

When they reached the top of the hill they paused to rest. Arnold ran a hand across his face, wiping away the perspiration. Carmela raised a hand, pointing towards the plateau just ahead of them. 'The Etruscan city of Veii dominated this plateau three thousand years ago. At the height of its power the city's sphere of influence extended for many kilometres. It has been calculated that the city was home to perhaps one hundred thousand inhabitants.' There was a wicked glint in her eyes as she glanced at Arnold. 'As Cosimo pointed out to me once, that means a lot of dead people.'

'So how did the *tombaroli* find the tombs?' Arnold asked, shading his eyes as he scanned the landscape.

'The Etruscans entombed their dead in *tumoli* – mounds of earth with carved stone bases. They were often laid out in the form of a town, with streets and squares and terraces. Over centuries, of course, they became more deeply buried, under the detritus of time . . . Sometimes it is easy to find them. Cosimo taught me how to identify promising sites. A circular depression, like that one over there, where the earth has subsided into the burial chamber. That is a likely site, possibly still unlooted. The experienced eye can identify other clues: you see that patchy stretch of grass near those olive trees? It grows with less density than the area surrounding it, because the ground underneath conceals a hollow space, and therefore contains less moisture. But you have to remember – generations of these men have spent their lives looting the graves. They built up experience. They probed the earth with metal poles, searching for passageways leading to central chambers where they would find the artefacts they hungered for. The excavations were done during the hours of darkness of course, but Cosimo told me with some pride that he and his teams knew these hills intimately.'

Arnold was visualizing what would have been a silent, sombre procession of men moving through the dark, moon-shadowed hills with their implements, roaming the plateau that they knew concealed thousands of ancient tombs. 'Did the police not try to stop the trade?' he wondered.

Carmela gestured to him to follow her, and began to climb once more towards the plateau. Over her shoulder, she commented, 'You must realize this whole area is like a vast, open-air museum. The remains of our ancestors in this land are scattered over hundreds of kilometres of open countryside: there are hundreds of Etruscan cemeteries, thousands of *tumoli*, many known only to the *tombaroli*. We are talking about a virtual sea of tombs.'

She paused, waved a hand to take in the hills about her. 'Can you imagine the difficulty? The Ministry has little money for excavation and without the constant on-site surveillance that you in your own experience know comes with archaeological field work, it is impossible to restrict the activity of thieves such as the *tombaroli*. What do we do? We place a policeman behind every bush? A member of the *carabinieri* conceals himself in every open field? It is impossible. That is why, seven years ago, the decision was taken at a high level to strike off the heads of the Hydra.'

'How do you mean?' Arnold asked, puzzled.

'The decision was taken within the Ministry to ignore the *tombaroli* themselves; instead, a concerted attempt was made to strangle the trade at its highest level. The organization itself. The big men. And to an extent, we were successful. In this area, the major player was a man I mentioned earlier, called Arturo Renzo. We finally accumulated enough evidence to bring serious charges. It was not just a matter of tomb-robbing and handling these stolen artefacts. There was murder, also: to control the trade they had always used violence. Arturo Renzo is now in jail; he will remain there for another fifteen years. Others were also arrested; several are in prison, like Renzo.'

Arnold nodded, understanding the strategy: if the organizers were imprisoned, the middlemen closed down, the men who haunted these hills would have no outlet for the artefacts they had disinterred. 'Where does Cosimo fit into this?' he asked.

'Ha! You will appreciate that once Renzo and his accomplices were arrested and imprisoned the system based here at Veii began to . . . how you say it . . . creak? It became more difficult for the *tombaroli* and their middlemen. Their incomes collapsed, their way of life was threatened, they became careless, desperate even. They sought new outlets, but did not have appropriate contacts, they took risks, and as is the way of new things, the control over information became less tight. The Ministry of Culture began to obtain a list of informants at the fringes, men who were now poor, with no other source of income, and who were prepared to sell information. We worked closely with the *carabinieri*; we learned of the separate raiding parties, and as the pressure came on, and arrests were made, the tender flowers and shoots of the new smaller operations were cut off, to wither and die.'

'You said Cosimo was a *capo*.'

'That's right. Here at Veii: he has boasted that no one could work on this plateau without his permission. Such positions of power can cause jealousy when sources of income dry up. He continued, in a smaller way, after Renzo was imprisoned. Eventually, three years ago, he was caught. It was somewhat ironic, the situation: he was on the point of leaving the tough business, the hard manual labour of tomb-robbing itself. He had trained his replacement. He was about to step down to become a consultant to the teams that operate on the site. The night he was apprehended, it would have been probably his last night raid. But he was betrayed. His team of raiders was intercepted up here in the hills; in the end, knowing it was all finished for him, he just walked home and the *carabinieri* were waiting there for him.'

'Was he jailed?'

Carmela stopped, hands on broad hips, her large bosom swelling as she breathed deeply, dragging oxygen into her lungs after the strenuous climb. She gestured with her hand towards a slope on the hillside. 'Over here, I will show you, it is one of the tombs that Cosimo himself looted, and of which he is very proud. We use it to explain and demonstrate . . . Jailed?' She smiled cynically. 'You must understand how these things work. While Cosimo boasts of his prowess, and his fame, and his reputation as *capo*, he has remained a relatively poor man.'

'The more hands the artefacts went through, the more the price rose,' Arnold commented. 'It's the way of the world.'

Carmela nodded in agreement. 'While his middleman drove a Mercedes, Cosimo himself drove a Fiat Panda. The artefacts which he might sell for fifty euros, they brought ten and twenty times that price to the middleman. And when they came into the market for the collectors, the prices gained were very high. But Cosimo saw only a fraction of that kind of value.'

'And when he was arrested?'

'When Cosimo was finally caught the threat of a jail sentence made him think hard. Renzo was already in jail. Cosimo knew that the tombs were going to be more difficult to loot: the area is now designated as a nature reserve so rangers patrol here now, as well as the military police, the *carabinieri*. And if Cosimo was to be held in jail, what would happen to his family? He was not a rich man like Renzo. So he was open to persuasion, prepared to enter negotiations with the Ministry. A degree of licence would be offered him, a brief sentence only, on condition that he provided us with information. It was a decision that appealed to him, in spite of the inherent danger.'

'Danger? How do you mean?'

She shrugged, put her hand up to shade her eyes, and pointed to the slope of the hill ahead of them. 'Over there, that's where we are heading . . . Danger? You must remember, though men like Arturo Renzo were serving long jail sentences, there was still *omerta*, the vow of silence, and those who broke the vow could be subjected to the long arm of revenge.' She glanced at him, frowning. 'There were a few killings, some legs were broken, faces scarred, but with the big men in jail it soon died down. There were just too many who were talking; Cosimo was one of them. So he was prepared to take the risk. Eventually, he became one of us. He now works for the Ministry, and has been able to tell us a great deal.'

She hesitated, grimaced. 'There are times when I think he does not tell us all he knows, and I wonder whether from time to time he still has some involvement in the illicit trade. You have a saying, do you not, about leopards and spots? But I have no proof of this. Of course, there will always be a demand for looted artefacts as there will be for drugs. Collectors, they have an addiction, you agree? But there is nothing we can prove, so we still use Cosimo, and he still assists us in our search, now that we at the Ministry have moved away from the phase when we arrested the *tombaroli* and their masters. Now, we focus on the demand end of the market.'

'And try to recover looted items like the calyx krater, when they emerge in the market place,' Arnold offered.

'That is correct.' She stopped, pointing. 'Now, this is the Etruscan tomb that we use to demonstrate to people like yourself, so that you have an understanding, a feel for the situation . . .'

They were standing at an iron-studded wooden door of modern manufacture. 'This door seals the entrance to the ancient opening of the tomb,' Carmela explained.

'How did the *tombaroli* find the burial chamber?' Arnold asked.

'From what Cosimo tells me, some years ago he led the team to what was to turn out to be a virgin site. They had probed at the surface of the hill with their long poles until they had found the entrance. They had chosen not to enter the tomb from the top for fear they might damage the artefacts located within. Also, there had been heavy rain for several days and they feared the tomb might be water-logged, so they had first installed some drains.'

'They knew their business,' Arnold murmured appreciatively.

'They had to wait for twenty-four hours after the draining, to make sure that any pottery inside the tomb dried out, otherwise the artefacts would be too fragile to move,' Carmela explained as she took out a heavy key and unlocked the wooden door. 'We had to put this door in for security, of course, although all artefacts had already been looted by Cosimo and his gang some years ago. But he and I are the only people holding a key at the moment.'

The entrance to the tomb was dank, the air fetid. Carmela took a torch from the pack she carried on her back and flashed a beam of light on to the walls. 'The tomb goes back about six metres into the hillside – a perfect example of the grave of a wealthy Etruscan nobleman. It's high enough for me to stand in – though you might have to lower your head a little. The tomb is empty, of course: all traces of its original inhabitant and the funerary objects that were ritually buried with him have gone. Cosimo was a bit reluctant to explain what he had done with all the items, and would supply us with no list, arguing it was so long ago he had forgotten, but in view of the other information he was giving us we did not press him on the matter. But,' she sighed, 'also gone for ever is the historical information archaeologists like you and I could have extracted.'

The beam of the torch played on the wall just inside the entrance. 'You see that engraving, cut into the wall? It is possible that it spells out the name of the deceased, the man who was buried in this chamber three thousand years ago.'

Arnold was paying no attention. He was staring deep into the cave.

'And you see there,' Carmela continued, 'the painted reliefs of cooking implements, and other household items?'

Something cold seemed to touch the pit of Arnold's stomach. He put a hand on her arm. 'Carmela.'

'It is sad, is it not? What you see here on these walls is all that is left of the people who –'

'*Carmela*,' Arnold said again, firmly.

She turned to look at him. 'What is the matter?'

'Give me the torch.'

She hesitated, then handed it to him as she saw the seriousness of his features. 'What is the matter?' she asked again.

Arnold stepped between her and the depths of the cave. The tomb consisted of a single vaulted chamber cut into the rock and the beam of the torch wavered as he sent it probing into the far end of the tomb. It settled finally on the thing he had glimpsed briefly as Carmela had been attempting to direct his attention to the wall engraving.

It was difficult to make out. It looked like a bundle of old clothes that had been thrown down against the far wall, deep inside the tomb. But cold fingers of anxiety touched Arnold's veins as he lowered his head, and slowly moved forward, his heart thudding in his chest. Behind him Carmela put a hand on his shoulder, peered past him, until she too caught sight of the huddled shape against the far wall.

'What is that?' she hissed in surprise.

'You said the tomb was empty. Everything looted from here years ago.'

'That is so. But what –'

Arnold moved forward, closer to the bundle on the ground. He knew now, as he stepped deeper into the tomb, that it was not a bundle of old clothes. He saw the hand, the arm flung out, fingers curled in a final relaxation. The air was thick, there was a sweetness in his nostrils, an old, familiar smell, an odour that made him gag suddenly, as the realization came to him, and he knew what lay at his feet. Yet almost in spite of himself he crouched, put out a hand, withdrew the tattered piece of shirt that lay across the shoulders. The sharp bile rose in his throat.

'*What is it?*' Carmela asked again, insistent, her voice wavering, scared.

'Go back,' Arnold ordered. 'We must get out, call the police.'

'But I want to see – oh, my God!'

Before he could stop her she had thrust past him, stared down at the corpse that lay huddled against the wall in the depths of the tomb. A gurgling sound came from her throat, involuntary, panicked. 'The *capo*,' she said, in a high, fragile voice.

'What?' Arnold asked, not understanding.

'I recognize him. It is Cosimo!' she cried out.

The sound of her voice echoed eerily around the narrow chamber, and was then followed by a silence that seemed to be almost tangible. Carmela dropped to her knees, put her hands to her face and then gave out a long, wailing sound that keened around the tomb, a sound that mourners would perhaps have made three thousand years ago. But she was not mourning: Arnold knew what caused her to utter the dreadful, shocked sound.

It was the horror of what she had seen there in front of her against the tomb wall. The man they had waited for at the Tiburtina train station had preceded them to the tomb, perhaps days ago. He lay there now with his throat cut. It had been done with the utmost savagery.

Carmela cried out in horror and terror not simply to mourn the man's death, but because Cosimo's head had been almost severed from his body.

3

Karen Stannard swivelled in her chair, giving Arnold a glimpse of her long slim legs. She was frowning slightly, a furrow of concern as she regarded him, one eyebrow raised in suspicious reflection. 'So you were delayed, then.'

Standing in front of her, Arnold nodded. 'It was inevitable. Once the *carabinieri* came on the scene at the Etruscan tomb it descended into chaos. We had to stay there in the baking sun for hours, then we were taken into the city and questioned. Interminably. The fact we were working under the umbrella of the Ministry only seemed to complicate matters. The whole of the delegation was then confined to the city for three days; each of us was questioned in detail, even though it was really only Carmela and I who were centrally involved, if that's the right way to describe it. We were all left with the feeling that we were individually under suspicion, even though none of the delegates, including myself, had ever met the dead man.'

'Cosimo,' she murmured. 'The former tomb robber.'

'That's right. And then, even when the other delegates were released I was still detained, because I'd been present when the body was discovered. So, in between the interrogations, for the next couple of days, all we could do was to spend the time as profitably as we could. My guide Carmela arranged for me to work with her, she took me to the libraries, gave me some books, which I was able to pore over – it was like giving me homework, really,' he suggested, managing a faint smile. 'But it became clear that the conference and training sessions had to be abandoned: the Ministry simply were unable to continue in the circumstances.'

'So do the police have any idea who was behind this killing?' Karen asked.

Arnold shrugged. 'There was no formal discussion of it with us, naturally; the *carabinieri* were not very forthcoming. But Carmela and I had a long talk. You can imagine she was badly shaken by the murder – after all, she knew Cosimo well, and had worked with him for several years after his release from his brief prison sentence. But before I left we had a long chat about it all. She's of the view it was a revenge killing.'

'Revenge for what?' Karen asked in surprise.

Arnold hesitated, thinking back over the conversation. 'The man who was murdered – Cosimo – had worked as a tomb robber for many years for an organization headed by a man called Arturo Renzo, who was finally jailed, some seven years ago. The police and the government cracked down on his organization: it was smashed. It would seem that a number of his lieutenants were also jailed, but inevitably some of the men who owed him loyalty remained free. They went on a vendetta for two years or more: there were some killings, some tongues cut out, legs broken, faces scarred. But the police continued to make arrests, and then eventually it died down.'

'But not completely?'

Arnold shook his head. 'Renzo is still in jail, but Carmela led me to believe there are members of his family still at large. It's been suggested that maybe old scores are still in the way of being settled. Cosimo, he was a *capo* who bought his way to freedom from a jail sentence by inform-ing. It seems he was very helpful to the Ministry of Cul-ture. There's the suggestion that maybe the Renzo organization, or what remains of it, was responsible for carrying out the killing as a reprisal, a reminder that their arm is long and their memories longer.'

'And he was murdered in one of the tombs,' Karen murmured.

'That's what points to Renzo, really, as far as Carmela is concerned. Using that particular site to leave the body was a heavy-handed reminder. The tomb was one that had been looted by Cosimo years ago. She thinks he passed the looted artefacts on through the Renzo organizational network. The tomb itself has been used for demonstra-tion purposes since, by the Ministry. Cosimo was well used to showing it, and was supposed to have shown it to me and Carmela that very day. He didn't turn up, as I've explained . . .'

'Because he had already been murdered.'

'That's right. He had a key to the security door – and that's where he was found, with his throat cut, locked inside the tomb. In Carmela's view it sends out a message, to anyone else who might be thinking of following in Cosimo's footsteps, and helping the Ministry in their war against the looting of ancient artefacts.'

'Did the police confirm any of this?' Karen asked.

Arnold shook his head. 'No, it was merely Carmela's view.' He was aware of a suspicious glint in Karen's eyes as she stared at him. Quickly, he added, 'She was the woman who acted as my field guide. Carmela Cacciatore. It's guesswork on her part, of course, but she was pretty convincing.'

There was a short silence. Karen looked away, her glance drifting towards the window. He was vaguely aware of a certain coiled tension in her body. But her tone was mark-edly casual. 'What is she like, this Carmela Cacciatore?'

The question surprised him, as did the sudden air of

barely veiled hostility in the room. 'She's a remarkable woman,' he replied. 'Educated at Milan and Bologna. She really has a tremendous knowledge of the Etruscan civilization. I admire her. And I like her.'

It seemed the answer was not what Karen Stannard really wanted to hear. 'Are you sure you didn't stay longer in Rome than you need have done?' Karen snapped, a frosty edge to her voice.

Arnold bridled at her tone. 'Of course not. I've already explained it to you. We were told not to leave the city while the police carried out their initial interviews. All the delegates were in the same boat. And unlike some of them I didn't waste the time I was held there, with Carmela's help.'

'I bet,' Karen muttered scornfully.

'She took me down to the archives,' Arnold said, his tone stiffening with resentment. 'We managed to do a hell of a lot of work together.'

Karen Stannard sat forward in her chair, reached out for the papers on her desk and began to riffle through them dismissively. 'That's as may be. But if you ask me this . . . escapade of yours has all been a waste of time. The Chief Executive has been asking what's happened, so I'll make a written report to him. Meanwhile, I suggest you get back to your desk and start dealing with the tasks that have accumulated during your absence on this little jaunt of yours.'

Unable to resist the question, Arnold asked coldly, 'And my . . . *retraining*?'

'The Chief Executive will probably regard the matter as at an end,' she sniffed. 'There's too much work piling up to spend any more time on this nonsense. Let's get you back into harness: Portia has been in it up to her pretty little ears since you left.'

Her tone was dismissive. She waved an elegant, imperious hand. Arnold remained where he was. After a moment she looked up at him, scowling. 'Well?'

'What I've reported isn't the full story,' he insisted doggedly. 'Far from my visit being a waste of time, it's been most productive. There's something else you need to know . . .'

A number of the other delegates had treated their enforced detention in Rome as something of a vacation, spending their time in the bars, or lolling on the sidewalk cafés in the sunshine. The more serious-minded had taken the opportunity to visit the Vatican and the Sistine Chapel, Keats's tomb in the Protestant Cemetery, Nero's Golden House or some of the Seven Churches of Rome. A few couples had paired off and taken part in the nightlife in the Testaccio district, enjoying live music and cheap drink, or strolled in the shade of the parasol pines in the park of Villa Borghese.

Arnold had not entirely turned his face away from such pleasures: Carmela had taken him to lunch at the tiny Grottino del Traslocatore, a seedy subterranean den which produced excellent *cucina romana*, but for most of the last three days during which he had been confined to the city under orders of the *carabinieri*, she had persuaded him that it was an opportunity too good to be missed. She sensed that he had become fascinated by the Etruscan civilization, as she was, and she was unwilling to release him to less esoteric mundane pleasures.

'So you can assist me,' she had argued. 'My work is never-ending, and I have undertaken much cataloguing, but there is yet much to do. So come with me, and feel and touch and hold the treasures that the Ministry possesses.'

As a consequence he had found himself working with her in the dusty atmosphere of the vaults beneath the magnificent floors of the Palazzo Spada. Above them was a well-regarded private collection that shared its space with the meetings of the Italian Council of State. Down below, in the dimly lit, shadowed vaults that retained the uncatalogued materials gathered by the Ministry in its drive against the tomb-robbers, he had laboured with the woman men still jeered at as DeeDee.

They worked there throughout the dusty afternoons, classifying, checking, noting, listing, and Arnold enjoyed the access it gave him to the artefacts of the ancient past, marvelling at the workmanship of the vases and pottery, the brooches, *fibulae*, torcs and buckles and *amphorae* that passed through his fingers. As they worked Carmela kept chattering, providing a flow of information, telling him of the likely provenance of many of the items, explained and translated for him the identifying tags, pointed out on the area maps the tombs from which many had been looted – a fifth-century mosaic piece, a collection of ancient ceramics, a group of funerary urns and pottery – and in the evenings she took him away from the vaults through traffic-choked streets to show him the baroque heart of the city with its natural architectural exhibitionism, its technical audacity, the ceiling frescoes, the antiquities of the carvings above the doorways of the *palazzi*. She invited him to some of her favourite cafés and restaurants in the Piazza Farnese, and the Piazza Campo dei Fiori, where she was welcomed with bear hugs and cries of 'DeeDee!' from fat, exuberant chefs and smooth-haired waiters. And always her enthusiasm bubbled over, her large breasts shuddering with delight as she waved her arms, exclaiming volubly about the cultural experience that was Rome.

But it was late in the afternoon of the third day, in the vaulted rooms deep below the Palazzo Spada, in her absence, that he came across the leather-covered volume on the lower shelf of the catalogue section.

The leather was worn, and water-marked, but when he opened the book, he saw that it was not an ancient volume: it had been published in 1884, a private printing, and it consisted of a compendium, a series of articles on various phases of cultural activity in the previous three thousand years. It contained no photographs but there was a series of line drawings of artefacts that had been discovered from time to time in the hills above the city, and elsewhere in Italy. But there was also a section on other areas in Europe.

Carmela had gone upstairs to get some coffee for them, so he was alone in the cool, dusty vault. He felt a little tired: it had been a long day, and the lights were dim in the archival vaults. Because of his weariness he almost missed the drawing in the European section as he turned over the pages of the volume, flicking through them in a somewhat desultory fashion. Then, after he had turned over several more pages, and was starting to look at a new chapter, something moved turgidly in his brain.

He sat there quietly for a few moments, his fingers splayed on the page, and then he frowned. His heartbeat had quickened; he turned back the pages slowly, with a deliberate care, inspecting each page, almost delaying the moment when he would reach the page he sought.

But there it finally was. He peered at the drawing, held it close to his eyes, checked each line and shading of the precise sketch, and then he sat staring at the Italian description of the object. It meant little to him, but the blood was pumping in his head. He was still sitting there silently, controlling his excitement, when he heard Carmela clattering back down the stairs with the plastic cups of coffee.

He accepted the cup from her and sipped at the hot drink. He had repeatedly told her he took no sugar with his coffee; she had repeatedly ignored the information. He said nothing now, sipping at the cup, trying to calm his nerves. She glanced at him, aware from his silence that something had upset him.

'What is the matter?' she asked. 'Did I forget again?'

He shook his head, and gestured to the book lying on the table in front of him. She leaned forward, inspected it. 'Borromini's *Antiquities*. I am aware of it. Borromini is a reference work, but of little assistance here among the

Etruscan antiquities. There are a few articles but . . .' She paused, eyeing him carefully. 'You have found something here of interest?' she asked quietly . . .

Now, in her office, Karen Stannard stared at him impatiently. 'So? What had you found?'

Arnold ran his tongue over dry lips, the way he had days ago, deep in the archival vaults of the Palazzo Spada. 'It was a line drawing of a Celtic cauldron. According to the supporting text it had been found in Denmark. It has been generally believed to be of Thracian origin. The imagery is eclectic, but Celtic motifs predominate. Borromini's notes suggest it might have been seen as a cauldron of knowledge: it made omniscient those who drank a magic potion from it, heated by the breath of nine maidens, so that in the quest for the lord of the otherworld –'

'Arnold,' Karen interrupted him. 'What the hell are you on about?'

He realized he had been almost babbling in his renewed excitement. He took a deep breath, steadying himself. 'The sketch of the cauldron would suggest that its design is very similar to the one we found at Avalon, which was stolen and –'

'– which was dismissed in the Evans trial as a forgery,' Karen interrupted testily. 'Yes, what about it?'

He hesitated. 'I have to accept that this one had certain differences in design, but that is to be expected, of course, and it displays none of the superior workmanship –'

'I trust this is taking us somewhere, Arnold!' Karen interrupted impatiently. 'I've got work to do.'

He paused, held her glance. 'I was unable to translate the description that accompanied the line drawing, but Carmela translated the text for me. The author stated that the object was made of unalloyed silver.'

'So?' Karen asked, frowning.

'She also pointed out that the author had quoted other

references in the text. Because I was clearly so interested, that evening she took me to the museum library at the Palazzo Barberini. We were able to check the references. They confirmed what the author concluded in Borromini's *Antiquities.*'

'And what was that?' she queried, though there was a glint of understanding in her eyes.

'There were a number of references, articles which any expert in Celtic art should have been aware of. I checked them. They all said the same thing. Celts *had* been known to use unalloyed silver in their artwork and artefacts. There are several examples of such work, noted in the 1880s. So don't you see? One of the main planks of the decision reached by the expert witness in the Evans trial was that the Celtic cauldron found in Evans's showroom was clearly a nineteenth-century forgery because of its construction.'

Karen Stannard regarded him quietly, a slight frown on her face. 'You're saying that Dr MacLean was wrong.'

'He held himself out to be an expert on Celtic artefacts, and he claimed the votive cauldron was forged. But I know now that he cannot have read all the literature. Or if he had, he'd chosen to ignore it. Yes, he was wrong.'

Karen took a deep breath. She shook her head slightly, expressing doubt. 'We all make mistakes from time to time, Arnold.'

He ignored the touch of sympathy in her tone. 'But we don't go into a courtroom and insist on something which is patently untrue. This changes things,' he insisted stubbornly. 'I think I should talk to DCI O'Connor.'

Karen grimaced, and shadows of uncertainty flickered in her green eyes. She drummed her slim fingers on the desk top, considering the matter. 'I'm not sure, Arnold . . . Disputes over detail between archaeologists don't rate highly with the public, and that includes the police. And in view of what happened at the trial, well, I'm not certain about this . . .' She wrinkled her nose, fixed him with a cool glance. 'But if you do go to see him, I'd better come with you.' Her gaze held his levelly. 'I don't want you making a pig's ear of this and dragging the department deeper into the mire. You've damaged our reputation enough already.'

He was forced to restrain the protest that came to his lips. Yet he enjoyed a certain satisfaction as with a degree of reluctance she picked up the phone and placed a call.

DCI Jack O'Connor stood by the window of his office at headquarters in Ponteland. He felt vaguely dissatisfied. At their last conference, ACC Sid Cathery still felt they should be pursuing their enquiries into Islwyn Evans, but as far as O'Connor could see they had come to a dead end. Farnsby was still checking through files on Ron Hamilton's operation and the only thing he had come up with had been the fact that Hamilton had certainly handled shipping for Gordon Portland.

'But that can mean nothing at all,' O'Connor had suggested. 'He's admitted to using agents to handle his sale arrangements. But then, Hamilton has clearly shipped stuff for Evans too, and the paperwork is all in order, so I don't see that we can make anything out of all that.'

'I'll keep digging,' Farnsby had replied, stiff-lipped.

And now their expert witness, Landon, wanted to talk about the Evans case. *Experts.* O'Connor grimaced in contempt: the word had come to have unpleasant connotations for him. He turned from the window as the phone rang. He picked it up.

'We have two visitors in reception, sir. Mr Landon and Miss Stannard.'

So he'd brought his sexy boss with him to hold hands. 'Send them up,' O'Connor grunted.

A short while later there was a tap on the door, and O'Connor's visitors entered. O'Connor smiled faintly and shook hands with Karen Stannard: he had met her several times before and remained impressed by her appearance, if a little over-awed. Unbidden, an image of Isabella Portland flashed into his mind: she too was stunning, but she also had a warmth, a sensuality that appeared natural. Karen Stannard was different: she was a beautiful woman but she was too aware of it, controlled it, maintained a cool professional air. She seemed to feel she should use it as a weapon in a constant war. He had no idea what that war was all about. Maybe just about men.

'Miss Stannard . . . Landon, take a seat.' He perched himself on the edge of the desk, one long leg swinging. 'I gather you want to talk to me about the Evans case.'

Karen Stannard glanced at her companion, then nodded. 'Arnold's just got back from Italy; a retraining course in Rome.' She hesitated. 'He got into a bit of trouble there.'

O'Connor raised an eyebrow. 'Trouble?'

Briefly, Arnold explained the circumstances surrounding the discovery of the dead Cosimo in the Etruscan tomb. O'Connor frowned, and nodded. 'We'd picked up something about it over the wires from Europol, but no names were mentioned, and I didn't know it was you who were involved.'

Landon seemed to squirm in slight protest at the word 'involved'. 'But that's not why I'm here,' he said quickly.

O'Connor nodded. 'I don't really see a connection established between this Etruscan thing and the Evans case. And it's that you say you wanted to see me about.'

'I'm not suggesting there is a connection between Evans and the murder of the Etruscan guide. It's what else I discovered, while the police were insisting I stay on in Rome, while they undertook further investigations. The fact is, Dr MacLean was wrong.'

A short silence descended in the room. O'Connor stared at Landon, puzzled. 'He was wrong. About the identification of the votive cauldron, you mean? You already told me that. You told the court that. But the court believed Dr MacLean. I don't see –'

'No, you don't understand,' Landon urged. 'I can understand how you – and the court – would regard this merely as an academic dispute, a disagreement between practising archaeologists about something of an esoteric nature. But my understanding of the Evans case is that it collapsed on a technicality, really, on the fact that there was a dispute about the provenance of the Celtic cauldron. But don't you see? MacLean was *wrong*, and I can prove it!'

'How?' O'Connor asked curiously.

'When I was in Rome I came across proof, literature on the subject. The Celts certainly did use unalloyed silver. This was known in the 1880s, over a hundred years ago! So MacLean was wrong: he claimed to be an expert, was used by the defence as an expert, but all the time he was talking through his hat!' Landon glared at O'Connor in subdued fury. 'And I can damned well prove it!'

Karen Stannard was sitting rigidly, staring at O'Connor. He gained the impression she was nervous, unwilling to be associated with something she did not entirely agree with, and concerned about what his reaction might be. After a short silence he held up a warning hand. 'Look, Mr Landon, I can appreciate your anger. And I've no doubt you feel you can prove that the defence expert was wrong, to your own satisfaction. But it all still comes down to a disagreement between two men over an artefact that may or may not be a thousand years old.'

'But –' Landon began.

O'Connor forestalled the interruption. 'There's no but about it, Mr Landon. You may well be right about all this, but I don't see what difference it makes to anything.'

'But of course it makes a difference!' Landon protested. 'The prosecution withdrew the case because it was believed I'd made a mistake! But it was MacLean who was wrong! The case need never have been stopped!'

O'Connor shrugged. 'That's water under the bridge. The fact is, the case *was* stopped prematurely. If you're suggesting that it should now be reopened because you believe you can prove that the defence expert was wrong in stating the votive cauldron was a fake, well, then I have to tell you that isn't the way things work. A hell of a lot of money was spent launching that prosecution. The case collapsed. Time, money lost. Evans walked free. Now there's no way that I could persuade the CPS to start the whole thing again, on the basis that you can prove MacLean was wrong on a matter of identification of an antique! I have to be frank – I'm not even persuaded myself!'

'But it's my reputation that's been damaged,' Arnold Landon gritted.

'And you have my sympathy,' O'Connor muttered, a hint of impatience coming into his tone. 'I'll admit there's no question of double jeopardy arising here: Evans wasn't found innocent of the charge of handling stolen goods – he was merely allowed to walk free because the CPS withdrew the prosecution. But believe me, they feel they got their fingers burned, and they're not going to be happy at the idea of sticking their hands in the fire again.' He hesitated, thinking briefly about Sid Cathery's displeasure, and his insistence that they still keep an eye on Evans, do more digging into his background and activities. 'And I have to say that I'm of the same opinion: I'd need a damn sight more to go on, before I made representations to the CPS to reopen the whole bag of worms again.'

'I still think –' Arnold Landon insisted.

'Enough!' Karen Stannard was rising to her feet. 'There's no more to be gained by continuing this discussion. I had my own reservations about coming here, and they've really been confirmed.'

DCI O'Connor stepped away from the desk. 'I'm sorry,' he said. 'No hard feelings, I hope, but I don't think we have enough to go on here with –'

There was a rap on the door. It opened quickly, and DI Farnsby was standing in the doorway. He glanced quickly at O'Connor's visitors, and then fixed his cold eyes upon O'Connor. 'I need a word, sir.'

O'Connor frowned, was about to say something to

Karen Stannard but she raised a hand. 'We won't hold you up further. We're leaving. Thank you for your time.'

She swept out of the room; Arnold Landon followed, frowning resentfully. O'Connor turned back to Farnsby. 'I think I should make it clear that when I have –'

'I didn't think you would want this to wait, sir,' Farnsby interrupted.

O'Connor hesitated, recognizing the tension in the man's voice. 'This had better be urgent.'

'It is. You know we've been continuing our investigation into the activities of Ron Hamilton, the dealer who ships stuff abroad? Well, suddenly it's got a whole lot more serious.'

'Why? What do you mean?'

'The call's just come in. I came straight up here with the news. Ron Hamilton's been found dead in his home.'

O'Connor's eyes widened. 'Circumstances?'

'I don't know too much yet. A scene of crime unit has been sent out there. One of his employees – a guy called Stanley – checked at his house because he didn't turn up at the warehouse yesterday. He gained entry. He had a key, it seems.'

'A key?' O'Connor raised his eyebrows. 'A key? Okay, he went in –'

'Stanley found Ron Hamilton in the sitting room downstairs. There was a lot of blood on the carpet.'

'How did he die?' O'Connor asked.

'Messily,' Farnsby replied. 'From the report in at the moment, it seems his jugular had been slashed. Very professionally, I understand. Just one stroke.' He held O'Connor's gaze. 'But with a throat wound like that, he just pumped his life away all over the floor . . .'

Chapter Three

Arnold knew that it was a matter of personal pride and he tried to fight against the feelings that overwhelmed him, criticizing himself for allowing the issue to gnaw at him constantly. Nevertheless he was unable to contain the continuing sense of resentment: he dealt with the files on his desk, the backlog of work which had built up during his absence in Rome, but he was unable to disperse the gloom that touched the back of his mind. The whole matter of his 'retraining' still annoyed him, even though he was forced to admit that he had actually enjoyed the time spent working with Carmela Cacciatore. Its conclusion had been unpleasant, of course, but he had been fascinated by the information he had acquired under her guidance during that period.

Yet in a sense it was that information that still irritated him. He felt a dark shadow of resentment that he had been made to look a fool; that his skills and experience and expertise had been called into question and held up to ridicule; and that in spite of what the courtroom had believed, he had been right all along.

Consequently, it was with a sense of relief that he finally managed to clear most of the pending files from his desk, complete the necessary committee meeting attendances required of him, and escape into the air of the Northumberland hills. It was time he visited the Avalon site again, not least because of the additional information that jostled inside his head. It was an interesting fact that in spite of the isolation of the Avalon site, it had nevertheless turned up a Celtic artefact similar to others found elsewhere in Europe, particularly in Denmark. It demonstrated the amazing journeys that ancient men had undertaken throughout Europe, and he was interested to learn whether anything more of a similar style and pattern had emerged from the mud of the gully at Avalon Island.

He did not proceed directly to the site: he drove inland towards the Cheviots for a certain distance, partly to make brief calls at two other archaeological investigations that had fallen under his supervision at the department, and partly just to enjoy the clean air of the hills, the salt-tanged breezes that swept in from the distant coastline, and see the buzzards drifting on the thermals above his head, dark predators scanning the heather and the moorland below.

The Romano-British burial pit at Cleator Hill had now been all but cleared, and there were only two students working with the site curator. Arnold spent a half-hour discussing the finds with him, before he returned to his car to drive over the hills to Scarp Moss, the extensive peat bog, high on the slopes of the Cheviot, where some skeletons had been discovered in the sandhole at the fringe of the moss. They had not been alone: a skeleton of a boar had kept them company, along with some stag horns and other animal bones.

The team leader at the site was more than happy to expound his views to Arnold when he arrived. 'Accidental, of course, with sheep and cows ranging for food, slipping into the pits and caught there in the bog, starving and suffocating. And finding human remains also is not surprising – maybe loaded with ale, carrying home their prey, slipping, falling, probably dying before morning . . . They were a peculiar lot, the men who lived on the margins of these ancient commons: buck-stealers, poachers with their traps and snares, living off what they saw as the natural and ready products of the country . . .'

Arnold had heard it all before and was familiar with the theorizing, but he found it impossible to get away from the garrulous team leader before lunchtime. It was another hour before he reached the coast, and made his way towards the headland below which was located the so-called island of Avalon.

Portia Tyrrel was already there: she waved briefly to him as he was parking his car at the end of the causeway, but by the time he had got out of the driving seat she had disappeared into one of the huts where the finds were being cleaned and catalogued. Arnold closed the security gate behind him and walked across to the dig itself. There was no one working there in the gully: he guessed they would be finishing their lunch break. A considerable amount of work had been done since his last visit and he wondered what they had managed to uncover. He glanced around him at the dark blue sea, white-capped, scouring the cliffs endlessly, and he turned, made his way across to the hut Portia had entered.

There were five people in there, three of them lounging around a small trestle table, coffee cups and flasks in front of them. Apart from Portia they were all students from Newcastle University who had been assigned to the site for project work: Portia was chatting to one of them at the far end of the hut, while the other three seemed to be arguing about something.

'Arnold,' Portia greeted him with a smile. 'A flying visit?'

He nodded. 'Just checking to see what progress has been made up here.'

She grimaced, glanced at her hands. 'A lot of scraping about, but nothing much to show for it. I'm of the opinion we've just about come to the end of our time here, as far as discoveries are concerned.'

Her windcheater had been unzipped, and the light sweater she wore underneath was sufficiently baggy to disguise the lines of her body. He had a brief, sudden

99

recollection of a different day, a warm afternoon on the high fells, when he had been close to that body. He thrust it to the back of his mind. Her black hair was windblown now, there were smudges of sandy mud on her cheeks, and her olive skin seemed chilled, but he could see that the young student standing beside her was badly smitten: the admiration shone clearly in his eyes. Arnold gestured past them to the table that took up the rest of the space in the hut. 'Are these the items that have been found since I was here last?'

'Nothing very exciting,' she answered carelessly. She slanted a wicked glance at him. 'But as far as I can make out, no fakes.'

He smarted at the barb, but made no comment. He walked across to the table and began poring over the scattered pieces of pottery, shards, so far unidentified metallic objects, and he began to come to the conclusion that Portia was probably right in her assumption that the Avalon site was very likely now cleared of most of what they might expect to find. As he inspected the objects on the table he began vaguely to be aware of the argument that seemed to be going on among the other three students. Portia was making her way out of the hut, zipping her windcheater; she was followed by her admirer, trotting along behind her like a love-struck poodle. The other students seemed almost unaware of Arnold's presence as their voices rose.

'Well, if you want my opinion, Charlie, you're a bloody fool! If she wants to hang out with a lecher like that bastard MacLean, let her get on with it!'

Arnold glanced over his shoulder, his nerves scratched again by the mention of the name that recurred persistently in his thoughts. Of the three young men, one was grim-faced, staring at the mug clenched in his right hand. The other two were leaning forward with their elbows on the table, almost browbeating him. The fair-haired, grim-faced young man they called Charlie was shaking his head, muttering. 'You don't understand. I hear what you're saying, but she's not like that. He's her bloody tutor, for God's sake, and it's perfectly understandable if she –'

'If she jumps into bed with him whenever he crooks his bloody finger?' the student facing him interrupted scornfully. He ran an irritated hand over his fashionably shaven head 'Aw, come on, Charlie, get real! Everyone knows what MacLean is like! It's common knowledge in the student bar, for God's sake. We've heard it all before: the guy's a stud, or thinks he is! He's been using his position to nail the girls in his classes for years. What do you call it . . . the sensuality of power? The stupid chicks fall for it every time – it's a well-known phenomenon. Look, as a postgrad student I've been at the university for five years now, and I've seen it all happen before. They come up from the country, thinking they're sophisticated, but they're wet behind their ears, and they go into his classes, they get to meet him in private tutorials and seminars, and suddenly they think he's God's gift, they get shagging with him and the next thing you know they think they're in love, and they're convinced they're going to end up as the wife of a don! But before you can click your fingers it's all over, they see some other idiot drooling over his attentions, and they get real!'

'She's not like that,' Charlie insisted stubbornly. 'We came up from Sheffield together. We've been together for two years now. We'll be getting married as soon as we finish at the university. This is all just innocent –'

'Innocent my arse!' The shaven-headed student glanced in desperation at his companion. 'Look, Fred here will tell you the same story. But, hey, if you don't want to see it, that's your problem. I'll tell you what, though, if she gets up the stick, Charlie, don't you go around assuming the brat will be yours! Take my advice and dump the stupid little cow.'

'That sod MacLean needs shooting,' his rubicund companion observed, nodding owlishly in agreement.

101

'Castrating, more like!'

Arnold moved away, past them, towards the door and the pale sunlight glinting on the sea. A bank of clouds had risen in the west, and the breeze had freshened, presaging a storm. He felt irritated again, annoyed, the resentment beginning to seethe in his chest. He had no interest in Dr James MacLean's sexual predilections or his predatory reputation among the students, but the mention of the man's name was enough to set off again the anger and the bitterness at the thought he had been wrongly derided.

Portia was standing near the hut, pointing out something on the causeway to her pet student. As he moved away obediently she turned, saw Arnold, came up to him. 'I say go fetch, and he goes. Why aren't all men like that?' She stared at Arnold, raised an eyebrow. 'You look pretty grim,' she suggested. 'You all right?'

He shrugged. 'The students there, they've been talking about James MacLean.'

'Oh, the gossip shop. Why do these young men talk about nothing but sex? Yes, I gather MacLean is something of a randy bastard. At least a girl a year, but he's got a roving eye outside the university as well, it seems. Not a bad-looking guy, though, I hear.' Arnold made no response. After a few moments Portia sidled up to him, and a mischievous glint came into her eyes. 'It's not that court business still, is it? Is MacLean's evidence in the Evans trial still getting to you?' She paused, eyeing him thoughtfully. 'Hey, Arnold, you ought to do something about that.'

He had already reached that decision. Whatever her motivation for the comment, he knew she was right. He had to do something, if he was to achieve peace of mind.

It was mid-afternoon before he returned to his office in Morpeth. He sat at his desk, and thought hard about what he was going to do. Finally, he picked up the phone, rang the university and asked to be put through to MacLean's department. There was a short delay, and at last a woman's voice answered him crisply. 'Dr MacLean? He's not in his office this afternoon, I'm afraid.'

'I was hoping to make an appointment to see him.'

The woman's tone was peremptory. 'I don't think this week will be a possibility. Quite apart from his usual class commitments, he's involved with a series of public lectures at the Literary and Philosophical Society in Newcastle this week. I would advise, perhaps, that you contact him sometime next week when the pressures on his time will have eased a little.'

'I can get to Newcastle next Tuesday –'

'Dr MacLean is a busy man,' she asserted. She sounded stiff, formal, somewhat protective.

Arnold took a deep breath, subduing his irritation. 'The Lit and Phil? He's speaking there tonight?'

'At seven thirty,' she replied. There was a short pause. 'Is there anything else I can do to help?'

There was nothing. Arnold sat back in his chair. He glanced at his watch. There was a dull ache in his chest. He had no intention of dancing attendance on the elusive academic next week. It was time he had his say with Dr James MacLean.

He left the office at five and drove to Newcastle. He found a parking place in the underground car park at Dean Street, and walked down to the Quayside to pass an hour or so. He took a seat in the Pitcher and Piano and ordered a drink and a salad. At the broad windows he sat gloomily watching the Millennium Bridge opening for the passage of a cruiser, coming in from the North Sea, and caught the gleam of the late sun glittering on the Baltic Centre windows. The salad in front of him was tired and unappetizing; at six forty-five he finished his drink and walked back up to The Side, to make his way up Dog Leap Stairs and along towards the Central Station, still uncertain what he was going to do. When he reached the Victorian building which housed the Literary and Philosophical Society and the Law Society Library he paused, uncertainly. A group of inebriated students came staggering out of the Station Hotel shouting excitedly. Arnold watched them lurch away towards the station portico erected by Dobson, then turned and entered through the doors of the Lit and Phil building, climbed the stairs to the first floor.

The library itself normally closed at five thirty but the building had been left open this evening for those who wished to attend the first of a series of lectures by invited academics from three universities. At the top of the stairs Arnold paused uncertainly. He stared at the tall wooden door where MacLean's name was highlighted for this evening, on a somewhat garish poster advertising the series. As people drifted past him, making their way into the lecture room, he hesitated, still uncertain whether he should go inside to attend the lecture, feeling that the sight of MacLean's lofty confidence would make him even more bitter. Frustration and indecision gnawed at him: it was unlikely he'd be able to speak with MacLean in any case and he decided it was a waste of time to attend the lecture. But as he hesitated, he heard someone speaking behind him, at the foot of the stairs. Their conversation echoed in the hallway, even though they spoke in subdued tones. He turned, looked down into the well of the staircase.

It was MacLean himself, talking to a fair-haired young woman who was gazing up at him with adoration in her eyes. He was saying something to her, his voice dropping confidentially, and she seemed to be about to make some kind of protest but he put his hand on her arm, muttered urgently, and looked about him, as though concerned that he might be observed. His glance turned upwards and he saw Arnold standing there; he turned away and spoke almost angrily to the girl. She frowned, nodded, then turned away, walking back towards the entrance. As MacLean turned his back on her and headed across the foyer towards the stairs leading up to the lecture room

Arnold stepped forward, coming halfway down the stairs to meet him.

'Dr MacLean.'

His way barred on the staircase, James MacLean glared at him, frowning, his handsome mouth set in an angry line, irritation from his previous conversation still affecting him. He stared at Arnold as though he failed to recognize him, then his brow cleared. 'Landon?' he said querulously.

'Could we have a word?' Arnold asked in a cold, measured tone.

MacLean hesitated, glanced back over his shoulder as though he thought it was going to be something to do with the girl he had been speaking to, and then shook his head. 'I'm sorry. I'm due to give a lecture. I don't have time for social conversations.'

'It won't be social,' Arnold snapped.

MacLean narrowed his eyes. He leaned back slightly, looking up at Arnold as though to measure him, weigh up his attitude. 'Then if it's a professional matter, perhaps you could make an appointment to see me at the university.'

'I've tried that,' Arnold said calmly. 'You're a busy man. This won't take more than a few minutes.'

MacLean seemed to be about to push past, but bit his lip in uncertainty, then shrugged. 'Well, what is it you want to talk about?'

'The votive cauldron.'

James MacLean's eyes widened. His lean, handsome features held a startled expression momentarily, and he scratched at his cheek, uncertainty touching his mouth. He had a folder under his arm; he shifted it uncomfortably. 'What?'

'The evidence you gave at the Evans trial, concerning the cauldron. You said it was a Victorian forgery.'

MacLean smiled as though in disbelief, shook his head in a bewilderment that might have been feigned, or was possibly real. 'I don't know what the hell you're on about.

105

That was weeks ago. I haven't got time to go over dead ground like that!'

'You held yourself out to be an expert on the matter,' Arnold ground out, 'and you called my own expertise into question. But what if I told you I can prove the artefact was genuine? What if I told you I could prove that *you* were the one who was wrong?'

Something moved deep in MacLean's eyes. He stood rigidly in front of Arnold, unwilling to proceed with the conversation, and yet making no move to brush past him. A nervous tic beat in his forehead, and his voice harshened, as though his mouth was suddenly dry. 'I don't know what you're talking about.'

'Have you ever heard of Borromini's *Antiquities*? Have you ever taken the *trouble* to read the literature annotated in that book? As an academic so-called expert in Celtic art have you ever really identified artefacts of this kind, made of unalloyed silver? You were wrong, Dr MacLean, badly wrong!'

'I don't need to listen to this, and I have no desire or time to do so!' MacLean blustered. He stepped past Arnold, thrusting him aside. Arnold reacted angrily, grabbing at MacLean's arm. The man stood just above Arnold, the elegant lines of his features contorted. He tried to pull away but Arnold's grip was firm.

'I want you to admit you were wrong,' Arnold insisted. 'If not in public, to me at least.'

MacLean's tone was contemptuous. 'You're crazy!'

'Obsessed with an injustice maybe,' Arnold snapped. 'But what I'd really like to know is, if you're the expert you claim to be, why exactly you claimed the article was a forgery. Was it just a mistake on your part?'

MacLean tugged at the restraining hand.

'Or was it a deliberate falsehood?'

Arnold could not have explained to himself why the words came out the way they did; unbidden, they did not essentially underpin his reasoning. The fact that MacLean might have deliberately lied on the witness stand had not previously occurred to him, but the effect of his question on MacLean was marked. The man's eyes glazed, Arnold became aware of the muscle of his arm twitching suddenly under his grip, and MacLean's fingers tensed, curling into a fist. He bared his teeth, glaring at his tormentor, and seemed to be about to say something when his glance slid past Arnold, and he hesitated.

Arnold felt a light touch on his shoulder. 'Is everything all right, Mr Landon?'

Arnold turned. He recognized the man standing casually just below him on the staircase.

'I think Dr MacLean has a lecture to give,' DCI Jack O'Connor suggested. 'Better let him get on with it.' He smiled. 'Why don't you and I go and get a coffee somewhere?'

Somewhat disgruntled, Arnold settled into the seat near the café window and stared out across the road towards the imposing porticoed entrance to the Central Station. The train from King's Cross had just arrived and travellers surged out through the archway towards the taxi ranks, mingling with others who waited to cross the road and make their way up into the town. After a few minutes O'Connor joined him, sliding a cup of coffee in front of him. 'Feeling a bit better now?' O'Connor asked.

'What do you mean?' Arnold asked suspiciously.

'You looked as if you were on the point of thumping the man.'

'It wasn't like that,' Arnold growled.

O'Connor smiled, relaxing his wolfish features. 'I certainly got the impression you were wanting to get something off your chest with Dr MacLean. I presume it was in connection with the evidence he gave at the Evans trial. The thing you came to see me about.' He paused, eyeing Arnold curiously, the presumption confirmed by Arnold's silence. 'Did you get him to retract?'

Arnold shrugged reluctantly. 'We didn't get to that point, really.' He grimaced, reached for his cup, sipped the hot coffee. 'But, yes, I suppose I did get rid of some of my bitterness. Just facing him, telling him . . . I guess that's enough. I needed to get the resentment out of my system.'

'So you'll take it no further?' O'Connor queried in a quiet tone that held a hint of warning.

Arnold shook his head. 'You've already made it clear to me that the Evans case won't be reopened. I can't imagine I'll get MacLean to admit his . . . error, not publicly. And I know what I know, anyway.' He sighed despondently. 'So I suppose it's time to put it all down to experience, and move on. I've got plenty enough on my plate, apart from worrying about the damage done to my reputation by bloody James MacLean.' He eyed O'Connor thoughtfully. 'But what were you doing there, at the Lit and Phil? I hadn't marked you down as a culture vulture.'

O'Connor was silent for a little while. 'It was accident, really. I've been in Newcastle for a case conference.' He paused. 'You'll have seen the newspapers: the killing of a man called Hamilton?'

'I read about it yesterday.'

O'Connor nodded. 'We need to co-operate with various forces, Newcastle, Teesside, Durham, so we had a briefing . . . Hamilton got around a bit, the kind of business he was in.'

'He had some kind of distribution business, according to the newspaper report I read. Have you found out who killed him yet?' Arnold asked curiously.

O'Connor held his glance levelly. 'We're making progress,' he replied. There was a short silence. Casually, O'Connor asked, 'He did some shipping of antique stuff, paintings, that sort of thing. Did you come across him at all?'

Arnold shook his head.

O'Connor was silent for a little while, watching Arnold

thoughtfully. 'I told you I was in town for a case conference. I was due to be picked up by my driver outside the station, and was waiting there when I saw you walking towards the Lit and Phil. I followed you.'

'Why would you do that?' Arnold asked in surprise.

O'Connor toyed with his spoon for a few moments. Then he shrugged. 'Impulse, I suppose. I don't know . . . it's just a matter of tying up loose ends, something like that. I told you when you came to see me at Ponteland that the Evans case wouldn't be reopened. That's true, as far as it goes. On the other hand, recent developments . . . the Hamilton killing, well, I need to look again at everyone who was involved in the Evans hearing.'

'Why?'

'Because of the kind of business Hamilton was in.' His mind drifted back to the bloodstained scene that had greeted him when he had entered the house owned by the businessman. There was little evidence of a struggle. The guess that the scene of crime unit had come up with was that Hamilton had allowed the killer entry, that he had been seized from behind as he walked into the living room, and been killed quickly. Ron Hamilton had been a slim man, middle-aged, his hair worn long, tipped with blond highlights. He had sported a soft moustache, over a delicate mouth now slack and black with blood. His blue eyes were staring at the ceiling, almost as though he was disbelieving of his fate. He lay on his back, in front of the settee, arms spread wide, and his throat had been cut professionally, in one wide sweep. 'Like a pig in a slaughterhouse,' one of the men had suggested. The blood had pulsed out, spreading, soaking into the carpet. The alarm had been raised by Hamilton's lover: it would seem the dead man had been in a homosexual relationship, and his partner had been concerned when he had not turned up for work, or answered his phone. He had called at the house, used his key to get in, found the body, and made a panicked call to the police. But there was little to suggest

109

the murder had anything to do with Hamilton's homo-sexuality, and his sexual partner was able to provide an alibi for his own movements. Hamilton had been dead for at least twenty-four hours before he was discovered. O'Connor was still waiting for a full report from the pathology laboratory.

'The distribution business, he shipped all sorts of stuff,' O'Connor explained, 'but a considerable part of the arte-facts he shipped consisted of antiques. There's no direct link between him and Islwyn Evans – other than the obvious professional one, because he handled stuff for Evans, as he did for other businesses in the north, from time to time – but there are occasions when one gets a *feeling* about things.'

'How do you mean?' Arnold asked.

O'Connor leaned back in his seat, tapped his spoon against the edge of his cup. 'Let's just say we're not deal-ing with the top of the range, Sotheby's kind of operation here. We're looking at the shady end of the business street, profitable certainly, but maybe a little bit dodgy, where maybe some of the transactions are not quite legitimate, shall we say? As you'll be aware, we've been looking at Evans for some time, and though we couldn't pin him down with the charges of handling the Celtic cauldron, we still feel he needs watching. And now there's Ron Hamilton: he's also raised a few suspicions in the past. He's been under investigation, insurance claims, that sort of thing. And now he's turned up dead.'

'But why would you want to talk to me about this?' Arnold wondered.

O'Connor shrugged. 'I hadn't intended to just yet, but when I caught sight of you going into the Lit and Phil . . . The thing is, you move in circles where ancient artefacts turn up; you know about the stuff that goes into museums. You're involved in the supervision of archaeological digs and I just wondered how much you might know about the dealers, the people who make a living out of buying, selling, collecting . . .' He eyed Arnold speculatively. 'And I hear the Ministry of Culture hauled you off to Rome to enrol you in their international team that's looking at the looting of artefacts from Italy.'

'Hardly a team,' Arnold responded. 'Points of contact, really. And it was supposed to be part of a *retraining* operation, after my performance at the Evans trial. But if you're asking me whether I'm familiar with the scene as far as dealers are concerned . . .' He shook his head doubtfully. 'I can't say I've had much to do with them. I hadn't come across Islwyn Evans before the trial, although I had occasion enough to observe him in the courtroom, and as for this man Hamilton . . .'

'And you say you've never met him?'

Arnold shook his head. 'Never even heard the name before.'

O'Connor hesitated. 'What about private collectors? Have you had much to do with them?'

'I'd recognize a few names, of course. And from time to time people come into the department for advice, but I wouldn't hold myself out as an authority on the antiques scene here in the north-east.'

O'Connor probed for a while longer. They talked about the Evans trial again, in a desultory manner, but it was clear to O'Connor that there was little Arnold Landon could say to assist him. At last both men rose, walked together to the café entrance. O'Connor watched Landon make his way back down towards Dean Street, and then turned, began to retrace his steps towards the station. He glanced at his watch: he had already contacted Farnsby on his mobile phone to arrange for the driver to pick him up. Now he hesitated, glanced back towards the building housing the Literary and Philosophical Society. He thought about the scene he had witnessed: Landon gripping MacLean's arm, the look on the academic's face.

He wondered whether MacLean would ever have had any dealings with Ron Hamilton. On an impulse he

111

decided to call in to listen to what Dr James MacLean might have to say. He hesitated, turned away from the café entrance and began to walk back towards the Lit and Phil building. He flicked on his phone, to call Farnsby again. He barely noticed the car until it slowed, slid in beside the kerb. It was a Jaguar. The driver's window rolled down.

There was a bright smile on Isabella Portland's features. 'DCI O'Connor. I thought I recognized you. Can I give you a lift somewhere?'

2

A week after his confrontation with James MacLean, Arnold left his office and headed for the car park: Carmela Cacciatore was due at Newcastle Airport at two in the afternoon, and Arnold drove down from Morpeth to pick her up. The plane arrived on time: he caught sight of Carmela, wearing an unsuitable low-cut flowered dress, coming through with her luggage trolley and he raised a hand. To his surprise she abandoned the trolley and hurried towards him, coming forward with a wide smile and arms extended. He found himself crushed against her expansive breasts, as she hugged him enthusiastically.

'I am so happy to see you!'

Slightly embarrassed, Arnold persuaded her to release her grip, recovered the trolley, collected his car park ticket and led the way out, as she walked beside him chattering excitedly.

Arnold drove her to her hotel in Alnwick; she registered, and went up with her luggage to her room. Arnold ordered himself a cup of coffee and sat in the lounge while she did some basic unpacking, and changed her clothes after the flight. When she came down to join him he suggested they might as well go immediately to the office in Morpeth so that she could meet Karen Stannard. Carmela was now more soberly dressed in a dark trouser suit. Arnold wondered how Karen would regard her.

'What brings you to the UK anyway? You didn't explain in your e-mail,' Arnold said as they swung out on the A1 towards Morpeth.

She flashed him a radiant, almost coquettish smile. 'To see you again, my friend, of course. But, more seriously, the arrangements have now been made for the Minister to visit again – he arrives in Newcastle in a few days' time – in order that the formalities are completed. You know how these politicians are.'

'Formalities?'

'The arrangements for mutual collaboration over the prevention of looting of artefacts. And the signing of protocols, and what do you say? Capitulations. The signatures for establishing the teams of experts, and the Italian government financing of the arrangements.' She settled comfortably into the passenger seat of his car. 'I managed to get myself invited to join the delegation, so I came early, in order that we might have some time together. I have more examples of artefacts to show you: they have been put on CDs, so that we can look at them together on the computer, and I can offer additional explanations regarding provenance.' She eyed him mischievously. 'You have the technology, I trust?'

'We have the technology,' he smiled.

'Italian?'

'Japanese.'

Karen Stannard did not indulge in her usual power games: Arnold was not left kicking his heels in the outer office when they arrived. He was invited in immediately he brought his guest to the appropriate floor, and Karen uncoiled herself sinuously from her chair, came forward to greet Carmela, extending her hand and smiling warmly. She was wearing a cool white shirt under the dark, elegantly cut jacket of her trouser suit. It was of a markedly better cut than Carmela's, though the contrast might have been due to their relative sizes. She introduced herself, but there was an odd look in her eyes as she took in Carmela's bulk, the broad hips, the heavy breasts, the peasant sturdiness of figure. When she turned to Arnold, she was at her most charming, making it quite clear to the visitor from Italy that she was the head of the department but condescending in the contribution she acknowledged had been made over the years by Arnold. She waved Carmela to a seat and ordered some coffee for them all: the two women spent several minutes chatting inconsequentially, hardly including Arnold in the conversation, Karen asking Carmela what she thought about the Northumberland countryside, and telling her of Karen's own memories of Tuscany and Puglia, Pisa and Siena and Florence.

'So you are much travelled in my country,' Carmela suggested.

Karen smiled deprecatingly. 'On the tourist tracks only, of course.' She flashed a winning smile in Arnold's direction. 'It fell to Arnold to make a professional visit recently: I would have loved to do it myself.'

Her tone sounded sincere, and her glance was warm and friendly. Arnold was taken aback, but when he looked at Carmela he thought he detected a certain amusement in her eyes. 'Sadly, I shall not have much time to enjoy your countryside,' Carmela said. 'And I fear that while I am here I shall have to monopolize Mr Landon's time, as a member of the European-wide team we have established.'

'I'm sure we can spare him to work with you during your stay. How long will you be with us?' Karen asked casually.

'Ten days only.'

'Will you be involved in the formal occasions?'

Carmela nodded. 'The Minister will be arriving in a few days' time; there will be some functions to which I have been invited as part of his delegation. He will be travelling but I will be based here in this area for the period of my stay.'

'Well, I hope that you'll allow Arnold to show you some

of the archaeological sites that are under our control,' Karen offered sweetly.

'Your Avalon site, certainly,' Carmela nodded, her enthusiasm clear, 'since I understand it was there that the Celtic votive cauldron was discovered.'

A faint shadow touched Karen Stannard's green eyes. She glanced at Arnold, raising one elegant eyebrow. 'So you've already been told that story.'

'Some of it, at least. There was a dispute concerning its provenance, I understand. But I would like to visit the site.'

'Tomorrow would be possible,' Arnold suggested.

'Why not?' Karen agreed magnanimously. 'Now tell me more about Rome . . .'

Half an hour later in Arnold's office Carmela took a seat and smiled, folded her arms over her ample bosom, regarding Arnold somewhat quizzically. 'She is a nice lady,' she suggested.

'Nice' was hardly a word he would have used personally to describe Karen, Arnold thought.

Carmela pursed her lips in reflection. 'You are lovers, no?' she asked mischievously.

Taken aback, Arnold shook his head. 'No, of course not.'

'Why do you say, of course not? She is a very beautiful woman.' Carmela cocked her head to one side, staring at Arnold reflectively. 'And possessive.'

'How do you mean?' Arnold asked, puzzled.

Carmela giggled. 'I think she had prepared herself for my appearance. I have entered her territory. She was ready to defend that territory.' Carmela assured him. 'But she is relieved.'

'I don't understand.'

Carmela grinned, spread her hands wide, looked down at herself. 'She was worried, I think, when she was told I was coming. An Italian girl. I am aware of the reputation Italian women have in English eyes. The hot sun, yes?

115

The warm blood. But when she saw me, she was relieved. I do not amount to . . . what do you say . . . serious competition?'

Arnold shook his head. 'I don't think –'

Carmela laughed. 'It is of no consequence. I may be mocked by my colleagues as "DeeDee", but I have a good love life! Indeed, there are men who appreciate my attributes! Many Italian men, they like their women to be . . . how do you say . . . voluptuous? However . . .' She extracted a thin cigarette from her handbag, lit it and regarded him seriously through the blue haze of drifting smoke. 'About the Avalon site. And the votive cauldron. Tell me in more details about the discovery, and about this trial you mentioned.'

They drove north to visit the headland and the Avalon site the next morning. Portia Tyrrel was already there: her oriental eyes widened slightly when Carmela almost lumbered into the hut, but she made no comment and she took over the task of showing Carmela the artefacts that were presently being catalogued and cleaned. She was also able to list the items that had already been removed and were held at the departmental archives in Morpeth. 'It will be some time before we'll be able to hold the planned exhibition, and naturally, we have to ensure historical accuracy in describing the provenance of the items.'

Carmela looked out of the window towards the so-called island. Two students were working there in the trench, behind the protective walls. She nodded slowly. 'It is interesting to consider how wide-flung were the travels of our ancestors. I come here by air in a matter of hours: how long would the men of old have taken to bring their goods to this northern coast from Italy?'

'We assume many of the European relics found in this area would have been traded here by later generations . . . the Romans probably,' Portia suggested.

'That is probably true. An antiquarian trade even then,

116

yes?' Carmela smiled. She glanced at Arnold. 'May we take a look at your island now?'

She nodded to Portia and made her way towards the entrance. Portia was walking in front of Arnold, and her step slowed. As Carmela stepped outside, Portia turned, looked at him archly, ran a hand provocatively down her slim body. 'Didn't know you liked them so big, Arnold.'

Arnold was still irritated when he joined Carmela on the causeway. She glanced at him; he gained the impression that she knew what was bothering him. She smiled. 'You work with too many women, my friend.'

He was inclined to agree.

They spent twenty minutes or so at the site: Carmela hoisted herself over the wall, and dropped down heavily into the trench to look it over with a professional eye. She talked to the students about their work. One of them was the man who had been teased at the hut, on the last occasion that Arnold had visited the site. Charlie . . . that was his name. The young man with woman trouble. In which, Arnold recalled grimly, Dr James MacLean was somehow involved . . .

Arnold walked with Carmela back along the causeway, and together they climbed the slope up to the headland, where they commanded a view of the crumbling cliffs to the north of the site and the ceaseless surge of the sea, foaming white against the dark rocks. Carmela sighed. 'It is so much more wild here,' she said. 'And the sea does not have the deep blue of my own country. But those centuries ago, my people came here . . .'

She was lost in reflection for a little while, and then she sniffed, shrugged, glanced sideways at Arnold. 'I detected a certain . . . atmosphere with Miss Stannard, when the Celtic votive cauldron was mentioned. What was it really all about?'

Arnold had spoken only briefly about the reasons for his being sent to Rome, to become part of the delegation team. Now, he felt sufficiently at ease with Carmela Cacciatore to give her the full story. He explained how he had originally seen the cauldron; how it had not been properly catalogued, and how it had been one of the items that had disappeared when the site had been raided.

'So you have problems similar to those we suffer from at Veii.'

'Not on the same scale, of course,' Arnold admitted. 'But in this instance, even though the robbers were never identified, when the cauldron came to light a year or so later at the premises of an antiques dealer, the police brought a prosecution, and I was asked to . . . assist.'

She eyed him speculatively. 'This was why you were so interested when you saw the drawings in Borromini's *Antiquities*.'

He nodded. 'It confirmed me in my beliefs, and showed me that the man who had disputed the provenance at the Evans trial was wrong.'

'This man you talk of . . .'

'Dr James MacLean. He works at the university in Newcastle.'

'What do you know about him?' Carmela asked curiously.

Arnold shrugged. 'Not a great deal, really. He works in the Department of Archaeology. He was called as an expert witness in the Evans trial. As I told you, he disputed my evidence.' Arnold hesitated, glancing down towards the Avalon site where the student called Charlie was still working. There seemed little point in telling Carmela of the student conversation he had overheard since it had no bearing on professional matters. 'I faced him recently, challenged his findings, but I got nowhere really. He wouldn't discuss it with me.'

Carmela shook her head in doubt. 'I find it strange, a man like that, a respected academic . . . why he would stake his reputation on a statement that was doubtful, to say the least. Unalloyed silver, you say?'

'He also argued from an aesthetic point of view.'

'Which would inevitably be subjective,' she argued.

'It seems he simply believed he was right and I was wrong.'

'Perhaps . . .' She nodded, and was silent for a little while. At last, she asked, 'And what is this about the murder of a man called Hamilton?'

'I know nothing about it,' Arnold replied, somewhat surprised, 'except what I've read in the newspapers, and heard on television. Where did you hear of it?'

'As you did. From the newspapers. His throat was cut, I understand.'

Arnold glanced sideways at her. A light offshore breeze lifted her hair, blew tendrils across her face. Her skin was perfect, unblemished, her eyes fixed on the waves below them. 'I've come across no details apart from that. The police seem to have made no announcements, regarding suspects or motive.'

'Cosimo's throat also was cut,' she murmured, almost to herself. 'You will remember.'

Arnold remembered.

She shuddered slightly at the memory. 'He was not a bad man, Cosimo. The fact that what he was doing was illegal, well, it did not seem that way to him. One must remember he had spent all his adult life in this activity; the way the villagers looked at things, it had always been done this way and always would be so. I got to know him, over the last few years. Cosimo. And his family.'

She fell silent. Arnold waited.

'I did not tell you before, but some days after we found him in the tomb, I went to see his widow,' she continued quietly, after a little while. 'We talked for a long time. She will move away from the village now, to live with a brother in Naples. She wants to break free from the past.'

'You gave me your views, but have the police been able to discover what really happened?' Arnold asked.

There was a short silence. Carmela grimaced. 'I went

back to the police eventually, after I had spoken with Cosimo's widow. What I had to tell them, from what she told me, it confirmed what they were already working on, it seems.'

'Confirmation of what?'

She turned her head to look at him: her eyes were serious, and troubled. 'It all certainly comes back to Arturo Renzo.'

The man who had run the international network, organized the illegal looting, and who had been jailed seven years earlier. 'You told me there had been some revenge killings, but they had died out.'

She nodded. 'That is true. But it seems they are beginning again.'

'Why?' Arnold asked, puzzled. 'If Renzo is still in jail, and those who have betrayed him have been eliminated, why was Cosimo killed?'

'The police believe they know who is behind it. As for the reason, it was Cosimo's widow who supplied me with the answer. It is what you would call private enterprise.'

'How do you mean?'

Carmela wrinkled her nose and shook her head sadly. 'When Renzo was jailed, and the organization collapsed, the looting ended for a while. The *tombaroli* had no outlet for their loot, no system to follow, no contacts by which they could sell what they found. But, as is the way of the world, where there is a vacuum it will soon be filled. In the case of Cosimo, it seems he was approached by men who were able to arrange shipment, purchase and distribution of his loot. He would not be able to get the same kind of prices, but he felt he had little choice. Either his trade collapsed, like the organization, or he began to trade with new men.'

'You mean he established another network?'

'He was a *capo*; he held the fates of men of his village in his hands. It is understandable, his attitude. He had responsibilities, to his family, to the villagers he led. Yes, he met others, made arrangements, established a small net-work of his own. Renzo was in jail; Cosimo had to live. That was how he saw it.' She paused, thoughtfully. 'Of course, that is not how Renzo himself would look upon it. He would see it as a betrayal.'

'Is this why Cosimo died?' Arnold asked. 'Because he had set up his own network?'

'I talked to the *carabinieri*. It is what they believe. Renzo is still in jail, but in the intervening years since his capture, his family, his nephews, slowly and carefully, they have been able to reconstruct some of his network. The police are watching them . . . and they believe that the family is now trying to re-establish the old organization. But in the meanwhile . . .'

'They've been facing competition from men like Cosimo.' Arnold paused, thinking. 'But you told me that after his original arrest Cosimo obtained a light sentence because of his co-operation. He was now actually working with the Ministry. You worked with him yourself.'

Carmela shook her head. 'That is so . . . but I had my suspicions from time to time. There were occasions when I wondered whether he had returned to his old ways, or had even ever relinquished them . . . However, there was nothing I could quite put my finger on. Now, Cosimo's widow confirmed to me, in her grief. She had tried to talk Cosimo out of it. But old habits die hard. Yes, even though he was working with the Ministry, he was at the same time following the old ways. He was still undertaking night raids.'

'Running with hare and hounds,' Arnold murmured. When he caught sight of her puzzled expression, he added, 'It's just an expression we have. So Cosimo was still rob-bing tombs, and had set up his own network?'

'This is what Cosimo's widow told me, and I told the police. This is why I think he was killed. The Renzo family is back in business; men like Cosimo need to be taught a lesson; need to be eliminated from the competition. And others need to be shown that setting up their own systems will not be tolerated. Cosimo was murdered because of his activity outside the system; and the location of his body was a warning to all who would wish to follow what he had been doing.' She turned her gaze away from the sea, to glance at Arnold. 'The widow, she told me that Cosimo had been working with an Englishman. The artefacts he had been looting, they were brought into England for distribution.'

'Not by way of the previous routes via Switzerland?' Arnold queried.

Carmela shook her head, brushed a stray tendril of blonde hair out of her eyes. 'No. Cosimo was linked to an Englishman who bought his artefacts, brought them direct into England. After that, who knows what happened to them? The United States maybe, or Japan.' She hesitated, her glance fixed on Arnold. 'You remember we talked about the calyx krater. It is an important piece, and it is believed to be here in England. It was originally looted by Cosimo.'

'I didn't realize that,' Arnold said soberly.

'And this man Hamilton. His throat was cut, like Cosimo, no?'

'I believe so,' Arnold replied, frowning.

'And he was involved in the antiques business?'

'I believe he ran a distribution business,' Arnold admitted, nodding. 'But are you suggesting . . .?'

'Who knows?' She turned away from him again, staring out to sea. 'But it is a possibility, is it not? That Cosimo had made arrangements with this man Hamilton? There is much at stake for the Renzo family. They wish to destroy the competition. And if the deaths of Cosimo and Hamilton are in reality linked, perhaps there are others who might be at risk. Do you not agree?'

* * *

Over the next few days Arnold worked with Carmela at his office, using the computer to look at the artefacts that had been photographed and catalogued electronically. From time to time Karen looked in on them, joined them for lunch at a local pub one day, and generally seemed to be on her best behaviour, although on each occasion that she joined them Arnold caught the same quizzical look in Carmela's eyes. He also gained the impression that Carmela went out of her way to display a certain overt affection towards him whenever Karen was present, as though she was seeking to tease Arnold's head of department. Arnold doubted whether it would have any effect: Karen Stannard was a beautiful, confident woman who drew all eyes in a room, and he was certain that their own relationship was nothing other than professional, whatever Carmela might believe. Certainly there had been occasions when a sexual tension had been generated between them, and one occasion when events had pushed them together, but almost by mutual consent Arnold and Karen had put the issue behind them. Carmela was not to know that, and seemed bent on teasing them into a closer relationship.

In the evenings, Arnold returned the hospitality that Carmela had shown him in Rome: he took her to dinner in Newcastle, down near the Quayside, and in the rolling Northumberland countryside at an award-winning pub. She enjoyed the experiences, and when mentioning it to Karen she rolled her eyes, and announced, '*Romantica!*'

Karen raised a cool, elegant eyebrow and made no comment.

But at the back of Arnold's mind a shadow remained. He found himself thinking about the death of the antiques shipping agent, Ron Hamilton: the newspapers seemed to be carrying no breaking news on the police investigation. And mingled with this were the comments that Carmela had made at the Avalon site – it left him wondering whether there was any real possibility of a connection between Cosimo and Hamilton. And then there was the Evans trial, and James MacLean. The university don had been called merely as an expert witness at the trial, but Arnold recalled his reaction when confronted on the Literary and Philosophical building stairs: the hazy question continued to shimmer in his mind. Had MacLean deliberately denied the provenance of the cauldron? What reason might he have for lying, and insisting the votive cauldron was nothing more than a Victorian fake?

And then there was Islwyn Evans himself. On one of the visits to Newcastle, to view some objects in the museum, on impulse Arnold decided to take Carmela along to one of the antiques premises from which Islwyn Evans traded. When they arrived at the shop front, it was to find that the building was locked. There were various pieces of highly priced Georgian furniture on display in the front window, but Arnold noticed that a litter of letters and local advertising materials were lying inside the front door. It would seem that no one had been in the shop for some days.

Arnold thought about the matter back in his office the next day. He got hold of a copy of the telephone directory yellow pages, and checked on the phone numbers listed for Islwyn Evans. The business operated from Newcastle, Kendal and Alnwick. He tried each of the numbers but received no reply, except for the premises in Kendal. The girl at the other end of the line seemed irritated.

'I'm afraid we're closed at the moment. The proprietor is away on holiday. No, I can't say when he'll be back. It should be next week, but I really can't say for certain. Perhaps you wouldn't mind calling back next Monday or Tuesday . . .' There was a hint of frustration in her tone.

Arnold caught Carmela Cacciatore watching him. As he replaced the telephone he wondered whether DCI Jack O'Connor would have been considering making contact with the man who might possibly have had dealings with the murdered Ron Hamilton.

124

Assistant Chief Constable Sid Cathery thundered into the room like an angry bullock looking for trouble. His brow was dark and both O'Connor and DI Farnsby knew that the discussion was not going to be a pleasant one. Cathery settled his bulk behind his desk and glared at the silent men in front of him. 'So,' he snarled, 'is there any particular reason why not a single sheet of paper has passed across my desk by way of a report?'

Jack O'Connor stiffened, aware of Farnsby's head turning in his direction, as though shifting responsibility. 'Regarding what, sir?' he queried.

'The bloody Hamilton killing, that's what!' Cathery almost shouted. 'Why the hell else do you think I called you in here? The Chief Constable's been on my bloody back; the newspapers are calling us incompetent clods; and I've got nothing in my in-tray that gives me any sort of answers!'

'I wasn't aware, sir, that we were required to keep you up to date with the day-to-day conduct of the investigation,' O'Connor commented quietly. 'Operational procedures –'

'Sod operational procedures!' Cathery's eyes bulged; with an effort he kept his simmering temper under control. 'Well, let me put it like this, DCI O'Connor. Maybe you weren't aware of my requirements, but like I said, I've been put under a hell of a lot of pressure just recently, and I'm not carrying cans for other people! Maybe you weren't aware, but you'd better be clear as of now! When I had to clatter someone in my rugby days I clattered him, and I expected the team around me to do the same. Take responsibility! Do the job! As far as I can make out, you two have been sitting on your arses, inspecting your bloody thumbs, filing your flaming nails, hoping something will turn up, and not getting out and about earning your corn. You, Farnsby – where the hell do we stand on any further information on that bastard Evans?'

'I wasn't aware that now had a high priority, sir,' Farnsby objected.

'What's all this *awareness* bullshit?' Cathery exploded, his face crimson. 'Are the papers right, and you really are a bunch of incompetents? Has it not crossed your mind that this character Hamilton was in the antiques business, and there might be a connection with that slimy Welsh bastard Evans? Are you going to tell me you haven't been chasing that up?'

Farnsby leaned forward to make an angry response, but O'Connor forestalled him. 'I think that's unfair, sir. Of course there's an ongoing investigation into Islwyn Evans, but the case against him collapsed as you well know, and when Ron Hamilton was murdered resources were pulled off the Evans investigation to concentrate on the rather more serious situation. Murder takes priority over fraud, and handling stolen goods.'

'Are you trying to teach your granny to suck eggs?' Cathery sneered. 'Don't give me that rubbish! Any copper worth his salt would be looking at all angles in a situation like this.'

'I think we're doing just that,' O'Connor countered, an edge creeping into his tone.

Cathery took a deep breath, and was silent for a few moments. He leaned back in his chair, his eyes glittering, a dissatisfied curl to his lip. O'Connor wondered just what drove the ACC, and he wondered again how much of Cathery's bluster was simulated, a deliberate goading to raise men's ire. 'All right, DCI,' Cathery muttered, sarcasm staining his tone. 'Why don't you tell me just what you *have* been doing since that bloody corpse was added to our list?'

'In the first instance, we've been waiting for the full forensic report,' O'Connor replied after a short silence. 'It's now in.'

'And it shows?'

'Essentially that it was a clearly professional job. One

quick, slicing slash, severing the jugular. Hamilton was taken from behind, and bled to death in a remarkably short period. The knife was wielded by a right-handed man – or woman, of course – and forensic suggest there is some evidence to show that Hamilton was grabbed by the arm, swung around, and the knife came in with one swift slicing. It would have been over in seconds.'

'Did this guy break in?'

O'Connor shook his head. 'We think not. There were no signs of forced entry. It would seem that Hamilton let the killer into the house; the visit was probably a short one – there's no sign that they maybe sat down, had a drink, probably nothing other than a brief conversation. The killer came in – sorry, was *allowed* in – did what he'd come for, and quietly let himself out.'

Cathery's eyes narrowed. 'So it could have been some-one he knew. You said man, or woman?'

'I was just being careful,' O'Connor replied grudgingly. 'Hamilton ran a male establishment; he lived alone but he had a lover – the man who discovered the body. Nothing feminine in the place, and no traces that would suggest the killer could have been a woman.'

'So why even consider that it might have been?' Cathery queried contemptuously.

O'Connor eyed him coolly. 'As I said. I was just covering all possibilities. For your report, sir.'

Cathery grunted, ignoring the edge to the comment. 'All right. That's forensics. What about this poofter friend of Hamilton's?'

'He had a key to the house. He let himself in, found the body, phoned the police immediately. He was in quite a state. But his alibi stands up. We can't link him to the killing. For the time being, he's discounted. Consequently, we've been following what other leads are currently avail-able to us.' He glanced at Farnsby.

DCI Farnsby was sitting in a very upright position in his chair, almost to attention. O'Connor found him a difficult man to deal with: he carried a chip on his shoulder that he made no attempt to dislodge. He had seemed to be heading for a swift, almost meteoric rise in the force under the previous Chief Constable's regime: the collapse of that regime under the disgrace of the Chief Constable and his consequent retirement had somewhat stalled Farnsby's career, not least with Jack O'Connor coming in from outside, above Farnsby's head. The detective inspector now wet his lips with a nervous tongue. 'We've been liaising with the insurance people, sir.'

'To what end?' Cathery barked. 'We don't want this investigation clogged up by outsiders!'

'You'll recall, sir,' Farnsby countered stiffly, 'that Hamilton had been under investigation because of a possible insurance scam, the firing of his warehouse some time ago. We'd already been talking with the insurers: with Hamilton ending up dead, it seemed sensible to get hold of all the information they might have regarding Hamilton. His business, his associates –'

'All right,' Cathery conceded grudgingly. 'And what have you come up with?'

'We've got details of all his contacts, as far as they appear in his books. The contracts he's fulfilled, those he was committed to, we have lists of all the shipping and distribution arrangements he's been carrying out. So far, we've found nothing of great significance. Many of the deals are with clearly reputable agencies overseas. The stuff he's been doing, the people he's been dealing with here in this country, well, we're still following up on these and maybe one or two of the firms concerned have a somewhat dodgy reputation –'

'Was Evans one of them?'

Farnsby nodded. 'Hamilton undertook shipping of artefacts for Evans. But so he did for most of the dealers in the north-east. There's nothing we can pin down, in particular. But the investigation is ongoing.' He flashed a quick glance in O'Connor's direction. 'It's what I've been concentrating upon. So to that extent, in spite of what you've assumed, sir, the Evans enquiry is still being pursued, albeit with a somewhat different slant.'

Sid Cathery grimaced, ran a thick, pudgy finger against the iron of his mouth. His glance slipped back to O'Connor. 'And you?'

O'Connor shrugged. 'We're still ploughing through an interviewing process. We've concentrated of course on all his personal friends – but have just drawn a blank as far as the investigation is concerned. We've trawled the known haunts, the gay bars, that sort of thing. And we've talked to most of the people he's done business with. The insurance people have been helpful in that respect. We're still working at it, sir, but you'll be aware this is a hard slog, it takes time, all these interviews to process, links to establish, documentation to plough through . . .'

Cathery raised a hand, silencing him. 'So, when we come down to it, we've got bugger all, other than a forensic report that gives us nothing other than suggesting a professional job, no motives, no suspects –'

'It's early days, yet –'

'Early days, my arse!' Cathery thundered. 'You know as well as I do, if we don't catch these bastards early, if an investigation drags on, every day that goes past makes it more difficult to get a conviction!' He glowered at them, but again O'Connor suspected there was something artificial about Cathery's attitude. It was almost a performance; there was a glint of triumphant satisfaction in the man's eyes even as he baited the two men facing him. Next moment, his suspicion was confirmed. 'So it's just as well you bloody incompetents have got someone like me to give you a kick up the stairs.'

In the strained silence that followed Cathery leaned back in his chair, folding his muscular arms over his broad chest. O'Connor waited. He was more than ever convinced that Cathery had been playing them along for his own malicious satisfaction. He had something to tell them.

'You're aware that we've got another visit here in the north-east, from the Ministry of Culture. The Italian delegation.'

O'Connor glanced at Farnsby; he nodded, frowning slightly. 'I'd heard the Minister himself was coming again. We've had to detail some officers –'

'A guy attached to the delegation came to see me this morning,' Cathery interrupted. 'We had quite a long chat. It was very illuminating. And then he gave me a contact to follow through on: I did that. A senior officer in the Italian *carabinieri*. And he, in his turn, put me on to another contact. A guy in Europol.'

The European-wide police information service. O'Connor wondered what was coming as he saw the self-satisfied smirk on Sid Cathery's features. 'It's been all the talk in the Ministry delegation, of course. They seem to know a damn sight more than we do about the whole thing. While you've been faffing around following non-existent leads, what we really should have been looking at has been right under our noses all the time. All we had to do was pick up a phone. And it had to be me to do it.'

O'Connor frowned. 'What's happened, sir?'

Cathery unfolded his arms, leaned forward on his desk and fixed O'Connor with a contemptuous glare. 'What's happened? We've got a new tree to bark up, that's what happened! A tree called Renzo.'

Farnsby shifted uneasily in his chair. 'We've not come across that name in the list of Hamilton contacts.'

'You wouldn't have done, son,' Cathery sneered. 'They weren't exactly the best of friends.'

'Who is this Renzo?' O'Connor asked quietly.

Cathery grinned mirthlessly. 'Big news in Europe, apparently. Especially in Italy. It seems Arturo Renzo was the head of an international smuggling ring that was supposedly smashed seven or eight years ago. They dealt with looted artefacts: that's how the Ministry of Culture hawks got involved, and that's why there's all this hoo-hah at the moment, setting up these bloody protocols, collaborations, all that stuff.'

'If the smuggling ring was destroyed, why is there some sort of excitement now?' O'Connor asked.

'Because the looting has still gone on, even though the distribution system collapsed. And more important, during this last seven years – while Arturo Renzo has been in jail – there's been a slowly increasing attempt to re-establish the system. Renzo might be inside, rotting in some Italian prison, but he's got family who apparently are in the business of setting it all up again.'

'That might explain why the Ministry wants to set up these collaborative teams,' O'Connor conceded, 'but what does it have to do with –'

'With Hamilton?' Cathery's grin was smug. 'Maybe nothing; maybe everything. What I've learned from Europol and the Italian *carabinieri* would suggest that it's likely to be linked to the recent killing of a man called Cosimo, just outside Rome. He was a tomb robber – supposedly reformed – but his killing sparked off an investigation that pointed to two nephews of Arturo Renzo. While their uncle is inside, they've been working to set up the network again, but that meant eliminating the opposition, the competition that had been building up while Renzo himself had been incarcerated. You'll no doubt get some of the details from an acquaintance of yours. Arnold Landon.'

'Landon? What's he got to do with this?'

'That's for you to find out, hey? On the face of it, not a lot – if you discount the fact that he was present when the Cosimo corpse was discovered.'

'He was in Rome as part of a delegation . . .' O'Connor considered.

'That's as may be,' Cathery interrupted impatiently. 'But it seems the killing of Cosimo was perpetrated because the Renzo nephews wanted to deal with competition, as I said – competition arising out of Cosimo's trading with some-one in England. There's been other leads of course, other

131

competitors who've been dealt with, but we're concerned only with the English end.'

O'Connor grimaced thoughtfully. 'Other competitors . . . You're tying Hamilton into a network?'

Cathery grunted non-committally. 'Network, pattern, call it what you will. What Europol are saying is that there's a real possibility that the Hamilton killing can be linked to a series of events in Italy.'

There was a short silence. Farnsby cleared his throat nervously. 'I'm still not clear. If the *carabinieri* know about the Renzo nephews, why are they still at large?'

'They're not,' Cathery responded bluntly. 'They've been arrested, on suspicion of involvement with two other killings, one in Florence, one in Padua.'

'When?'

'Six weeks ago.'

'But Hamilton –'

'Died since then.' Cathery fixed O'Connor with a cold triumphant glance. 'Of a knife wound. His throat sliced open. Just like Cosimo and the others.'

'Yes, but –'

'The mark of a professional hitman. One who specializes in the knife. One who takes a professional pride in his work. A man who's already been paid to undertake his assassinations, and will keep to his contract no matter what happens to his patrons. A matter of pride. The worst kind, don't you agree?'

There was a short silence as O'Connor digested the implications. At last he looked up. 'You have more information.'

'The murders in Florence and Padua bear the same modus operandi. Europol think they've identified the killer,' Cathery nodded emphatically. 'They think he was the guy who might have knifed Hamilton. And they've warned me that there might be more killings to come.' There was a grim satisfaction in his voice. 'The suspicion is that Ron Hamilton was one of the people who had set up deals with Cosimo. The tomb robber provided the arte-facts; Hamilton arranged the shipment. Now Cosimo is dead. And so is Hamilton. Both died under the knife. As did men in Padua and Florence.'

'And you're suggesting that Europol believe that Hamilton wouldn't have been alone, in dealing with Cosimo,' O'Connor said slowly.

'Damn right. He was probably only one of a group.' Cathery glowered at the two men facing him. 'So you two have a problem. If Europol and the *carabinieri* are right, Hamilton was offed by a contract killer. And he's in England with a mission. So you got to identify just who was working with this Hamilton character. You need to get to them before it's too late. Get to them, or get to the hired killer who's still intent on completing his bloody contract, come hell or high water.' He paused. 'His name is Rakoff. Europol are convinced he's in this country. So you'd better start checking airport and sea entries. If he is here, he'll be after anyone who was connected with the network set up by Cosimo. Hamilton was the first. You better concentrate on finding the others.'

'And if Hamilton wasn't murdered by this man Rakoff?' Farnsby asked.

Cathery scowled. 'From all I hear, he's our best bet, our front runner.' He stood up, headed for the door. 'I'm getting one of the clerks to prepare the dossier that Europol have sent over the wires. O'Connor, you'll get it on your desk shortly. Maybe it'll help you buggers to sort yourselves out, refocus yourselves, stop blundering about to no effect.' He grinned in malicious triumph, shook his head contemptuously. 'I'm pulling your irons out of the bloody fire. Get working on this Rakoff character. And find out whether Hamilton had partners in crime. But it all makes me wonder: just what the hell you idiots would do without me to kick your arses, I fail to comprehend!'

An hour later O'Connor sat staring at the dossier in front

of him. It had made interesting reading. There was a tap on the door. He looked up, motioned to DI Farnsby to enter. He waved him to a seat.

'I've had a quick look again at the files from the insurance company and Hamilton's own business documentation,' Farnsby said. 'I've trawled through the lists, checking on individual names, and also on the kinds of materials and artefacts that Hamilton was dealing in, on behalf of clients. I've run a quick computer check, trying to match up the two. I've come up with a list of names.' He eyed the dossier in front of O'Connor. 'Is that the stuff on Rakoff?'

O'Connor nodded. 'Constantine Rakoff. Lithuanian by birth; spent his formative years in Latvia, earned his criminal spurs in Chechnya. A man who kept moving around, probably for good reason. He spent five years in a German prison: convicted of attempted murder, robbery. But he was then only twenty-two years of age. After that he seems to have dropped out of sight for a while: the dossier seems to suggest he had begun to work for an assassination bureau operating out of Poland. From that he graduated into special assignments. He became a loner. His prices went up. Europol believe he was responsible for the elimination of that property tycoon whose corpse was found on a yacht on the Italian Riviera; then there was the ambassador in Austria; they think he also knifed a French politician in Nice. They're convinced he has close Mafia connections, but works almost exclusively as a freelance. He's not exclusive regarding the weapons he uses, but he prefers the knife.'

O'Connor sighed. He extracted a crisp copy of a photograph from the dossier and passed it across to Farnsby. 'This is a mug shot they've provided of him. The *carabinieri* arrested the Renzo nephews and one of them at least was prepared to give out information in the hope that he'll save his neck. The authorities believe he was paid by the nephews – with Arturo Renzo's backing – to deal with

Cosimo as he had already dealt with similar competition in Florence and Padua. They're also convinced he was then contracted to follow through with the people Cosimo was dealing with.'

'Of whom Hamilton may be the first.' Farnsby stared at the photograph thoughtfully. He saw the image of a man of perhaps forty years of age, somewhat hollow-cheeked, dark-haired, heavy-browed. His jaw was pugnacious, his lips thin, his eyes marked with suspicion. 'When was this taken?'

'Maybe five years ago. He'd been hauled in on a murder charge, but he escaped from custody. The investigating magistrate has since been jailed for corruption. Since then Rakoff has been underground, but he's been active too.'

Farnsby handed the photograph back to O'Connor. 'So our instructions are clear.'

'The Almighty has spoken,' O'Connor agreed sarcastically. 'We need to concentrate on finding Rakoff – if he's in the area – and we need to work out just who Hamilton might have been working with. Catch a killer and solve a murder, and prevent other murders occurring. Piece of cake, hey?'

'We start with Evans?' Farnsby queried.

'We do,' O'Connor concurred. 'Maybe we've been going too easy on him. Given him too much slack. But now, if we put some pressure on him, maybe even tell him about the threat posed by Rakoff, maybe he'll cough up what we want, about his own activities and any accomplices he might have. You said you've got a list of names from the Hamilton shipping dealings.'

'That's right. We can work through that.'

'Starting with Evans. Let's put the fear of God into him. Get talking to the other dealers as well – anyone who might be looking to be too busy with Hamilton, or too friendly.'

'And other people?'

'Such as?'

Farnsby shrugged. With a deliberately casual air, he said, 'I don't know. Maybe people who just used his services. No apparent connection. Maybe guys who worked with him through agents.'

O'Connor felt a prickling at the back of his neck. 'Just who are you thinking of?'

Farnsby chewed at his lower lip. 'Well, there's that guy Portland, for instance.' His eyes fixed on O'Connor's then slid away again, evasively. 'You think we should take a look at him? I mean, he had dealings with Hamilton, used him to ship some goods to the States. Worked through agents, he says, and never dealt with Hamilton on a personal basis, but his name is in the files. Should we talk again to him? See if he's tied in with Hamilton, in any way other than the obvious?'

O'Connor slipped the photograph back into the dossier, closed the file cover. He felt a slow flush rising to his face. He looked up, stared at the man standing in front of him.

Farnsby knows, he thought. *He knows.*

Chapter Four

1

The reception for the Minister of Culture was held at the Gosforth Park Hotel. There was a short speech from the Minister himself, delivered in heavily accented, halting English, to an assembly that included most of the local politicians from Northumberland, Teesside and Wearside. The Chief Executives had turned out to a man and there was a heavy police presence in view of the fact that three Members of Parliament were also present to lend support to the Government Minister who had flown in from Whitehall to make a brief appearance.

Karen Stannard looked stunning in her pale blue, off-shoulder dress and she did not lack for attention. Arnold noted the way in which Powell Frinton himself hovered from time to time in her vicinity: Arnold could not be sure whether the somewhat controlled Chief Executive was attracted, or protectively nervous that one of his subordinates might be exposed to moral danger. He had come across to talk with Arnold for a while, somewhat stilted in his conversation as usual, and acknowledged Carmela in a guarded manner. He seemed more at ease with her, after a few minutes, perhaps because he felt she presented no threat: she had made an effort as far as her appearance was concerned, but she still remained broad-hipped, generous in her curves and a marked contrast to Portia Tyrrel, who remained at the edge of the small group that included

Arnold and who received more than her fair share of attention from middle-aged admirers.

Arnold himself made little attempt to circulate in the approved cocktail party fashion. He stayed close to Carmela, watching with a jaundiced eye the bees that clustered around the Stannard honey-pot. She was in her element, of course: Karen was always aware of herself on occasions like this, and she played the game to her best ability, particularly with those politicians who might at some stage have some impact upon her career. But he noted also that she kept a wary eye on who was talking with Portia: the element of competition still glinted like a knife between the two women. Arnold sighed, and turned to Carmela, asked her if she would like another drink.

'Not just yet. Maybe later,' she smiled, 'when the Minister has left. One has to be careful on these occasions: unlike many Italians he believes that only Bardolo or Chianti is good for the health. Champagne is too French and whisky is too Scottish.'

'And beer?' Arnold asked, grinning.

Carmela shuddered in mock horror, and her bosom quivered dramatically. She sipped her glass of champagne and looked about her. 'There are many important people here,' she murmured. 'The Minister will be pleased, and honoured: it will be a successful conclusion to his visit.'

'The protocols have all been signed?' Arnold asked.

'While we have been slaving away over the CDs in your office, the officials have been hard at work,' she said with a hint of cynicism in her tone, 'drinking their coffees and brandies, having lunch, checking a document here, a document there, and genuflecting to their political masters. It is how one gets on in the world, is it not? In my country, and yours?'

'I suppose so.'

She waved her champagne glass vaguely to take in the wide confines of the room. 'The civil servants and the politicians are all here. But what of the trade, the people who are active in the world of antiques and artefacts? Are they also present?'

Arnold nodded. 'I believe so. As far as I can make out from the guest list there's been a pretty wide trawling for the traders and businessmen also. Most of them are local bigwigs, of course, unconnected with antiques, but important socially. But the list includes a number of academics, there's a few faces I recognize from Archaeology Departments, there's a small group of trustees from the Laing Gallery, the Baltic Centre, and one or two individuals who we've had dealings with from time to time, in Karen's department.'

'She is very beautiful tonight,' Carmela said softly, eyeing him with a degree of arch amusement.

'Yes.'

'You are positive you are not lovers?' she teased.

He frowned at her in mock annoyance. She fluttered her eyelashes at him, theatrically, and then glanced around the room again. 'And what of your nemesis? Would you like to introduce me to him?'

'Nemesis?'

'The man who disputed your findings in regard to the votive cauldron.'

'Dr MacLean.' Arnold shook his head. 'I haven't seen him. His name was on the list but as far as I'm aware he's not put in an appearance.'

'What about the man whose premises you showed me? The man at whose trial you gave evidence.'

Arnold grimaced. 'Islwyn Evans. No, he's not here either. I rang again, by the way, this morning. I spoke to the girl in Kendal, left a message which she said she'd pass on as soon as Evans returned. But she seemed a bit puzzled herself at his continued absence. He was supposed to have attended a trade fair in Kendal a few days ago but he just didn't turn up.'

A shadow seemed to touch Carmela's eyes. She lifted

a shoulder in a slight shrug. 'Perhaps he has become nervous.'

Arnold was silent for a few moments, as the chatter swirled around them like eddies in a rippling lake of conversation, a rising crescendo of voices, groups of people meeting, breaking up, reforming, the clink of glasses, the rattle of laughter, some false, some genuine. It was the kind of gathering that wearied him with its political manoeuvring, its false posturing. He turned his thoughts back to more serious things. 'You really think there's a possibility of a link between the killing of Hamilton here, and Cosimo back at Veii?'

She shook her head. 'It is a guess only, but in my bones I feel there is a possibility. And the *carabinieri* . . . well, as I have already said, if such a link exists, it requires no great stretch of the imagination to wonder whether this man Evans might also be in danger. Do you not agree?'

Arnold shrugged. It was a possibility, he considered. And there was the fact that Islwyn Evans seemed to have gone to ground during this last week or so. Perhaps he also felt it was safer to disappear, in view of what had happened to the shipping agent Ron Hamilton. Pushing such thoughts aside he glanced around him. He caught sight of a familiar face: standing near the doorway, hands locked behind his back, was DCI Jack O'Connor. Their eyes met briefly; Arnold nodded. He received a somewhat bleak nod in return.

Ordinarily, Jack O'Connor might have experienced some pleasure in an occasion like this. He was not averse to a glass of champagne, relaxing in the company of powerful men and beautiful women, even if it was with a certain cynicism as he observed the manoeuvrings, the manipulations, the general grovelling that went on behind the air of false bonhomie. But this was different: he was on duty.

The thought gnawed at him somewhat. It was not that he objected to being on duty in such surroundings – there would be the possibility of relaxation later, maybe, when most of the politicians had gone. It was the fact that he felt it a waste of time: Cathery had insisted there should be a senior police presence apart from himself – the ACC was certainly not on duty, as he stood, dinner-jacketed, in close attendance to the Lord Lieutenant and cosying up to the Chief Constable, while he quaffed his champagne with a degree of abandon. But, with Cathery's sarcastic comments still rankling, O'Connor felt he had better things to do than dance attendance on a bunch of local and national politicians, in the interests of security.

But there was another reason why he felt irritated and uncomfortable. He had already been forced to face the problem, when Gordon Portland had made his way through the throng to come across for a brief word.

'DCI O'Connor.' He stood there, cold eyes flickering glances around the room. 'You're not drinking.'

'I'm on duty, sir.'

The glance was uninterested. 'I can't imagine there'll be much thuggery among this gathering to worry you. So, how is the investigation into the Hamilton business progressing?'

'We're following up a number of leads, sir,' O'Connor replied reluctantly, locking his hands behind his back.

'This whole antiques business seems to be riven with problems recently,' Portland muttered sourly. 'I've been involved for some years now as a collector, as you know, but I'm seriously thinking of getting out of it, disposing of my own collection, and ending any association with the people who operate in the trade. First of all there was this Evans trial: it shook my confidence, O'Connor, I tell you. And then, when you came to interview me in relation to this Hamilton business, I was even more concerned. I've no wish to be involved with people who . . . are fraudulent. People one can't trust . . .' He frowned, glanced around the room, as though seeking for villains. 'And when a murder occurs . . .'

His voice died away. O'Connor had avoided meeting his eye, but now he glanced at him, curiously. Portland was looking away from O'Connor, across the room. His skin had a pallid tinge; his mouth was slack. His pouched eyes were heavy and listless. O'Connor thought he looked ill, and was clearly not enjoying the occasion. And yet there was a coiled tension in the man still; his muscles seemed to be quivering, like a cat about to spring. O'Connor felt distinctly uncomfortable in his presence, and he followed the man's glance.

Isabella Portland was standing at the edge of a small group some twenty feet away. She wore a black sheath dress; the plunging neckline revealed the swell of her breasts to the two middle-aged men who were hanging on her every word. Her head was back, she was laughing merrily, and as he watched her a cold ache, like a lump of ice, lay heavy in Jack O'Connor's chest. As he stared at her, her glance slipped sideways. It was as though she was aware of his eyes on her, and she looked directly at him, still laughing. Then she turned back, said something to her companions, making an apology. She moved away from the group, began to walk towards her husband, standing beside O'Connor. She was still smiling, a light in her eyes.

O'Connor felt the tension rise inside him; he turned to Gordon Portland. 'I believe your wife is about to join you. You'll excuse me, sir,' he muttered and moved away, heading towards Arnold Landon.

He was losing control. He knew it. He was losing control, had been, ever since that afternoon near the Central Station in Newcastle . . .

He was still unable to explain it, even to himself. It had been like a cataclysmic explosion in his personal life. Jack O'Connor knew what he was: born in Lancashire, descendant on his mother's side of three generations of weavers, he had grown up in a society where it was important to control one's feelings, set aside displays of emotion, exercise an iron control over one's reactions to disappointments and disasters. His father had been a big man, an Irishman who had come over from Kilkenny to work in the pits of Yorkshire, but who had later joined the police, rising to the rank of sergeant before failing health sent him into retirement. Now, it was a dreary nursing home in York, senility and incontinence, a memory that had long since crumbled away so that he barely recognized his son. It had happened too soon for Jack O'Connor; the death of his mother, the mental and physical collapse of his father, and the demands of his job when he himself joined the police had left him with little time to develop his own relationships. He was known as a somewhat taciturn, committed copper who kept his head down, pursued his career with a doggedness that brought results, and that had finally led to his transfer further north, to take over the role formerly held by DCI Culpeper. Whatever people thought about Culpeper and his dinosaurian ways, Jack O'Connor knew that he had large boots to fill.

So Isabella Portland had arrived like a bombshell in his life.

He had little experience of women, sexually. There had been a girl, a trainee accountant, when he had started out at York: it had been a fumbling, unsatisfying relationship that had ended when she had moved away to pursue her own career in Leeds. There had been arch offers from prostitutes, hoping to obtain favours when he was on patrol, and he knew there were colleagues who took advantage of such offers, but he had been uninterested. There had been a time when he wondered whether his libido was in fact low, his sexual drive barely existent, but that had been proved wrong with the thirty-year-old local actress with whom he had had a torrid three months, until she had moved away to London with the offer of a place in a West End play. The relationship had stuttered on for a while, but gradually faded as she met other men, more

143

glamorous men, who wined and dined her in smart clubs in the city. But even then he had found a certain relief in the situation: it meant he could concentrate on what he saw as his first love – his job.

Till that afternoon when Isabella had wound down the window of her car and asked him if he wanted a lift.

He had been very aware of her, of course, that first time they met, in the hallway of Gordon Portland's house. He had admired the lines of her body, the lithe sensuality of her walk, the provocative lilt of her voice. But it still could not explain the speed at which their relationship had blossomed into a passion that kept him awake at night, that made his body move almost involuntarily, that made her image intrude upon his waking thoughts and his fingertips tingle at the memory of her.

Time and again he had gone over in his mind every step of the way, every memory of that first encounter. He had phoned his driver immediately, almost without thinking, cancelling his pick-up as he got into the Jaguar. She had been animated, happy, and when she had suggested they stop off at a country pub for a drink on the outskirts of Ponteland he had agreed almost without thinking. They had sat there for two hours, and he listened fascinated as she told him about her early life in Lucca, her time as a model for a fashion house, and in her he almost saw and felt the warm atmosphere, the bright sunlight, the coursing heat of the Tuscany countryside. Then she had asked him about his own life, and maybe she had sensed the loneliness that lay at the centre of it, the personal void in which he was entombed. He had found it easy to talk with her, quietly, but at the same time aware of a growing warmth that gradually stole over his whole body.

And when they left the pub it was by a wordless consent. She had driven away from the village and deeper into the countryside: as they drove neither had spoken. The farm track that led under the overhanging trees was darkened, secluded, and almost before she switched off the car engine her arms had reached out for him, her lips had been eager, and thereafter each movement, each sensation had remained with him. He could recall the sensuality of her mouth, the thudding of her heart under his hand, the long, slow progression towards intimacy, the final shuddering drive that consummated their desire. That first occasion had been followed by others, each more passionate than the last: they had torn at each other in their excitement, bruised each other, locked in a swirling heat and excitement that neither seemed to want to ever end.

He was besotted. In his cooler moments he knew he was in trouble, that she was beginning to dominate his thoughts, drag his mind away from reality, induce fantasies that could never be realized. They never spoke of her husband, they never spoke of her marriage. They were in a whirl of passion that was egocentric, confined, shutting out the world beyond their own demanding closeness. But when he was apart from her, still longing for her, he could still remember, occasionally, that she was the wife of a rich man, that passion cooled, and he knew that there was no real future for what they had. They both knew it, he suspected, so they did not talk about it. But as the weeks passed, the guilt inside him grew, an amalgam of inability to concentrate on his work and awareness of the existence of Gordon Portland – yet it was never enough to drown the excitement that rose in his loins at the thought of her, and never enough to deny the realization of his dreams . . .

'Landon.'

'DCI O'Connor.' Arnold Landon turned, extending a hand towards his companion. 'I don't think you've met Miss Cacciatore.'

'Carmela,' she said, extending her hand.

O'Connor could not help but compare her appearance with the svelte, sensuous figure of Isabella Portland, talking to her husband not fifteen feet from where he stood.

He hardly heard what Carmela was saying as she chattered sociably about her visit to the area, and how much she appreciated the English countryside. It was only when Landon said something about duty that he dragged back his concentration.

'I'm sorry?'

'I said I guessed you were on duty here tonight,' Landon repeated.

O'Connor grimaced. 'I suppose it's better than slaving over a desk, although I'm not exactly turned on by occasions like these. But yes, I'm on duty, though I don't imagine there's much chance of catching many criminals here.'

'Like Islwyn Evans, you mean?' Landon suggested.

O'Connor glanced at him in sober reflection. He smiled sourly. 'I suppose you still think we should have nailed that man when we had the chance.'

Landon shrugged. 'I just regret having been involved at all, in the circumstances. But it wasn't your fault.' His gaze travelled around the room. 'He's not here tonight.'

O'Connor frowned. 'No.' He was on the point of saying more, but held back.

Landon glanced at Carmela Cacciatore. He hesitated. 'Carmela and I . . . you know that it was we who stumbled upon a murder at the Etruscan site north of Rome?'

'I had heard. Outside our jurisdiction, of course,' O'Connor added, 'but the way things work in Europe these days, a deal of information gets circulated.'

There was a short silence. 'Does that mean you will have told the *carabinieri* about the murder of this man Hamilton?' Carmela asked curiously.

O'Connor stared at her. He was reluctant to discuss the progress of the Hamilton investigation in this manner. He shrugged. 'As I said, we tend to feed information into Europol, and its gets disseminated.' He paused. 'Why do you ask?'

Her glance fixed his. 'Arnold and I . . . we have

been talking. We wonder whether there is any connection between the death of Cosimo and the killing of Hamilton.'

O'Connor was silent for a little while, uncertain how to respond. 'Do you believe there might be?' he countered evasively. Before she could answer, he became aware of someone standing just behind him, moving into the group. The back of his neck prickled.

Isabella was moving into place beside him, extending a hand. 'You must be Miss Cacciatore. I was with the group attending the Minister earlier, and you were pointed out to me. Forgive me, gentlemen . . .' She nodded to Landon, smiled at O'Connor as her shoulder brushed his, teasingly. 'I cannot resist meeting someone from my own country.'

'You are from Italy?' Carmela asked, glowing.

'I was born in Lucca.'

'Ha! Such a beautiful place!' She launched enthusiastically into Italian and within moments the two women were laughing, exchanging memories, talking of the things women usually talked about, O'Connor guessed, and he stood there awkwardly, keenly aware of Isabella's nearness, catching the hint of her perfume, finding his mind flooding with memories that he was unable to control, or limit, or deal with dispassionately.

Landon also seemed to be shuffling in embarrassment. Carmela Cacciatore suddenly cried out. 'Ah, Mrs Portland, we are being so rude! Neither of our friends here understand our language, and this is a social occasion.'

O'Connor hated the word 'friend' in the context of Isabella Portland, and as she turned to him and smiled knowingly he felt that she understood what was going through his mind. His pulse was racing, he was on edge, he was too aware of her presence and terrified that others in the room would see what lay between them. He glanced at Landon, wondering if he could feel the tension, and he avoided Isabella's luminous glance.

He looked back over his shoulder. Gordon Portland was

standing alone, where first O'Connor and then Isabella had left him. He was staring at his wife. His body was stiff with resentment. There was a fixity about him; he glared at the small group as though anger was boiling deep in his veins. O'Connor felt a hand touch his arm lightly. Isabella was smiling at him, saying something, but he was unable to hear what she said. Beyond Gordon Portland there was a man, striding urgently into the room. His eyes met O'Connor's. He came forward, hurriedly.

'Pardon me.' It was with a degree of relief that O'Connor stepped away from Isabella and the rest of the small group. 'Farnsby! What are you doing here?'

Farnsby's glance slid past O'Connor for a brief moment, recognizing the woman who stood beside him. His mouth tightened in disapproval, and then he turned back to O'Connor, thrusting aside the thought in his mind.

'The car's outside,' he said urgently. 'You'd better come back to headquarters.'

O'Connor frowned. 'I'm on duty here. Cathery insisted on a presence –'

Farnsby cast a contemptuous glance around the noisy room. 'Forget Cathery. He'll agree this is more important. You'd better get back with me. It looks like Rakoff –'

He grabbed O'Connor by the sleeve, pulling him away.

O'Connor resisted, almost automatically. 'Rakoff? What do you mean? What the hell's this about?'

DI Farnsby's mouth was grim. 'It happened about thirty-six hours ago, at a guess. Another knifing.' He jerked his head, began to lead the way out of the reception. 'We better get back immediately. We've got another body on our hands!'

2

Raindrops chased each other, coursing down the window-pane, racing, merging, subsiding, and the light drumming of the storm on the roof was the only sound to be heard within the four walls of the sparsely furnished, green-painted cubicle. The young man seated in the interview room was clearly scared. His eyes were unhappy, he had a hangdog air, there was a line of perspiration on his upper lip and he was unable to keep his hands still. O'Connor watched him impassively, DI Farnsby seated beside him. At last O'Connor said quietly, 'You've been buggering us about, son.'

The young man licked his lips, hunched forward in his seat, blinked nervously but said nothing. O'Connor waited patiently. Several days had passed since Sid Cathery had raged into the briefing room set aside for the scene of crime unit, and ignored protocol and discipline by yelling at the two senior officers involved in the investigation. 'Are we servicing a bloody charnel house here, or what?'

Silence had fallen. The other officers assigned to the case had kept their heads down while Cathery stabbed an irate finger in O'Connor's direction. 'You seen the papers this morning? You heard that snotty reporter on TV? With this second killing they're getting hysterical, screaming on about the prospect of gang wars; they're shouting about a collapse of law and order; they're reckoning Armageddon, a bloody third world war, the end of society as we know it is descending upon us! The flaming *Church Times* will be getting involved next!' He had glared furiously around the room, as though seeking for anyone prepared to offer a word of dissent. When the silence remained unbroken he had homed in on the senior officer present. 'DCI O'Connor. My office, right now.'

'This is a briefing meeting, sir –' O'Connor protested angrily.

'Briefing be buggered! I said my office. You, and Farnsby. *Now*!'

Within the confines of the ACC's office the two men had been forced to endure a twenty-minute tirade, during which everyone lost their tempers. Cathery prowled around the room, raging about the pressure that was being put upon him, the inferences being assumed by the media, the incompetence of the team and their failure to come up with answers, and O'Connor had argued angrily that with the resources they had they were doing the best they could. Farnsby had stuck his oar in and suggested that if the ACC was so concerned, with two murders on their hands they should maybe seek the assistance of other forces, and Cathery had bawled back that he was not going to have his people seen to collapse under a bit of pressure: it was their patch, and they were going to handle both cases themselves. It became bitter and personal when O'Connor launched his own attack, saying that interference from the top was going to do nothing to assist in the swift completion of enquiries, and they had to be given some slack, some time to come up with answers, but finally, when things had calmed down somewhat, and some of the aggressive vituperation had been blown away, Cathery had growled reluctantly, 'Well, all right, but it's been days and nothing seems to be happening. Just how far along are we?'

Calmly, O'Connor had explained. There were forensic reports to be completed; video footage to be analysed; documentation to be inspected; phone calls from the house to be checked and logged . . .

'How did you know it was me?' the young man facing the two officers suddenly asked, his tone edgy and nervous.

O'Connor leaned forward, a grim set to his mouth. 'We didn't, not straight away. But it would have helped if you'd just come forward immediately, told us what you knew, instead of us having to waste time chasing up phone numbers. We knew there'd been a couple of calls placed from the house: once we'd got the second number from the phone company it meant we had to go through the process of finding out the location. And the fact it was a student phone, in the hall of residence, meant it was still difficult. We had to narrow it down between about thirty of you youngsters. We wasted time talking to the wrong people. Till your name came up as a possibility. And it turns out that it *was* you. Charlie Davis. Archaeology student.'

Charlie slumped in his seat, worried and uncertain, a line of anxiety on his brow. He brushed back the hair that was falling in his eyes.

'And we can guess who called you. We've been talking to some of the other students in the department. We've heard what's been going on.'

'You don't want to listen to what they've been saying,' Charlie Davis replied quickly, irritation staining his tone. 'They don't understand. They don't really appreciate –'

'One of your mates, he was quite forceful about it. Says he's been telling you for weeks to dump the girl. Says he told you MacLean was sleeping with her. But you wouldn't take good advice. You still stuck with her. And it was her; it was Jenny Sanders, wasn't it?'

Faced by a stubborn silence, Farnsby intervened. 'It was she who phoned you from Dr MacLean's house.'

Charlie started to bite at the nails of his left hand. While he waited for a response, O'Connor's mind flicked back to the house in Gosforth. Flies had buzzed noisily in the kitchen. When he entered the house O'Connor was aware of the sweet sickly smell of death. Uniformed officers had been kept outside while the forensic team went in, photographs were taken; along the quiet, expensive residential street neighbours were being questioned in a door-to-door enquiry. Dr James MacLean had died in the hallway. He had been dressed in a light sweatshirt and slacks, clearly dragged on hurriedly because he wore no underpants; he was wearing no shoes, his feet were bare. The knife wound in his chest was horrific: the weapon would seem to have been plunged straight into his heart, then ripped downwards. The shock had probably brought on immediate

151

cardiac arrest. James MacLean had died very quickly. There was no sign of the murder weapon.

There were smears of blood on the carpet in the hallway and on the front step; forensic quickly established it was MacLean's blood. They surmised that someone had left the house carrying traces of that blood on their shoes. When O'Connor had gone upstairs there were signs that the bed had been recently used: the duvet was thrown aside, the pillows disarranged, some stains on the undersheet. Later, when the place had been dusted for prints there were several sets that they could use for matching. And when they checked the phone records it was clear that around about the time of MacLean's death two phone calls had been made. One to a mobile; the second to the phone number of a university hall of residence.

'She tried your mobile first, didn't she, Charlie?' Farnsby asked.

Charlie Davis twitched, but made no reply.

'But you must have had it switched off,' O'Connor added. 'So she had to try to get you on the hall phone. What was it all about, Charlie? Did she want you to help clear up the mess she'd got herself into?'

'It wasn't like that!' Charlie protested suddenly, shaking his head violently. 'All right, I got this phone call but you've got to realize she was panicked, she was sobbing, she was in a flat spin, begged me to help her get out of there. What the hell was I supposed to do? She'd been my girl, I'd been with her years and all right, she'd been persuaded by MacLean . . . that bastard,' Charlie half sobbed bitterly. 'That bastard *needed* killing.'

In the short silence that followed, Charlie suddenly realized the implications of what he had said. He raised a trembling hand. 'Hey, it wasn't like that! Look, she called me, so I got the car out and I drove around there to MacLean's house like a bat out of hell. When I got there the front door was open. I went in and there she was, on her knees in the hallway, beside the phone. She was like, spaced out, you know what I mean? She was *gone*! She'd been hysterical on the phone, crying a river, but by the time I got there it was like she was shocked. She sat there silent, just staring. It was weird, man, I tell you – weird.' He sighed heavily, shook his head. There was a hint of tears in his eyes.

'Was the knife still in MacLean's chest at that point?' Charlie stared blankly at the two officers.

'Did you remove the weapon, Charlie?' Farnsby asked quietly. 'Did you pull it out, get rid of it somewhere in case her prints were on it?'

Charlie Davis shook his head in denial. 'Hell, I didn't even look! I saw his body stretched out there, and her on her knees beside him, and the blood all over the place, and I just flipped! I just grabbed her, pulled her to her feet and shook her till she started to come around. We went back upstairs to get her clothes and then we got the hell out of there.'

'Bad mistake, Charlie,' Farnsby said soberly.

'Why didn't you phone us, call for help?' O'Connor asked.

Charlie Davis stared at him as if he was crazy. 'You kidding? I couldn't think straight! She was there, my girl, and she was falling apart and there was that bastard lying there dead, so what was I supposed to do about it? I didn't know what the hell had happened, didn't know what had gone on in that place, all I could think of was to get the hell out of there, get Jenny out of the house before she completely fell apart . . .'

'And before the police got there?' Farnsby asked gently.

Charlie Davis gave him a stubborn, resentful glare. 'I didn't want to be involved. I didn't want Jenny to be involved.' He hesitated. A contemptuous twist came to his mouth. 'Bloody hell, you don't think Jenny could do something like that, do you? You don't seriously believe she stuck a knife into that randy bastard?'

O'Connor leaned back in his chair. 'If someone can get

153

mad enough . . . if someone finds out she's no longer important, that her lover has been cheating on her . . .'

'That's crazy! You don't know her!'

'Or maybe it wasn't the way you say it was,' Farnsby offered, almost casually. 'Perhaps it was you who stuck the knife in MacLean, because you were jealous of her involvement with him, got out of there, went back to your digs and when Jenny arrived and found what you'd done, she rang you and you were forced to come around, return to the house –'

'That wasn't the way it was! I disliked that bastard, and hated what he was doing with Jenny, but I was never near the place in Gosforth until she called me! I told you the way it was.'

'Well, that's something we have yet to ask your friend Jenny, isn't it?'

Charlie Davis glowered, lapsed into a bitter silence, hands between his knees.

Jenny Sanders was waiting in the second interview room and she was just as scared as Charlie Davis. She was small in stature, with blonde hair that was in some disarray. Her eyes were large, smudged with pain. Neither she nor Charlie had asked for legal representation, so O'Connor knew he had to tread carefully.

'How long have you known Charlie?'

She blinked, as though the question was unexpected. 'We were at school together. We came north to university the same time. We've been hanging out a long time.'

'Until Dr MacLean arrived on your scene,' Farnsby suggested.

Distress crept into her eyes. 'He . . . he was my tutor.'

'And you slept with him.'

'He . . . it wasn't . . . I was –'

'Did you love him?'

The question disturbed her; O'Connor could not be certain whether the panic that twisted her mouth was due to memories of the last time she had seen MacLean, lying in the hallway. She was silent for a little while, then she nodded. 'I guess so. I was . . . flattered, I suppose.'

'And what about Charlie?'

She shook her head, sniffed. 'I don't know. He'd always been around. He was my mate. I was always comfortable with him. But James was different, mature . . . he was exciting. I was all confused. Charlie . . . James . . . he was so . . .' She began to sob, a catch in her throat. O'Connor waited, as Farnsby shifted uneasily at his side.

'All right. So why don't you just tell us what happened that night?'

Her voice was small, and shaky. 'I'd arranged to go around to his house. I'd been there before. We couldn't really be together at the university, because lecturers dating students, it was kind of frowned upon. But I'm old enough to know what I was doing,' she added, with a flash of defiance, 'in spite of what Charlie said.'

'He tried to persuade you to break away from MacLean?'

She nodded miserably. 'He told me people were talking about it.'

'MacLean had a reputation, I understand,' Farnsby suggested. 'You were only the latest in a line of student conquests. And other women too, apparently.'

She raised her chin, with a hint of anger in her features. 'I don't believe all that. All right, he told me he'd recently had a relationship with a woman older than me, but he said it was over. I didn't care. He was . . . exciting. Different.'

'So you went around to his house that evening,' O'Connor prompted.

She nodded. 'He'd always warned me to be discreet, because I was a student, so I had my hood up, kept my head down. He said he had nosy neighbours . . . When I got there he let me in, but he said I couldn't stay long.'

'What time was it?'

155

She shrugged diffidently. 'About seven thirty. It was dark. He said I couldn't stay long because he had work to do so we went straight upstairs.' She looked at O'Connor defiantly. 'We both wanted to make love. We went to the bedroom. We undressed. Then he turned out the light, had just got into bed with me . . . then there was the door bell. It rang, kept ringing. James was angry. He told me to wait there, and he shoved some clothes on and he went downstairs. He closed the bedroom door behind him. I just waited there. I didn't know who it might be, so I just waited. Then I heard voices in the hallway.'

'How do you mean? Just talking?'

She shook her head. 'No, there was shouting. Sort of an argument. Then I heard a kind of thud – I think maybe that was when James fell.' She sucked in her breath, holding it, her teeth gritted in emotional pain. 'It was a while before I decided to get up. I was a bit scared. Apprehensive, like. Everything had gone quiet. I couldn't hear any movement downstairs. I put on James's bathrobe, called out to him. There was no answer. I went to the top of the stairs: the light was on in the hallway but I didn't see him at first. I think the front door was partly open. I can't really remember. Then . . .' There was a catch in her throat, and her eyes were wide, staring as though she was visualizing the scene again. 'Then I saw him lying there. I screamed. After that . . .' Tears glistened in her blue eyes as she stared at O'Connor. 'After that, I don't know how long it was. I think I went down beside him, I saw the blood, I knelt down and held his face in my hands . . .' She looked down at her hands, as though she could still make out the stains of MacLean's blood there.

'When did you decide to make the call?' Farnsby asked gently after a short interval.

She shrugged. 'I don't know. I was there on my knees, crying. I was panicked. Time . . . it just wasn't important. But when I knew he was dead, I sort of flipped. I didn't know what to do. I was falling apart, you know? So

156

I grabbed the phone there in the hallway, and I phoned Charlie's mobile number. I knew he would help me. I knew he'd know what to do. But I couldn't get an answer.'

'He'd switched it off. So what then?'

'I tried his digs – the hall of residence at Leazes Park. I was sobbing. Someone got him for me. Then Charlie told me to stay there, wait for him. He came round to Gosforth. He took control. He got me dressed. He helped me out of there. He took me away . . .'

'Was it Charlie who persuaded you to say nothing about it?' Farnsby queried.

She nodded. 'He said I needed to stay out of things. I think he was panicked too, shocked. He just wanted to protect me. From myself, he said.'

'What happened then?'

'After I was dressed we went off in Charlie's car. We . . . we went back down south, stayed at a friend's house in Sheffield – Charlie had a key while he was away in France on an exchange – and Charlie stayed there with me, said it would give me time to get my head around things. Give me time to recover.'

She needed more than time, O'Connor guessed. She was shaking now, an involuntary trembling of her limbs; she seemed to be in a bad way.

The questioning continued for another half-hour until eventually O'Connor nodded to Farnsby, and they gave up. Jenny Sanders seemed alarmed, but when they told her she could go home and that Charlie would be waiting, her mood lightened and she left quickly.

The two men returned to O'Connor's office. O'Connor picked up the videotape on his desk and inserted it into the VCR. He sat down behind his desk, gloomily, while Farnsby stood with folded arms, staring at the screen of the monitor. 'Their story seems to stand up,' Farnsby observed.

Jack O'Connor nodded. They watched the video silently, for the fourth time.

It had been taken by a widower a few doors down the street. Obsessed with his garden, and convinced that local vandals had been damaging his fence, he had installed a video camcorder on a tripod in an upstairs window. He left it switched it on for several hours each evening. He had yet to catch anyone attacking his fence or garden, but he had fortuitously captured some movement on the night James MacLean had died.

It made frustrating watching. The house owned by MacLean appeared in the top left-hand corner of the screen, hazy, a little out of focus, and the light was not good enough to produce clear pictures. But what could be seen was the arrival of a ten-year-old Fiat parking near the house. The figure of what seemed to be a young man emerged, and ran into the house. Several minutes later the man re-emerged, his arm wrapped protectively around a huddled female figure.

'Charlie Davis and Jenny Sanders,' Farnsby muttered. 'Their story hangs together.'

O'Connor ran the tape in reverse; the jerky movements came and went, the car disappeared, a man walked his dog backwards, the counter picked up speed as the dark images flashed by. At the appropriate moment O'Connor slowed the tape and then stopped it. He pressed the button to begin running the videotape once more.

It was as unsatisfactory as it had been the first time they saw it, after the constable on door-to-door enquiries had brought it in triumphantly, thinking he had solved the case. It showed the scene some half an hour before Charlie Davis had made his appearance. The fuzzy outline of a big car was there, parked sideways on to the camera, almost directly outside the house where the camera was operating. It was impossible to make out who might be inside the vehicle, and the registration number was not visible. Two people walked past; a cat skittered across the road. Then, a few minutes later, the figure of a hooded woman could be seen hurrying down the street, head bent. She entered the front garden of MacLean's house; a brief wait, and then the door opened, and she entered.

'From what we know, that must be her, Jenny Sanders,' Farnsby muttered, 'but the way she's muffled up it would be impossible to identify her.'

'She wasn't keen on being identified, going into her tutor's house,' O'Connor murmured. 'She knew their liaison needed to be kept quiet. But it's not helpful to us.'

'Half the student body knew about the damned affair,' Farnsby grunted.

The tape whirred on, displaying the eerie half light of the silent street. There was no movement from the car. Then the light in the bedroom flicked on. O'Connor leaned forward, frowning, peering at the screen. There was a delay of several minutes where nothing moved in the street, and then, suddenly, the bedroom light flicked off again, and the house was in darkness.

'Now,' O'Connor murmured.

There was a faint glow from the courtesy light inside the car. It was quickly extinguished. The driver's door opened, and a man got out. O'Connor squinted at the screen, desperately trying to make out something of consequence but it was the same this time as it had been on every previous occasion: all he could distinguish was a squarely built man, dark-clothed, walking across the street, towards the house.

'Rakoff?' Farnsby queried.

'Who can tell?' O'Connor snapped. 'It's not clear enough for a positive identification. It could even be Charlie Davis.'

'Do you think they can enhance these pictures down at the lab?' Farnsby asked in irritation.

'To some extent, but my guess is it'll show us little more than what we've got,' O'Connor replied.

Sourly, he watched the replay of scenes that had become

familiar. The man from the car turning into the front garden; the wait on the front step; lights appearing on the ground floor, the door opening, the man stepping inside, one hand pushing against the door. A brief interval when all that could be seen was a faint lance of light shining down into the front garden, then a man emerging again, hurriedly, almost running back towards the car. A slamming car door, headlights flicking on, and the car moved away, out of shot.

At last, after a while, the bedroom light flashing on again, behind the drawn curtains.

O'Connor turned off the tape, leaned back in his chair. He locked his hands behind his head and stared at the ceiling. 'So down she comes,' he muttered, 'finds MacLean in the hallway, as she said. Then she phones Charlie Davis, the faithful slave. Twenty minutes after she places the call, he comes tearing around in his old banger, gets her dressed and together they flee into the night. They go to ground, and we spend days, wasted days, trying to find who the hell they were.'

'We've got Charlie's shoes, and there's traces of MacLean's blood on them, but he's already admitted he was there. If only we could get a fix on that bastard who entered the house when MacLean and the girl were upstairs!' Farnsby exclaimed bitterly.

'Life is never that simple, is it?' O'Connor sighed. 'I think we have little chance of identifying him from this tape. But at least, we've got evidence that more or less lets the two youngsters off the hook.'

'Jenny Sanders still could be the one who killed MacLean,' Farnsby argued cautiously. 'We see the stranger going in; we don't see him committing the act. He could have left while MacLean was still alive; she could have come down and planted the knife in MacLean's chest after he'd left.'

'But we don't really believe that, do we?' O'Connor muttered in frustration. 'And we can make a pretty good guess who that character in the car is. If the information from Europol is correct.'

'Constantine Rakoff,' Farnsby agreed, nodding. 'And if it is, there are likely to be more killings. Anyone connected with the Italian network. First Hamilton, and now MacLean . . .'

'Have we obtained MacLean's bank statements yet?'

Farnsby shook his head. 'As usual, the banks are being difficult. But we've been promised them soon.'

'Did we find anything more on MacLean's computer?' O'Connor asked.

'I've got people still working at it,' Farnsby replied. 'But there's certainly a list of items there which seem to match up with stuff that was later shipped by Hamilton. There's nothing we can use to pin things down precisely, but there's enough for us to make an educated guess that James MacLean certainly had some connection or other with Ron Hamilton. And now both of them are dead. Tying that in with the Europol information, and the killing of that man in the Etruscan tomb, it's beginning to look more and more certain that Hamilton might have been linked with a smuggling network.'

'What would have been MacLean's role?'

Farnsby shrugged. 'Identifier. Evaluator. Checking on the validity of items that were shown to him.'

'Advising Hamilton, who fenced the stuff onwards, after receiving it from Cosimo . . .' O'Connor rose, retrieved the videotape from the VCR. 'It's a hypothesis, anyway. Gives us something to work on.'

Farnsby hesitated. 'Of course, with a connection established between MacLean and Hamilton, we've got to remember that MacLean gave evidence at the trial. That may be a link between him and Islwyn Evans. It could mean that he was protecting one of the group . . .'

'But we won't know that until we get that Welsh bastard here at headquarters for questioning. Any sign of him yet?'

161

Farnsby shook his head. 'He seems to have gone to ground. We'll find him, hopefully. If we don't, and Rakoff finds him first . . .' He was silent for a little while, his eyes fixed on O'Connor. The silence was uncomfortable, an edge of tension intruding into the room. 'We'd be warning Evans, of course, if he was a member of the smuggling group. Warning him he was in danger.'

'If he was tied in,' O'Connor grunted, 'the deaths of Hamilton and MacLean will have been warning enough. It's my guess that's why he's gone to ground . . .'

'I was just wondering,' Farnsby said quietly, 'whether we should be warning other people.'

'Such as?' O'Connor asked, as he felt a nervous ache beginning in his chest.

Farnsby shrugged diffidently. 'I don't know . . . anyone, really, who appears to have had dealings with Evans, or Hamilton.'

'There are plenty of those,' O'Connor admitted reluctantly, knowing where this was going. 'We can't get around all of them, and they can't really be at risk.'

'But we don't know, do we, sir?' Farnsby insisted. 'If there is any chance of involvement, maybe we should be talking to them . . .'

'You got anyone particular in mind?' O'Connor snapped, staring directly at his colleague.

Farnsby hesitated. His face was smooth; his features unreadable. At last, faced by the challenge, he admitted, 'No one in particular, sir.'

But he was lying and they both knew it. O'Connor thrust the videotape into his hand. 'Let's just leave it as it is,' he suggested harshly. 'Meanwhile, get this tape down to the lab and see what they can do if they play around with it.'

After Farnsby had gone, O'Connor groaned aloud in the silence of his room. He put his face in his hands, rubbed at his eyes. Life was getting too complicated. Farnsby hadn't had the courage to come out with what he was thinking, but O'Connor knew that it was nothing to do with the Rakoff targets. Farnsby knew about Isabella, or at least suspected an affair. He was trying to warn O'Connor, and the bitter taste in O'Connor's mouth emphasized that Farnsby was right: getting involved with a married woman was a dangerous game to play . . .

O'Connor scowled at the ceiling. Cosimo, Hamilton, MacLean: he had to concentrate, and yet these days he found concentration difficult. Constantly in his mind was an image, a woman, red-gold, luxuriant hair spilling over the pillow, warm flesh, soft thighs, a river of excitement coursing through his veins . . .

Two murders to investigate, and all he could think about was Isabella Portland.

3

In the darkness of the hotel room his skin was cool, a light sheen of frustrated perspiration covering his naked body. The woman lying beside him was very still; her breathing was light and steady as though she were asleep but he guessed that, like himself, she was awake. After a while he slipped his hand across to touch her, sliding his fingers along her thigh, reaching for her hand. Her slim fingers lay in his and he said, 'I'm sorry, Isabella.'

She sighed lightly. 'There's nothing to be sorry for. These things can happen.' She turned slightly, so that she could see his face in the dimness. 'It's understandable. You're preoccupied. You've got too much on your mind.'

It could have been that; it could have been thoughts of the killings that had caused their lovemaking to fail for the first time. It was true that things kept revolving in his mind, affecting his body, almost irrelevant things, like the meeting with the pathologist, Dr Carter, who had stopped him as he was about to leave headquarters late that afternoon.

'Ah, DCI O'Connor. You got my report?'

Eager to be away from the building to keep his rendezvous with Isabella Portland, O'Connor had been brusque. 'We're still looking at it,' he replied attempting to push past.

Carter was a short man, squarely built, with a bald head, flyaway eyebrows and a dogged disposition. He barred the way in the narrow corridor, one hand on O'Connor's arm. 'I've been spending time making a further analysis of the wound on that corpse you handed over to us,' he said, almost beaming in satisfaction, 'and I think I've got some more information that might be useful. You ever read anything by Paul Wellman?'

'What?' O'Connor snapped, dragging at the restraining hand.

'Wellman. I was quite a fan of his years ago. He used to write histories of the American West, then novels based on those histories. One of them was filmed. *The Iron Mistress*. Alan Ladd. You ever see it?'

'It rings no bells for me,' O'Connor growled. 'Now if you'll excuse me –'

'Wasn't a woman, of course. Good title, though, *The Iron Mistress*. Came to dominate his life, as mistresses often do.'

O'Connor stared at the pathologist, suspecting for a moment that this was a direct gibe. Then he forced himself to relax. He was beginning to get paranoid. 'Who are you talking about?' he demanded.

'Not Wellman, of course – the character played by Alan Ladd.' Dr Carter cocked a knowing eye at O'Connor. 'The title actually referred to a weapon.'

O'Connor grunted in exasperation. He was in no mood for small talk in the corridor. 'Look, I've got a meeting to attend and –'

'I've been looking closely at that wound in MacLean's chest.' Dr Carter purred in self-congratulation, little eyes gleaming proudly behind his round-rimmed glasses, stolidly unaware of O'Connor's urgency. 'Interesting exit wound. One thrust into the chest, then a ripping with-drawal . . . I think I know the kind of weapon that made it.'

'A knife,' O'Connor interrupted impatiently. 'You already made that clear in the report. It was obvious anyway.'

'Ah, yes, but a special kind of knife,' Carter smiled knowingly. 'I think I can tell you precisely what it was like. *The Iron Mistress*, the film, it was about a man who invented a special kind of blade. It became famous, was widely adopted in the American West. They named it after him. He died at the Alamo, you know, along with Davey Crockett. They made a film about that too, the stand against Santa Ana. You ever see that film – *The Alamo*?'

O'Connor was disinclined to stand discussing old films that he had never even seen. 'Dr Carter –'

'Yes, he died alongside Davey Crockett at the Spanish mission called the Alamo but he's also remembered because he made this special kind of knife, sharp, slightly curved blade, serrated at the back. His name was Jim Bowie. They called the knife after him. The Bowie knife.' Carter clucked his tongue in admiration. 'Special design, useful for hunting. Could rip an animal open, skin it swiftly. A hunting knife.'

O'Connor stared at him, his interest finally aroused.

Dr Carter shuffled sideways, to allow O'Connor to pass. 'It's the kind of knife used by the man you're looking for. A knife initially designed, I believe, for hunting purposes. But an effective man-killer, as well. And that's what it was used for this time.' He made a thrusting gesture with one pudgy hand. 'Driving in, ripping open on the withdrawal. Very effective, for a man-killer.'

A man-killer; a hunter of men.

Constantine Rakoff.

Dr Carter went on his way down the corridor whistling happily.

O'Connor twisted uneasily on the bed. He was unable to

dismiss the image from his mind, the ripping, serrated edge of the murderous knife blade. Ever since he had heard what Dr Carter had said, it had remained with him, the thought that he was missing something, an important piece of a jigsaw, lurking just out of reach in the dark recesses of his mind. He was aware of Isabella, turning, moving closer, her left arm stealing across his chest, caressing his shoulder, sliding down to his waist. 'You must relax, Jack. Dismiss work from your mind: forget these things that are bothering you. We should try again,' she whispered. 'Why don't I –'

'I haven't talked to you about what's happening,' he muttered.

'Why should you?' she whispered seductively. 'Everything we need exists for us only inside this room. We don't need to worry about the world outside. You're here beside me, I can feel the hardness of you –'

'There's a man on the loose. A dangerous man. He's called Constantine Rakoff.'

She paused, her fingers stilled on his thigh. 'Do we have to talk about this now?'

'It was Europol who first alerted us to this man's existence – and his presence in England,' O'Connor went on doggedly. Then he hesitated, uncertain after all whether he should continue, aware of Isabella's softness lying close against him. But even that was different: things seemed recently to have changed subtly between himself and Isabella. Their first meetings had been like a rage, a passion that had driven everything else from their minds: in the following weeks it had continued, it was as though they could not get enough of each other, their lovemaking was almost violent in its urgency, and their waking hours were clouded by both memories and anticipation. He resented every evening he lay in his own bed, without her; their meetings were necessarily snatched occasions, in darkened hotel rooms located outside the city, and their longing for each other, for the act that welded them together in a crazed whirl of tangled limbs and driving lust, made everything else in the world fade into insignificance. But just as he now found other things intruding into his consciousness, other anxieties, so recently did Isabella seem different. There were times when he felt that she too was preoccupied, an element of tension creeping into their lovemaking on occasions, as though she too was worried about something. It could have been something to do with her husband, the fear of exposure of her betrayal of her marriage with O'Connor. Perhaps it was the realization that it could all evaporate, be blown away if their relationship was discovered.

She was tense now, but it was probably a degree of resentment because he seemed unable to relax.

'We've been looking for this man Rakoff,' he continued. 'We've been checking points of entry, and because Europol were also able to give us details of the pseudonyms he's sometimes used in the past, the false names he's used on passports, we finally struck lucky. We know that he entered England a month ago. And credit card checks have shown us he came up from Harwich, first to the Middlesbrough area, and then a bill was paid at an hotel in Gateshead, which shows us Rakoff is in the area.'

'Why do you feel the need to tell me this?' Isabella asked, shifting petulantly, rising on one elbow, a hint of querulousness in her voice. 'The time we have together –'

'We've developed a theory,' O'Connor interrupted, ignoring her reluctance to listen, 'and we think that Rakoff has a mission. He's a contract killer; he's been paid to undertake a task that is part revenge, part elimination of competition, his employers have been arrested but that makes no difference to him. It's a matter of professional honour. He'll finish the job, even if his paymasters are inside.'

She shifted away from him slightly, removing her hand, and he was aware of her growing impatience. But he felt he had to continue.

'He's probably the man who killed an Italian tomb robber north of Rome. He came to England to continue the job he'd been set. In this country, we think he murdered a man whom the tomb robber had been dealing with: Ron Hamilton.'

Reluctantly, she murmured, 'I read about the killing in the newspapers.'

'We're now pretty certain it was Rakoff from a scrutiny of Hamilton's dealings in Italy. And we strongly believe Rakoff was also responsible for the murder of James MacLean.'

She stiffened. She remained very still for several seconds, then her head turned, so she could stare at him.

'MacLean?'

'You'll remember him. He gave evidence at the Evans trial. You'll have seen him in court, when you came with your husband.'

Her tone was underlain with disbelief. 'He killed James MacLean? But why would he do that?'

'Because MacLean was involved with Hamilton: we've been through MacLean's computer records and it's clear he had dealings with Hamilton. And that could mean there could be a third person in the frame.'

'What on earth are you talking about?'

'You'll recall that MacLean gave evidence in favour of Islwyn Evans. There's a strong possibility MacLean and Evans worked together: that's why MacLean stuck his neck out over the expert evidence he gave. We suspect that Hamilton, Evans and MacLean were tied in together as a group, smuggling artefacts from Italy. If they *were* involved, and Rakoff killed Hamilton, and then MacLean, well, we think that Evans will be the next target. We also think that's why Evans has dropped out of sight.'

'Because with this man Hamilton, and . . . James MacLean dead, Evans is aware of the danger?' She sounded rattled now, nervous. The thought of the man hunter out there in the northern streets had affected her;

she was trembling slightly. He suddenly regretted the necessity to talk to her about all this, and he reached out, put a protective arm around her shoulders, pulled her towards him, sliding his fingers over the warmth of her breast. His lips were close to her hair, spread luxuriantly on the pillow. He was aware of her perfume, overlaid with the musky scent of their lovemaking. 'Evans is lying low, but he's not used to such a game. He's been careless, and we've managed to trace him to an hotel in Berwick; we've got him under surveillance; and we're just waiting now for him, or the man who's looking for him, to break cover.'

'You're using Evans like a sacrificial goat,' she murmured.

'I guess so.'

The callousness of it seemed to have a rousing effect upon her; she moved closer to him suddenly, sought for his mouth. Her lips were demanding, and her body strained against his. When she broke away, she was breathless, and she writhed against him as his body moved, aroused at last by her closeness. 'You're a bastard,' she murmured thickly, as her hands sought him out. 'A hard bastard.'

And then it was as it had been at the beginning. Suddenly, all the dark thoughts that had been swirling about him faded, and he was on fire: the familiar passions were aroused, their eagerness thrust them into a driving urge that made them claw at each other's bodies, seek out the dark places, struggle for conclusions and yet hold them off, breathlessly, until they were lost, aware only of the heights of desire, the trembling climactic surge and then the long, slow loss until they drifted, spent, breathless . . .

Half an hour passed as they lay, damp, cooling, the sheet tossed lightly aside, until she stirred, muttered something and curled closer to him. 'That was good . . .'

It was an understatement.

'Perhaps you should talk to me more often of your

ruthlessness,' she said, and he caught the hint of a smile in her voice.

'I wasn't trying to frighten you,' he replied, a little uneasily.

'I wasn't frightened,' she murmured, snuggling closer to him. 'Aroused is a better word.' There was a short silence. He could feel the light touch of her breath against his chest. 'But I still don't understand why you wanted to talk to me about this man Rakoff.'

O'Connor tensed. 'It's because . . . Hamilton, MacLean, Evans . . . we think they were involved in a smuggling group. Rakoff's task is to eliminate them. But there's the chance, maybe, that there are others also involved.'

'Others?' she asked, a cautious curiosity marking her tone.

He hesitated. 'My colleagues . . . we've wondered. At the Evans trial, your husband was present, watching proceedings. And after the trial, he asked me to see him, to advise him on the progress of any further investigations into Evans's activities. It gives rise to the thought. Maybe he wasn't just seeking advice, as he said he was. Maybe he was trying to find out whether the smuggling group was safe from further interference.'

'Why would he do that?'

'There's the possibility that your husband was also involved with the smuggling group.'

'What?'

'If so, he too could be in danger from Constantine Rakoff.'

Isabella pulled away from him. He was aware of her eyes staring at him, and then her body began to tremble. He thought it was anxiety, fear, and he tried to pull her closer to him. But he was mistaken; a moment later, as she resisted him, he realized he had completely misread her feelings. She was giggling; the sound came, she began to laugh, and he gripped her arm, annoyance touching his mind. 'You must take this seriously –'

'*Gordon?*' Her giggling became almost uncontrollable. 'You think Gordon would get involved in a scam like that? That's unbelievable, ludicrous! You don't know him the way I do!' She turned over, evading his arms, lay on her back, trying to control her laughter. When she recovered somewhat, still gasping, she said, 'You think Gordon might be a criminal mastermind? That's hilarious! Gordon is a collector; it bores the hell out of me, but it is an obsession with him. But don't for a moment think that his obsession would lead him into criminal activities . . .' She took a deep breath, controlling her giggling, aware of the tension in his body. She wiped her eyes, and turned back to him. Her hand reached out, caressed his mouth. 'I've been married to Gordon Portland for a long time,' she murmured softly. 'I know him well. Believe me, there is no way he would have got involved with little people like the men you mention.'

'You can't be certain –'

'I am,' she said firmly. 'There are two things in his life that he values, obsesses over: his collection, and me. But the emotion that lies in both is one of possession only.' She was silent for a little while, her head on his chest. Her tone became sober, somewhat reflective. 'He has his collection of artefacts, which he moons over; when he tires of individual items, he sells them, obtains something else. As for me . . . I also am one of his possessions. I was perhaps aware of it from the very first time, the early days when we met at my home in Lucca. He wanted me, he was wealthy, and I was perhaps dazzled by what he could offer . . . My family encouraged the match. I went along with it. I was very young. But there was never real desire on his part, other than the desire of possession. He owns me, I am a desirable object, but he would never get rid of me as he does with other things in his collection. He makes no attempt now to do anything other than own . . .'

She fell silent. O'Connor found his mind drifting back to the first time he had met Isabella, at Gordon Portland's house. He recalled her appearance that day in the hallway, standing casually at the foot of the stairs; he remembered the way she had looked, striding towards him from the stable block; and he saw again the movement in the window, Gordon Portland looking down, watching the woman he owned . . .

'When did it begin?' he asked quietly, as other, unbidden thoughts entered his mind.

'When did what begin?' she said almost sleepily, pulling back from old memories.

'Other men.'

There was a short silence. At last, she murmured, 'What makes you think there have been other men?'

He detected a certain wariness in her tone. 'Logic. Reason. I don't think . . . I can't imagine I am the first.'

She shifted, uneasily. 'Is it important to you, to know?'

He was silent.

'You must understand,' she said at last, lying on her back, an arm flung across her eyes. 'I was young when we married. I soon discovered that marriage was not what I had expected it to be. We made love, of course, but that part of the marriage soon ended. Gordon was . . . is . . . not a passionate man. His desires are . . . subdued. Controlled.' She hesitated. 'His life is controlled.'

She had not answered his question. But he needed no answer, in reality. Their own relationship had developed explosively; there had been no circling in subdued awareness, no hesitancy. When the reality had thrust upon them it had been raw, an urgency that demanded fulfilment. They had both reacted swiftly, grabbed for what they saw in each other, eager to sate the passion that rose in each of them. But he could not believe it had been a unique experience for Isabella. These were meadows she had walked before: he would not have been her first lover, beyond the confines of her marriage to Gordon Portland. But did it matter?

172

'Something is bothering you,' she remarked quietly. 'Is it really the thought of other men?'

'No,' he sighed. 'What you might have had before me is irrelevant. We didn't know each other then. No, it's not that.' He hesitated, touched her shoulder lightly, traced a finger down the swell of her breast. 'It's the fact that I don't want anything to damage what we have . . . and if the relationship gets known, is talked about, that damage can arise. What would happen if your husband discovered you and I are lovers?'

Her fingers laced into his. 'He doesn't know about it.'

'We can't keep it this way for ever. It's almost inevitable it will come out.'

'Why should it? We are careful; we are discreet.'

He hesitated. 'I think my colleague Farnsby suspects.'

She turned to him, her eyes large. 'How could he know about us?'

O'Connor made no reply. His mind slipped back to the way Farnsby had been observing him these last weeks. There had been suspicion in the man's eyes; a resentful silence when they were working together. O'Connor knew it would have been difficult for Farnsby to raise the issue. But just two days ago he had clearly been trying to summon up the courage to confront his senior officer on the matter. He had stood squarely in front of O'Connor's desk, dogged, troubled. The two men had not become close even though they had now undertaken several investigations together: Farnsby still harboured a degree of resentment that he had been overlooked for DCI Culpeper's job when O'Connor had been drafted in. O'Connor had tried to bridge the gap from time to time, and they had developed a grudging respect for each other; they had a workable relationship but one that was still liable to spill over into irritated resentment on occasions. But they certainly had failed to achieve any great ease in their relationship. Which was why Farnsby found it difficult to deal with the issue now.

173

'I've been unable to raise you on your mobile a few times recently, sir.'

O'Connor raised an eyebrow, and shrugged. 'So?'

Farnsby frowned. 'It's important that we stay in touch, with these two separate investigations going on. In case anything breaks.'

There was a short silence. O'Connor regarded the younger man coolly, in spite of the quickening of his pulse, as he guessed what was coming. 'You got something to say, let it out.'

A slight flush stained Farnsby's neck. 'I saw you getting into that Jaguar a few weeks back, when we were supposed to pick you up.'

'I'd phoned you to cancel the pickup,' O'Connor replied.

'But we were already there, at the Central Station by then. I saw you getting in.'

'As you've already informed me.'

'I was puzzled – and thought it best to check. I ran a check immediately. The car belonged to Gordon Portland.' Farnsby ran his tongue over dry lips. 'I get the impression recently you've got things on your mind, sir. And a . . . relationship with Mrs Portland is unwise. You know that Gordon Portland had dealings with Hamilton; you know he wanted to find out what we were going to do about Evans –'

'There's no evidence to link Portland with the deaths of Hamilton or MacLean, nor have we found anything that ties him in with the smuggling group set up by Cosimo. So just what's your point, Farnsby?'

'It's none of my business, sir, I know –'

'Then why are you raising it?' O'Connor snapped, unable to keep the defensive note out of his voice.

Farnsby had not had the courage to continue . . .

In the dimness of the hotel room O'Connor turned, moving away from the woman beside him. He sighed, glanced across to the bedside table and the digital clock. 'I'm going to have to leave,' he said.

'I know. Duty calls.' There was just a hint of sarcasm in her tone.

'You know I don't want to go.'

'I know.' She moved close to him again and he held her. They stayed like that for several minutes, neither moving, content merely in the nearness, and then he gently disengaged himself.

'You want me to leave first, as usual?' she asked in a matter-of-fact tone.

He shrugged, careless. It was a pattern they had fallen into. She would arrive after he did, she would leave before him. They never used the same hotel; he always paid for the room in cash, even though it often caused difficulty since hotels tended to dislike dealing with anything other than credit cards. But he had no intention of being trapped, in the way that Constantine Rakoff had been traced. He watched her as she rose from the bed, walked across to the bathroom. When he heard the shower turned on he rose also, followed her and stood in the open doorway, watching her while she showered. He wondered whether her husband ever watched her like this.

Ownership. Possession. Indifference to love.

And yet as he saw Isabella glance over her shoulder, smile at him, beckon to him to join her with her naked skin glistening with water, he knew that Farnsby was right. It was not merely the fact that O'Connor was having an affair with a married woman; it was with someone who might be connected to an investigation that was ongoing. Yet he was unable to break the spell; the time they spent together was urgent, desired, and when he was away from her memories of her lingered in his mind.

After she had dressed, kissed him goodbye and left the room he remained for half an hour, sitting on the edge of the bed as a vast depression washed over him. He felt empty, seized by a vague desperation. This relationship fired him and yet it was going nowhere: it could go nowhere. He had no illusions. The reasons that had caused Isabella to marry Gordon Portland would be the same reasons that would continue to bind her to him. There was nothing O'Connor could offer her to change that.

He closed the hotel room quietly behind him. He glanced at his watch. It was eight in the evening; there was no one at the reception desk when he walked past. He made his way to the car, got in, and then switched on his mobile. He was in no mood to return to headquarters, but it was wise to check in. If only to keep Farnsby off his case.

When he read off the numbers he realized it was the detective inspector who had been trying to contact him. He rang through immediately.

'Farnsby?'

'DCI O'Connor.' Farnsby's voice held a cold anger. 'We've been trying to contact you.'

'You've got me now.'

'You're the senior officer in charge. I wasn't prepared to take a decision until I'd spoken to you,' Farnsby said, making no secret of his resentment.

'What's happened?' O'Connor asked quickly, a surge of anticipatory anxiety running through his veins.

'Islwyn Evans has broken cover.'

'What do you mean?'

'Evans has made contact with someone, trying to arrange a meeting.'

'What exactly has happened?' O'Connor demanded, angry at Farnsby's prevarication.

'A message came in three hours ago. It was from that archaeologist Arnold Landon. He wanted to speak to you, but the desk sergeant couldn't get hold of you so took the message. Landon says that Evans has been in touch, wants to meet him in Berwick. Landon says he's driving up there, to meet him on the town ramparts, at Brass Bastion.'

176

'The hell he is! Didn't you try to stop him?' O'Connor rasped.

'The message was for you, sir,' Farnsby replied coldly. 'The desk sergeant couldn't reach you. I only received it personally an hour ago. And I couldn't raise you either.'

O'Connor was silent for a moment, his mind racing. He thrust aside his resentment at Farnsby's justified anger: the position was serious. They had Evans under surveillance; they knew that Rakoff was in the area; and if Evans was coming out to meet Landon . . .

'I'm coming in,' he snapped. 'You say Landon phoned some time ago?'

'At least three hours ago.'

'Meet me at Ponteland. And get us a helicopter. We've got to be up there at Berwick before Landon walks into more than he expects. And Farnsby –'

'Sir?'

'We'll need the support of an Armed Response Unit.'

Chapter Five

1

When the phone call had come in to Arnold's office in Morpeth, Carmela had been insistent: she wanted to come with him to Berwick.

They had just returned to the office from a session spent in the County Archives where he had been showing Carmela records of the artefacts that had been discovered in Northumberland over the years. She had been particularly keen to see photographs of the items with whose discovery he had himself been involved: while the artefacts themselves had now been taken for display at the British Museum in London, and elsewhere, the archives retained photographs of them – the Viking sword *Kvernbiter*, the *sudarium* he had discovered in the gateway to a castle wall, the shamanic cave paintings they had found in the sea cave at Hades Gate. She was naturally interested in Roman remains gathered over the years from Hadrian's Wall and Hexham, Vindolanda and Housesteads and Whitley Castle. They discussed the seemingly impossible distances the ancient people had travelled, given the state of the roads and the availability of transport: Syrian women operating shops in Wallsend, serving the Roman garrison; German soldiers commemorated as standard bearers in the XVth Legion; tombstones and pottery, medical instruments for trepanning and cataract removal and limb amputation.

When they returned to the office Carmela commented

178

on her reluctance to end the visit. 'The Minister has already returned home, and although I managed to get an extension to my visit, in two days' time I also must take my leave of you, Arnold. But I am sorry to go. It has been most instructive, this time here with you: I have enjoyed working with you, and while I cannot come to terms with your English weather, the countryside you have shown me is quite beautiful.'

The phone had rung at that moment.

'Is that Landon?' The voice was almost a whisper; the tone husky with caution.

'It is. Who's that?'

There was a brief pause; he could hear shallow, irregular breathing at the other end of the line.

'This is Islwyn Evans.'

Arnold was taken aback. Evans would have no reason to make professional contact with the man who had acted as an expert witness for the prosecution against him, and he could not imagine why he would now be calling. 'So you're back in circulation,' Arnold commented.

'How do you mean?' The man's voice seemed distant, and edgy.

'I've called at your premises . . . and I've tried ringing you a couple of times. You were expected at a trade fair in Kendal but didn't turn up. I was told you were out of contact.'

'What did you want of me?'

Arnold hesitated. 'It's not something I would want to talk about on the phone. But it was sort of connected with your trial. And . . . you'll have heard that there have been two killings. One of them was –'

'I know,' Evans interrupted testily. 'I've heard about all that. Look . . . I would like us to meet.'

'What about?' Arnold asked, puzzled.

'I understand from the newspapers you've been involved with people from the Italian Ministry of Culture.'

'That's correct,' Arnold replied, mystified. 'But what's that got to do –'

'I've got something they might be interested in.'

Arnold frowned. He glanced at Carmela. 'And what might that be?'

'An ancient artefact, of some considerable value.' Evans's voice dropped, conspiratorially. 'It was taken from an Etruscan tomb. It found its way into my hands. The calyx krater.'

Arnold sat up in surprise. There was a short silence. Arnold frowned, saw Carmela raise her head curiously as she became aware of the tension in his body. He was silent for a while as he considered the matter. Cautiously, he asked, 'What is there to discuss concerning the artefact?'

Carmela was watching him, a slight frown on her brow.

'I . . . I want to negotiate.'

Arnold felt a slow burning of anger in his chest. 'Negotiate? You know damn well that the calyx krater was stolen, so what's there to negotiate about? If it ended up in your hands, it was because you were somehow involved in the dirty business of –'

'Listen to me!' The antiques dealer's tone was harsh. 'Things have moved on for me recently. I'm not interested in discussing moral issues with you, or ownership, or even how the calyx krater came into my hands. All that is irrelevant. I understand you have the right connections within the Ministry, and I'm in a hurry. I haven't got time to put it on to the open market. The fact is, it's in my possession, and I'm prepared to negotiate its return. At the right price. And under the right conditions.'

He fell silent. Arnold bit his lip, considering. He could understand why the antiques dealer could be in a panic: he would know about the murders of Cosimo in Italy, and Hamilton and MacLean in England, and it was clear he was contemplating an early disappearance from the scene, to avoid the possibility of a similar fate. But he wanted to get rid of at least one valuable possession first. Trade it back to the people who owned it, and were looking for it in England. 'All right,' Arnold agreed at last. 'There's no reason why we can't talk about it. Where shall we meet? And when?'

'The sooner the better,' Evans replied crisply. 'Tonight. You can get here in a couple of hours.'

'Where are you?'

There was a slight hesitation. 'You know the site of the Citadel, at Berwick? I'll meet you nearby, on the ramparts, close to the Brass Bastion there. Nine o'clock this evening. We can talk then.'

'I'll be there,' Arnold agreed, and Evans rang off. Arnold looked at Carmela.

She was staring at him, wide-eyed with excitement. 'I heard you mention the calyx krater.'

Arnold nodded. 'The man who was prosecuted – the one who seems to have dropped out of sight – he says he's got it, and wants to talk to me about it.'

'Talk?' she asked, frowning.

'I think he wants to sell it. I've agreed to meet him tonight.'

She stood up, her face alight with anticipation. 'The calyx krater! That's wonderful! I'll come with you.'

Arnold did not think it was a good idea. It was clear that Evans was nervous, in view of what had already happened. He might be scared off if Arnold did not arrive alone. Carmela argued otherwise: Evans would hardly object when he saw it was a woman accompanying the man he was to meet. And besides, she was an expert on Etruscan artefacts – she would be able to support Arnold in his identification of the object, make sure that Evans was not trying to pass off a fake.

'Moreover,' she added intensely, 'I can be of assistance in the negotiation itself. I am, after all, a representative of the Ministry of Culture. It's the Ministry he wants to sell it to; I might be able to put pressure on this antiques dealer.' Passion flared in her eyes. 'I might, perhaps, even be able to force him to give up the calyx krater without payment.'

Arnold was still doubtful. He glanced at his watch, calculating the time it would take to get to Berwick by car. 'There's something else you're forgetting,' he reminded her.

She was suspicious, anxious that he should raise no further issues to dissuade her from coming with him. 'What?'

'The things we discussed earlier. The fact that Cosimo would seem to have established a smuggling ring. The likelihood that Evans was involved in it. The fact that two men are already dead . . .'

'So what do you suggest?' she flashed at him, folding her arms over her generous bosom. 'That it is dangerous to meet him? If so, why do you go alone?'

'I've thought about that. I don't want you to get exposed to danger – and it's maybe unwise that I go to talk with him. I think it would be sensible to inform the police.'

'Of what?'

'Of the fact Evans is prepared to meet me in Berwick.'

'And what will happen to the calyx krater then?' she argued passionately. 'Will Evans hand it over if the police arrive there, instead of you? Or if he sees them, will he run? And then will it merely disappear, remain hidden for decades, fall into the wrong hands? Arnold, it is important that you negotiate with this man. You must go, and I must come with you.'

He was still doubtful, but he understood the force of her argument. He thought about it for a while, as she sat there, glaring at him, her large bosom heaving in her barely controlled excitement. At last he nodded, reaching for the phone. 'All right, we'll compromise. I'll go to Berwick to meet him as arranged. But I'll call DCI O'Connor first, to tell him about the meeting. If we can get to Berwick ahead of O'Connor, talk to Evans, we might get what we want before the police arrive . . . if they arrive. After all, we can't be certain they're looking for him, in connection with the two murders.'

'You'll go, then.'

'Yes,' he replied, placing the call to Ponteland.

'And I'll come with you,' she insisted, breathing hard.

There seemed no point in further argument.

They left the Morpeth office in Arnold's car twenty minutes later. He had calculated they would reach Berwick in good time to keep the appointment. As they left the town on the A1 running north, Carmela settled into her seat with a comfortable sigh. 'This place, Berwick,' she said. 'What is it like?'

He was pleased to talk about it; it was something to take his mind off the possible dangers inherent in the impending meeting. 'You'd find it interesting, from an historical point of view,' Arnold explained. 'It stands on the north bank of the River Tweed: it was a frontier town that was fought over for generations.'

'Fought over? Who by?'

'The Scots and the English, throughout the early medieval period. The border between Scotland and England – two separate kingdoms – was constantly shifting. As a consequence, the town itself changed hands with monotonous regularity. It finally settled as part of England, but it still has strong Scottish affinities. Of course, there's not much of the castle or the medieval walls left now – the coming of the railway ended all that, except for a bit of the medieval quay. But there's still a sixteenth-century circuit of ramparts and bastions that were erected to meet the threat of artillery. You'll be interested, because the system of defence was developed by your countrymen.'

'Italians?' she exclaimed in surprise.

'The principal engineer was English, beginning the massive works in 1558, but he was advised by Giovanni Portinari and Jacopo Contio.'

'They were a long way from home,' she murmured.

183

'But very important to the design of the works, it seems. They were there until 1569, when the work was brought to a halt. Only two sides of the fortifications were finished.'

'But they remain?'

'They do. And it's in that area that we're going to meet the elusive Islwyn Evans.'

She lapsed into silence. The evening was drawing in, dark clouds piling up in the east, and when they caught glimpses of the coastline it was vaguely marked by the flicker of distant lightning, far out to sea. Arnold felt a subdued excitement at the prospect ahead of them: the chance to get his hands on the calyx krater, examine it, with Carmela available to confirm its provenance. And Carmela had been correct: it would be useful to have her along, to use her position with the Italian Ministry, and to help identify the artefact as genuine. He could appreciate her excitement also: the calyx krater was endowed with a certain symbolism in her Ministry, and its recovery would be regarded as a considerable triumph.

It was just after eight fifteen when they finally crossed the Royal Tweed Bridge and entered the town. Arnold turned left and parked the car near Scotsgate. It was only a short walk from there to Church Street, and then up to the Brass Bastion, but they had time to spare so he suggested they might as well walk along the ramparts, while they waited the arrival of Islwyn Evans at the appointed time. Carmela agreed, so they crossed past Meg's Mount and ascended the Quay Walls, which gave them a good view of the surrounding area: he was able to point out to her the seventeenth-century Old Bridge, and beyond, towering above the river upstream, Robert Stephenson's great railway crossing, the Royal Border Bridge. As they stood there the lights of a train departing for the south glittered through the darkness as it crossed the bridge. They walked slowly towards Palace Green and then swung around the curve of the town towards King's Mount. A distant murmuring in the sky turned to a muted, beating roar: offshore, in the distance, they saw the lights of a helicopter, chattering its way northwards. After a few moments it disappeared north of the town.

'If this was a tourist stroll,' Arnold explained, 'I'd be showing you the Governor's House and the old Custom House but there's hardly much point as it is, in the dark. If we just head up here now we'll reach the eastern defences of Berwick: King's Mount is the first bastion, then we walk along the Elizabethan ramparts past Windmill Bastion. Evans wants to meet a little further along at Brass Bastion – presumably because it's close to Cow Port, the sixteenth-century gateway leading into the town.'

She linked her arm into his affectionately as they made their way along the ramparts. He was aware of her suppressed excitement, from a slight quivering of her arm. They were not entirely alone: a young couple stood embracing, leaning against the wall of the rampart, lost in each other, seemingly unaware of the presence of others; a tramp sat on one of the seats, head almost between his knees, a dark bottle in his hands, singing vaguely to himself. He was swaying slightly to the rhythm of the old song, oblivious to their passage. Murmurs of sound came from the town itself, traffic in the roadways, and they caught occasional glimpses of the streets beyond Ravensdowne Barracks, the earliest built in Britain in the eighteenth century. When they finally reached the Brass Bastion they were alone. They waited. The sky seemed to be getting even darker: offshore, the flickers of distant lightning were accompanied by occasional faint sounds of thunder. Arnold raised his head: there was a hint of rain but he doubted whether a storm was on the way. Yet the evening air was oppressive, heavy.

He still caught the occasional distant murmur of the helicopter that had earlier crossed seawards, flying north: it was possibly a military activity, from the base at RAF Boulmer, the camp based near the cliffs beyond Seahouses and Bamburgh, he concluded. It seemed to be hovering beyond their sight, the sound of its clattering rotors beating towards them intermittently. He glanced at his watch in the faint light: Evans should be putting in an appearance soon. Carmela still clutched at his arm: she shivered slightly, perhaps from nervousness, perhaps from the oppressiveness of the evening. He turned his head slightly, looked down past the church behind him, towards the Cow Port, and he thought he caught a faint movement down there in the dim shadows of the gateway. He screwed his eyes, staring, and a few moments later made out the dark figure detaching itself from the shadows.

'This might be him,' Arnold murmured.

The man came through the gateway with a slow, hesitant step. He reached the Elizabethan ramparts and stopped, peering around, taking in the ramparts themselves, looking towards the Windmill Bastion before he turned and began to walk slowly in Arnold's direction. Carmela was at Arnold's side, half hidden. When the approaching figure was some twenty yards away she moved, and the man stopped, crouching slightly as though ready to turn and run.

'Evans? Is that you?' Arnold called.

A distant rumble of thunder came rolling in from the horizon. It was matched by the faint chatter of helicopter rotors, still hovering north of the town. The man standing there in the darkness straightened, then called out in reply. 'Landon. I thought you'd be alone. Who's with you?'

'A member of the Ministry of Culture,' Arnold replied.

'Carmela Cacciatore,' she added.

The man facing them remained still, tense, as though debating whether to walk away. He hunched himself in his dark jacket, the upturned collar almost covering his head. 'I didn't expect two of you,' Evans grumbled in doubt, but then after a moment, with a nervous glance over his shoulder, he came forward until he was standing just ten feet away from them. 'Why did you bring her?'

'She has an interest in all this,' Arnold said firmly. 'She

knows the artefact you possess. She'll be able to confirm that what you claim to have is the real thing. She's an expert in Etruscan art.'

'Experts,' Evans sneered contemptuously.

Arnold's tone hardened. 'You wanted to talk, to negotiate. You say you have the calyx krater –'

'You don't expect me to carry the bloody thing with me here, do you?' Evans snapped. 'I've got it safe, don't you worry. What I need to know is whether you're prepared to pay for it: I am, you might say, in the position of needing to liquidate my assets.'

'You're running, you mean?' Arnold queried in a quiet tone.

There was a short silence. Arnold could barely make out Evans's features. The man was bareheaded, but Arnold could now see that he was wearing a heavy duffel coat, with the collar turned up, fastened across his throat. His hands were thrust deep into his pockets, and his stance was marked with tension. 'My motives are irrelevant,' he muttered. 'All you need to know is that I'm prepared to be reasonable, reach a bargain with you. I'll let you have the calyx krater, provided we can agree a figure –'

'I will need to see the artefact,' Carmela interrupted firmly, stepping forward in an attitude of defiance.

Evans dragged a hand out of his pocket, held it up as a warning. 'Stay right there. I'm in control of this meeting. You'll get to see nothing,' he snarled. 'You know what I'm talking about; and if you're really from the Italian Ministry you'll know how valuable it is. But let's be clear about one thing: I'm not going to be stupid enough to bring it out of the safe place where I've got it stashed away. We need to talk about an appropriate figure. And then I'll not be bringing the damn thing out until you've arranged a transfer of money to an account number I'll give you –'

He stopped suddenly. He cocked his head to one side, peered past them towards Lord's Mount, some three hundred yards distant. Then he glanced back behind him, to

187

the Cow Port. He said something under his breath; it was almost unintelligible, but Arnold guessed it was an obscenity. Slowly, uncertainly Islwyn Evans began to back away.

Arnold put out a hand. 'Where are you going? I thought you wanted to negotiate –'

'Not here,' Evans muttered, an edge of panic in his voice. 'This was a mistake. I'll be in touch with you again . . .' He backed away anxiously, then turned, quickening his step as he hurried along towards the ramparts. From behind him Arnold caught the sound of feet, running towards them from the Lord's Mount. Beyond Evans's retreating figure he saw further activity: someone moving swiftly along the ramparts from the direction of Windmill Bastion. Evans spun on his heel, glaring wildly along the ramparts and then back to the running figure converging upon the small group from Lord's Mount. He was uncertain, hesitant as to which direction to run, and then he seemed to make up his mind as he headed back towards Cow Port. He was brought up short momentarily as the distant chattering they had heard in the dark sky was suddenly rising, swelling into a loud, rushing clattering sound as the helicopter came sweeping in from above the town, a bright light playing across the Church of the Holy Trinity and the Ravensdowne Barracks, homing in on to the ramparts, and Evans yelled loudly, picked up speed again, broke into a run and headed directly for the Cow Port gateway. He was only halfway there when he skidded to a halt again, almost falling as he saw someone coming through the gateway towards him.

Arnold himself broke into a run, half-dazed though he was by the brightness of the light sweeping across the rampart. Carmela caught at his arm, hindering him, but staggering along beside him as they heard Evans scream in terror, turn back, rush towards them. It was a wild, chaotic scene: the harsh stabbing light, the sound of a man's voice booming an incomprehensible warning through the night, the drowning sound of the rotors of the police helicopter, and staggering at the edge of the darkness was the antiques dealer, locked in a struggle with a man taller than himself, big, dark-clothed. Then Evans fell backwards on the rampart, and the figure of his assailant was running towards Arnold and Carmela, throwing something aside, reaching inside his coat for a weapon as he ran.

Arnold shouted as the man bore down on him, held out his arms while the voice thundered at him from the circling machine in the sky. He was confused, his senses in disarray, and the man who had attacked Evans was suddenly on him. As the heavy figure darted past Arnold tried to grapple with him but was thrown aside, and he saw the flash, heard the cracking sound of a pistol shot, and Carmela fell beside him, screaming. Entangled with her he tripped and fell also, lying across her body as she clung to him. The confusion became greater, the noise indescribable as the chattering rotors thundered close above their heads, but Arnold thought he could hear other shots.

He lay still, with Carmela's body shuddering under him, her arms clasped about him, holding him close to her panicked body. Someone came running up, knelt beside them. Arnold blinked hard; in the white, throbbing light from the circling helicopter the man he had taken for a tramp down near the King's Mount seemed huge yet almost ethereal for all his bulk.

A hand gripped his shoulder. 'Are you all right?'

Arnold nodded, then shifted to one side, as Carmela struggled to rise beneath him. 'I felt something,' she muttered, 'like a pulling at my coat . . .'

The tramp reached for her, felt at her shoulder. He grunted. 'You're okay,' he said, and rose, began to move off towards where the helicopter now hovered, hanging like some monstrous bird of prey in the sky, its white lights pinning down the people caught in its bright pool, air-lashed, noise-battered.

There were three of them: Arnold thought he could

make out a man and a woman, the young couple who had been seemingly lost in each other near Palace Green, and another man, staring down at a dark bundle near their feet. Others were converging, uniformed men, yellow-jacketed.

'What is happening?' Carmela asked wildly.

'Are you all right? I thought he'd injured you,' Arnold said.

'My coat, I think, the shoulder . . . but I am not hurt.'

Evans. Arnold turned his head, began to rise to his feet, holding out a hand to assist Carmela. There was another small group at the edge of the pool of light, near the Cow Port gateway. Even as he looked down to them headlights edged into the gateway, flashing lights, a police car, an ambulance. Arnold began to walk towards the group, Carmela just behind him, until a man detached himself from the huddle, began to make his way towards Arnold, one hand outstretched.

Carmela tugged at his arm. 'I think he wants us to remain here,' she said in a quiet, shaky voice.

Down at the Cow Port gateway, the police officers were lifting a man to his feet. Evans. He was staggering, so it appeared he had escaped death. But when Arnold looked across to the other group, the armed men surrounding the figure huddled on the ground, he guessed that Evans's assailant had failed in his mission, and had paid for it with his life.

The noise of the rotors clattered in his ears, insistent, raucous, until finally the machine began to lift and the battering wind about their heads eased.

2

Assistant Chief Constable Sid Cathery entered the room rubbing his hands vigorously, a gesture they had come to associate with the expression of pleasure on his part. When he saw that O'Connor and Farnsby were seated in front of the television monitor, replaying the grainy scenes of the video footage from outside the house in Gosforth, where James MacLean had died, he treated them to a broad grin of approval. 'Hey, lads, that's what I like to see, devotion to duty. Reviewing the evidence, is that it? Making sure everything's in place when you make out your final report. Good, good, that's what I like to see.'

O'Connor glanced at him indifferently, and made no reply. Farnsby leaned back in his chair. 'Are the interviews all over now, sir?'

Cathery's eyes narrowed a little, wary, his ears attuned for criticism. Then he relaxed. 'Aye, all done and dusted.' He eyed the men in front of him with a degree of cunning. 'I thought it best that the interviews were conducted by others in the section, under my supervision. You two, you've done enough. You needed to rest up, back off a bit after that chase up to Berwick. Bit Wild West, wasn't it? Knifing . . . gun play, lot of shouting and yelling and that bloody helicopter. Like the punch-ups I used to get involved in back in my rugby days in the south-west. I tell you, they were hard buggers down there. Kick anything that moved above the grass, they did. Getting the ball was a secondary consideration.'

He perched his bulk on the edge of the desk, one leg swinging, glanced briefly at the videotape playing, and then turned back, regarded them with satisfaction. 'Aye, I wouldn't have minded getting stuck into that shindig myself. Mind, it didn't go with the kind of precision we might have hoped for.'

Wearily, O'Connor rubbed a hand over his eyes. 'We didn't have much choice, sir. Farnsby and I were in the chopper and we were just north of the scene when the call came in that things were moving. We'd had Evans under surveillance, we had people posted on the ramparts, undercover officers, and we got the message that Evans was moving out of the house in Northumberland Avenue. We'd had intelligence that Rakoff was probably in the area,

191

and even that he possibly knew where Evans was hiding out. Just biding his chance, waiting for the opportunity to get at Evans. Fulfil his contract.'

'And he almost bloody made it!'

O'Connor ignored the hint of criticism. 'As Rakoff made his way past the Bell Tower and cut through the streets towards the Brass Bastion he was picked up, we had him under surveillance from vantage points all the way. We had people on the ramparts, down near Cow Port, and the ARU in readiness. But there was no way we could know for certain whether Rakoff would make his play then, nor exactly how he intended making his attack.'

Cathery frowned, scratched his cheek with a pudgy forefinger. 'Aye, that was the dicey part of the operation, it seems to me, and one we'll have to play down a bit, at the press conference I've called. The media don't like the idea of gun play in public places. And no doubt some smart bastard will suggest we should never have allowed things to get that far.'

'I don't think there was much choice,' Farnsby replied evenly. 'We'd temporarily lost surveillance on Rakoff. We got the radio call that Evans was on the move, keeping his rendezvous with Landon and the Cacciatore woman, but when we picked up a signal of unauthorized movement on the ramparts we felt we had to go in. If we'd gone in earlier we might have lost him; if we'd held back, waited longer to see how events might have unfolded, we'd have had more than one dead man on our hands.'

Cathery nodded, in reluctant acceptance. 'As it was, Evans was saved only by that heavy coat he was wearing. When Rakoff slashed at his throat, he penetrated the cloth, but not deeply. Evans's throat wound was superficial and he's been able to sing. Quite sweetly, in fact.' Cathery grinned, nodded his head in grim satisfaction. 'He's been able to confirm that it was all set up a few years back, after the Renzo organization Europol told us about had collapsed. During the interregnum, with Arturo Renzo in the nick, the man they called Cosimo had entered into new arrangements. It was Hamilton who went to Rome and made the first contact, and set up the system. He supplied the distribution network to the UK, Japan and the States. Evans acted as the procurer, developed provenance for the stuff they had, and ran the warehousing arrangements, while MacLean was a more marginal figure, but involved nevertheless, usually simply to provide information of the kind they needed to supply false provenance for individual artefacts. Things began to unravel, of course, when we put Evans on trial over that cauldron looted from Avalon.'

'It brought MacLean out into the open, certainly,' Farnsby suggested.

Cathery nodded his bull-like head. 'Evans has now admitted that the cauldron was stolen from the Avalon site, but when he was caught and charged with handling stolen goods he insisted that MacLean involve himself, agree to act as defence expert witness and deny the cauldron was genuine. MacLean resisted it, because it put him in the limelight, but in the end he went along after he was threatened by Evans. And Hamilton was backing it too: the smuggling group would have collapsed if Evans had been found guilty.' He rubbed his pudgy hands in satisfaction. 'But there you go. The Renzo organization was in process of being re-established. Rakoff was contracted to eliminate the opposition of small groups like Cosimo's, and put the fear of God into anyone else who might even think of working outside the Renzo empire.' He shook his heavy head in reluctant admiration. 'You got to hand it to that bastard Rakoff: he was a committed killer. When he agreed to do something, there was nothing going to stop him doing it. Except a bullet.' He paused. 'Which brings me back to his getting downed.'

'He pulled a gun,' Farnsby explained. 'He fired the first shot.'

'He almost hit the Cacciatore woman,' O'Connor added quietly.

Cathery grimaced. 'Like I said, Wild West stuff. Well, as long as we've got evidence that he started the gunfight, I suppose it was inevitable that our own people had to open up.'

'I believe the men from the Armed Response Unit have put in their own report,' Farnsby noted.

Cathery considered the matter for a little while. 'I suppose he pulled the gun when he realized we were closing in on him.'

'He'd already attacked Evans,' O'Connor replied quietly. 'Left him for dead, because he had no time to finish him off properly. He discarded the knife, made a run for it as we came around in the helicopter and the ARU people closed in. Landon tried to stop him, got knocked aside as Rakoff fired the first shot. After that, our people didn't have much choice.'

'And neither Landon nor the woman were hurt. They've made statements?'

'The same evening,' Farnsby nodded.

Cathery nodded and swung his bulky haunch off the desk. 'Right. Well, like I said, it was good work. Ended well. And you got the knife?'

There was a short silence. Farnsby looked at O'Connor expectantly. O'Connor nodded. 'He'd thrown it aside. We found it just below the rampart, in the grass. Nasty weapon.' He looked Cathery directly in the eye. 'A flick knife.'

Cathery grinned. 'Excellent. So we can close the whole thing. I'll be holding a press conference later today. No need to involve you two. Evans is in custody, and he'll face trial again, slimy Welsh bastard. And we can tell Europol that we've got their killer for them, even if he did manage to nail two of his intended victims. And even if we did have to execute him in the process.' He made his way towards the door. Then he looked back at the two silent officers. 'Hey, you guys stick with me, follow my lead and I'll make good coppers of you two yet.'

O'Connor slumped back in his chair, after the door closed behind the Assistant Chief Constable. After a few moments' silence he switched on the video again, and the grainy video images began to replay. The two men sat there watching scenes they had already gone over time and again. At last, almost impatiently, O'Connor pressed the button, and the machine clicked to a halt. He picked up the sheaf of papers lying beside him on the desktop. He shook his head. 'Bloody banks. They take their damned time producing statements. We should have had these MacLean account statements in our hands days ago.' He stared at the top sheet gloomily, read once more the entry marked with a yellow highlighter pen.

Farnsby watched him, frowning. After a while, he asked, 'Do we pull in Charlie Davis and Jenny Sanders again?'

O'Connor nodded. 'I think we have to,' he agreed gloomily.

'And after that . . . you want me to do it?'

O'Connor hesitated, then shook his head reluctantly. 'No. This is down to me.'

'I think it best that I come along with you.'

O'Connor shrugged. It was a matter of indifference to him.

3

The same grave-visaged butler opened the door, and when O'Connor flashed his warrant card he stepped aside without a word. O'Connor looked back to Farnsby, seated in the car, and then entered. As he stood there in the hallway he could hear the sound of raised voices in the library. He glanced at the butler; the man's eyes met his expressionlessly. He said nothing, merely raised a hand in the direction of the library and stalked away towards the rear of the house.

195

The library door was ajar and O'Connor didn't bother to knock; he pushed the door wider and walked in. The voices stopped abruptly as he did so and both Gordon Portland and his wife turned to look at him in surprise. They were standing at the other side of the room, near the end of the display table. Gordon Portland had been glaring at his wife, hands clenched at his sides, stiff with anger and resentment. Isabella was some two feet away from him, her face pale apart from red marks of fury in her cheeks. At O'Connor's entry she had turned, her eyes wide in shocked surprise. He knew what she would be thinking: he should not be here, coming to see her in her own home.

'Marital tiff?' O'Connor asked ironically. He had difficulty keeping his tone level. His heart was hammering against his ribs as he moved slowly forward.

'DCI O'Connor.' Gordon Portland almost ground out the words. His features seemed drawn, his eyes red-rimmed, pouched with fatigue, and he seemed to have grown older since O'Connor last saw him. 'What brings you here?' His tired eyes narrowed as he looked at Isabella, and jerked his head in her direction. There was a sneering tone in his voice. 'Have you come to see me, or is this a social visit with my wife?'

Isabella flashed a surly glance in his direction, her lip curled in contempt, but she made no comment. The three of them stood there silently, awkwardly, for several seconds, as though waiting for something to happen. At last, O'Connor said, 'You'll have heard that an attempt was made on the life of Islwyn Evans.'

'The missing antiques dealer,' Portland muttered. He raised an eyebrow, shook his head as though trying to clear it of unwelcome thoughts. 'I'm not surprised. I heard it on the news. Are you here to advise me on my future investments, tell me that he's the scum we all suspected he might be?'

O'Connor nodded slowly. 'Something like that. We now

196

have confirmation that Islwyn Evans did indeed have links with Italy; he was involved in an antiques smuggling ring, along with Hamilton and MacLean. Their activities were unwelcome to certain criminals in Rome, who were seeking to re-establish their own organization. A contracted assassin from Italy was employed to wipe out the men in the group. Evans was to be the third man to die, but we managed to get there in time to prevent that.'

'And you killed the assassin in the process of rescuing Evans, I understand,' Portland said, his eyes holding a cold challenge as he stared at O'Connor. When O'Connor made no response, Portland too was silent for a little while. But he seemed edgy. He extracted a flat silver case from his pocket, took out a cigarette, lit it from a lighter on the table. His hand was trembling slightly. 'I saw the televised press conference held by Assistant Chief Constable Cathery. He was boastful, lavish in his praise, for the men who had trapped this man Rakoff, responsible for the killing of those villains.' There was a contemptuous note in his voice. 'Overlying his comments, of course, was praise for himself. He was overcome in my view by what the Greeks called hubris.'

'Cathery always was a pompous ass,' O'Connor replied in cold agreement. 'And if he wants to stick his neck out and make a fool of himself, why should I try to stop him?'

Silence fell again. Isabella's body was stiff, her eyes now fixed on her husband, as though she was still waiting for an explosion, which was nothing to do with what the men were discussing. But after a momentary uncertainty, Portland seemed to have regained his composure. He eyed O'Connor quizzically. 'So, if this isn't a social call what is it you want with us, now that you've dealt with these murders? I can't imagine we have anything else to discuss, between the three of us.'

Isabella shuddered slightly at the sneer in his voice; her glance flicked between the two men. She was on edge, nervous. O'Connor's eyes were drawn to the glass-topped cases on the long oak table. He remembered clearly admiring the display of medieval weapons there. He became aware that Isabella had turned her head, was watching him. There was something dark in her eyes, a pleading, a slow-moving anxiety. He stared at her without expression and saw the anxiety grow. She wanted him to leave. She wanted no damaging disclosures. She wanted to be left alone to sort out things with her husband.

'You should have told me about MacLean,' O'Connor said coldly.

Her eyes widened. 'MacLean?' She hesitated, confused. 'How . . . how could I tell you about MacLean? I had no idea he might be involved in a smuggling ring!'

He had hoped for better from her. 'That's not what I'm talking about.'

She looked quickly at her husband and then moved around the end of the table, approaching O'Connor. Her mouth twisted slightly, emphasizing her nervous uncertainty, but her eyes were blank. She shook her head, and a wisp of red-gold hair flicked across her eyes. Impatiently, she brushed it away. 'I don't understand –'

Gordon Portland moved also, leaning against the table. 'Surely you do, my dear,' he sneered. 'Your little secret is out. That's it, isn't it, DCI O'Connor? You've finally discovered that you're not unique: you're only the latest in a long line. And no doubt you've become aware that your immediate predecessor was none other than the libidinous Dr James MacLean.'

Isabella grimaced involuntarily, her eyes still fixed on O'Connor. She moved again, closer to him, but there was a jerkiness about her movements that underlined the tension in her body. He thought briefly about the last time he had touched that body, in the darkness of the hotel room . . . She was standing just a few feet from him now. Her tongue flicked out to touch dry lips. 'I . . . I didn't expect

. . . I didn't think . . .' She took a deep, shuddering breath. 'How did you find out?'

O'Connor's voice was dull with disappointment. 'I've spoken again to the girl who was with MacLean the night he was murdered. Jenny Sanders. She knew that there had been other women, before she entered MacLean's bed. Her own boyfriend, Charlie Davis, had warned her, as had other students in the faculty. The gossip was that he had just come out of a relationship with a married woman.'

'But that could have been anyone!' she burst out angrily.

'True. MacLean was a serial womanizer. But there's other evidence . . . for instance, entries in a bank statement of MacLean's. He was a meticulous man. He annotated his statements, marked each item. So it's been easy to identify all of them – payments from time to time from Evans, who handled the money side of things. But there was another entry that stood out, different from the rest. It amounted to rather a large sum of money. Payment from your husband.'

His eyes held hers, coldly. 'And there's also some video footage taken from a house just across the road from MacLean's in Gosforth. A nosy neighbour.'

She blinked, uncomprehending. Then, slowly, realization dawned upon her. 'You can't be serious! You're not suggesting that I had anything to do with the death of James MacLean! This man you told me about –' She bit her lip suddenly, glanced at her husband as she understood what she had let slip, and then ploughed on, regardless. 'This man Rakoff, it was he who killed Hamilton, and then MacLean, and he was seeking Evans! You *told* me that! So how could I have had anything to do with MacLean's death?' Anger stained her eyes; she was breathing quickly. He guessed she was feeling a sense of betrayal and it caused her to throw caution to the winds. 'How could I have had anything to do with his murder? You know damn well that the night he died, I was with you!'

Gordon Portland moved slightly but said nothing, and a strained silence settled about them. O'Connor held Isabella's glance for what seemed an age: he saw the fear and the anxiety there, but he remembered also the trembling of her body in darkened rooms, the way they had made love, wildly, the night that MacLean's life had ebbed away. Slowly, he nodded. 'That's right. I know very well that we were together that night.' He raised his eyes, glanced past her towards Gordon Portland, leaning stiffly against the end of the table. 'But you didn't know that, did you?'

The older man was very still. He was silent for a little while, then a slow, cynical smile touched his lips. It carried no warmth, no mirth. It was the acceptance of a reality that had soured his life, an admission that whatever he did or said would make no difference. 'No, I did not. In fact, your relationship with my wife did not become clear to me until earlier today. It's strange the admission people will make when under stress.' The faint smile turned into a bitter twist of the lips. 'You might have heard part of our . . . ah . . . discussion of the matter as you entered the house. But such discussions are not new.' He raised the cigarette to his lips, drew on it thoughtfully, narrowing his eyes against the smoke. He gestured towards her, in weary dismissiveness. 'You must know by now that my wife is nothing but a whore. Over the years I have come to . . . accept her sluttish indiscretions, until they become too indiscreet, too obvious, begin to damage my peace of mind, humiliate me, bruise the enjoyment of my possessions. Of which she is one.' He slid a vicious, reptilian glance in her direction. 'But the problems go away, in the end. A quiet word here; perhaps a gentle warning there; a trip abroad to take Isabella away from the source of her latest lust and my discontent. And on occasions, the payment of a sum of money if necessary, as it seems you've discovered.'

'You didn't . . .' Isabella's angry intervention died away almost before it really started.

Portland's tired glance returned to O'Connor. 'But none

of these actions will be necessary as far as you're concerned, I imagine. You're an intelligent man. You're probably aware by now that Isabella will never leave me. And certainly not for you. A penniless policeman with few prospects; someone who could never give her the kind of life she enjoys. The reasons why she married me still remain. What would you have to offer, other than a short-lived sexual gratification until she moves on to the next man who excites her febrile imagination? No, I think not: she would not leave me for you. Is that what you came here to hear today? Is that the confirmation you seek? Or did you think you might yet persuade her to give up this house, this life, for you?'

O'Connor shook his head. He kept control of his voice. 'So you are able to confirm the entry in MacLean's bank statement – it was the sum you paid to buy him off, end the relationship, persuade him to stay away from your wife.'

'I've no reason to deny it,' Portland replied coldly.

Isabella glared at him in silent protest, but perhaps she also had wanted to hear the answer. It provided the reason for the end of one affair, and sparked the beginning of a new one. Gordon Portland shrugged. 'I arranged to meet him, and yes, we came to an agreement. He was a remarkably greedy man, you know.' His lip curled in contempt. 'He actually *bargained*. Even though I was under the impression that he was tiring of her in any case.' His eyes betrayed the lie; his glance slipped away from O'Connor, and he straightened, ground out the cigarette in an ashtray, moved away from the table. He faced O'Connor squarely, folded his arms across his chest with an air of defiance. 'Yes, I bought him off.'

'But then,' O'Connor said slowly, 'shortly afterwards, you began to believe he had reneged on the deal.' When Portland made no reply, O'Connor went on, 'You became suspicious at Isabella's absences, you began to realize she was meeting someone.'

201

'It was a pattern I was already familiar with,' Portland replied in a dismissive tone.

'You didn't know it was me: it occurred to you that maybe MacLean had gone back on his deal with you, that in spite of the payment you'd made to him, he was still secretly meeting Isabella. So that evening, when Isabella told you she was going out, you drove to his house, parked in the street, waited for the evidence you wanted. And when you saw a woman enter the house, shielding her face, you assumed it was Isabella. Or maybe you didn't even care. You waited, you saw the light in the bedroom come on . . . and when the bedroom light was switched off, you could stand it no longer, you got out of the car in a murderous rage at what you saw as a further betrayal.'

Isabella Portland stepped forward in protest, shaking her head in disbelief. She put a hand on O'Connor's arm. 'But you said Rakoff –'

'The death of James MacLean had nothing to do with Rakoff,' O'Connor said woodenly. He disengaged his arm, and stepped forward, walking the length of the table. He rested one hand on the glass of the display case.

Arms still folded, Gordon Portland held his glance. He grimaced. 'A fanciful tale. But I saw the report on television of the press conference held by your Assistant Chief Constable Cathery. He announced that the murders of all three men had been solved, and the killer, the man called Rakoff, had himself been killed at Berwick, by armed police. So why are you trying to raise these stupid issues now? Is it because your own judgement is warped? Because you want to attack me, knowing that Isabella will never cleave to you, in the long run? Is it because you realize just what she is, and how she will never leave me, for all I can give her?'

O'Connor's tongue was thick in his mouth. But he controlled himself, ignoring the taunting note in Portland's voice. 'Cathery was wrong,' he said. 'He made a mistake.'

'Ha!' Portland's amusement was cynical, and hollow.

'He identified the wrong killer, you mean? What you might call a *grave error*, perhaps?' He shook his head, his tired, cynical eyes fixed on O'Connor. 'It won't work, you know. All this supposition . . . people will see it for what it is. A bank statement, a payment . . . what is that worth? No, this will be seen merely as an attempt by an embittered man to revenge himself. You want to revenge yourself for the shortcomings of the woman you bedded, revenge yourself upon me. You don't have a hope in hell of proving –'

'The video footage is blurred, and I doubt whether it's good enough to prove the man is you,' O'Connor admitted, 'but I think with enhancement we'll make a pretty good case out that it's your car that was filmed outside the house in Gosforth. And one thing is clear: the man entering the house . . . it certainly wasn't Rakoff.'

'My lawyers will strip such an argument bare,' Portland sneered. 'And I'll get the best lawyers, believe me.' He shook his head dismissively. 'I think now this interview is over. Isabella, I consider it might be appropriate if you saw DCI O'Connor out. You may even embrace him, out of my sight.' He glared at her fiercely. 'It can be by way of a last, fond goodbye.'

O'Connor slid his hand along the glass top of the display case. 'No, the interview isn't yet over. There is one other matter which you'll find might clinch things. I remember this collection, from my last visit. I remember admiring the flintlock pistol, the medieval stiletto, and your special pride in your nineteenth-century Western collection, the Colt 45 and the Buntline Special . . .' He stood looking down at the case and the exhibits placed there. 'Ron Hamilton's throat was slashed professionally as was Cosimo's in Italy; and when Islwyn Evans was attacked, Rakoff tried to cut his throat also, but Evans was saved by the heavy duffel coat he was wearing. After Rakoff was downed, we found the knife he used. It was a very nasty kind of weapon: an extremely sharp flick knife.'

He paused. Portland was standing very still.

'It's clear it was Rakoff's preferred mode of attack,' O'Connor went on softly. 'Clean, quick, quiet. Of course, he also carried a gun. If he hadn't, he would probably not have died. He would then have been able to tell us the truth. He would have been able to tell us that he had not killed James MacLean. If it *had* been Rakoff, he would have slit MacLean's throat in the good, old-fashioned Italian manner. But MacLean died when a broad-bladed knife with a serrated edge was thrust into his chest, and then ripped out.' His fingers strayed over the glass top of the display case. 'It wasn't a flick knife that killed him.'

O'Connor leaned over the display case, inspecting the contents. 'The pathologist, Dr Carter, he told me about the kind of knife that was used to kill MacLean. I didn't pay too much attention at the time. But later, after Rakoff died, and we found his preferred weapon . . . I remembered what the pathologist told me. Dr Carter reckons it was something similar to a Bowie knife that was used to kill James MacLean.'

O'Connor tapped the glass of the display case. 'Very much like this one here. The special knife designed by Jim Bowie in the nineteenth century. I imagine you probably cleaned it pretty thoroughly before you returned it to its position in the case. But you know, Mr Portland, it's almost impossible to remove all traces of blood, or skin, or other matter from which we can extract samples of DNA, from a knife like this, however much you think you've cleaned it. My guess is, we'll not only be able to match the serrated edge of this knife to the wound, but we'll also find traces of MacLean's DNA . . .'

There was a long silence. He looked up. Portland had turned his back, was walking stiff-legged towards his desk. He leaned over it, opened the desk drawer. When he turned back he was holding something in his right hand. His voice was thick. 'This isn't exactly part of my display collection, but it's of some historical interest nevertheless.

A .38 Special. American issue.' He raised it, pointing the muzzle directly at O'Connor. 'And still very much usable. For the destruction of vermin.'

O'Connor heard Isabella gasp.

'The laws in this country against the possession of hand guns are not very effective,' Portland remarked shakily. 'Not if one is wealthy, and a collector . . .'

'This is stupid,' O'Connor said coldly, controlling his voice even though adrenalin was pumping through his veins. 'Put the gun down. There's a car outside. My colleague –'

'Gordon, don't be crazy!' Isabella cried. 'You can't do this!' She stepped away from her husband towards O'Connor, gripped his arm, pulled herself close to him, almost protectively. O'Connor tried to disengage her, push her away out of the line of fire but she clung to him, glaring frantically at her husband.

The muzzle of the gun was rock steady in Gordon Portland's hand. But there was a wavering of his glance: his eyes moved from O'Connor to Isabella and a fog of uncertainty seemed to fill them. Perhaps it was a realization that his world was crumbling about him, that his wealth would no longer protect him, that the woman who had constantly betrayed him might for the first time not come back. Or maybe it was another kind of loss that he faced, and one he would not be able to contemplate.

'Portland –' O'Connor began, extending one hand.

The man facing him twitched, stared at O'Connor as though he was seeing a stranger. He blinked. His finger tightened on the trigger but something was happening to his face. His skin seemed leaden in colour, his mouth sagged: the muzzle began to waver, drop, as various emotions ran through his mind. Isabella was clinging to O'Connor still. He would lose her. There might be the horror of an existence in prison. Humiliation, public cuckoldry . . . He blinked again and then in one slow deliberate movement Portland turned the muzzle of the gun away.

O'Connor grunted in relief, sighed, stepped forward with hand outstretched to take the gun from the older man. But he was too late. Staring at him fixedly, Portland placed the muzzle of the .38 against his own temple and pulled the trigger.

The explosion was sharp in the room. Blood, bone, flesh and skin flew sideways, spattering across the room as the man dropped. O'Connor heard Isabella scream in terror and denial, but he himself was rooted to the spot, dazed, his senses in uproar. He could hear Isabella's crazed voice, but he was unable to move.

He had no idea how long he had been standing there, immobile, before he heard the door open behind him, became aware that it was Farnsby rushing into the room.

Isabella Portland was seated on the floor at his feet. She was clinging to his legs, sobbing hysterically. He looked down at her, a sour taste in his mouth, a slow, agonizing ache in his stomach. He could no longer recall with clarity the way they had clung together in the darkened hotel rooms; what they had shared seemed distant, faded, something that had happened to two other people. Farnsby had tried to warn him. And O'Connor knew that for him, too, it was as Gordon Portland had earlier said. It had all been a bad mistake.

A grave error.

'Italian sunlight,' Carmela Cacciatore said. 'I have missed it.'

Arnold stood beside her as she hesitated before proceeding through to the departure lounge at Newcastle Airport. 'You'll soon be back home again,' he said.

'And none the worse for wear, apart from a bruised arm.'

Arnold nodded. The bullet from Rakoff's gun had ripped through the arm of her coat, but had not opened a wound: they had both been lucky that night.

'When do you expect the return of the Celtic votive cauldron?' she asked.

He shrugged. 'The police expect to have it returned to the department in a week or so. It's not really essential evidence, because when Evans goes on trial again it'll be in respect of the smuggling operation he ran with Hamilton and MacLean, and of course it's likely he'll get off fairly lightly in view of the way he's co-operating with the police in their enquiries. And in any case, they wouldn't want any more disputes about its genuine nature, or its provenance. They'll quietly let it come back into our hands at the Department of Museums and Antiquities.'

'And the calyx krater?'

'It will be released sooner rather than later, I would imagine,' he assured her. 'It'll be a while, of course. But now it's in the possession of the police I'm pretty sure your Ministry will be making the necessary representation for its recovery, and its return to Italy.'

'Well, when it is ready for return, perhaps I will be able to persuade my superiors that I should be allowed to come back, so I may formally accept the artefact. And when it is handed over, I shall make a speech, praising you.'

'I would like that,' Arnold said, laughing. 'Your return, I mean, not the speech.'

'And I.' She smiled at him, then suddenly threw her arms around him, planted an enthusiastic kiss on his lips. After a few seconds she pulled back, looked at him, smiling. 'On the ramparts at Berwick, when you lay across me, protecting me on the ground, I enjoyed that. I *wriggled* a bit, you know.'

Arnold smiled, recollecting. 'I . . . er . . . I was aware of that.'

'Actually, I wriggled a lot. So who knows? Perhaps when I return we will wriggle a bit again, no?' She held his glance, archly. 'And when I do return, I think I will not object if you were to call me DeeDee. When others say it, I find it . . . boring, an old joke. But with you, perhaps

I would like you to call me DeeDee. In appropriate circumstances.'

She turned away, began to walk towards the baggage check. She glanced back, and waved. 'Remember, next time, DeeDee.'

Arnold grinned. 'I'll think about it, I promise.' He waved. 'I'll think about it . . . Carmela.'